Guardian Angel

———◆———

Nick saw commotion in the direction from which the last gunman had come. A man was chasing a boy, a four-foot-tall bundle of flailing arms and legs.

"Get back here, you!" the man grunted.

Nick caught sight of the little boy's face and was drawn to a pair of wide, terrified eyes. The boy's mouth hung open in a silent scream. His pursuer reached out to grab him. His gun arm bent at the elbow, allowing him to fire off a quick hipshot. The bullet blazed through the empty air, forcing Nick to duck.

As he rushed toward the boy and his attacker, Nick saw another armed man close in on the kid from behind.

"Look behind you!" Nick shouted.

The kid flinched and huddled down, rooting himself to the spot.

Nick swung his arm around to fire at the second man, just to buy a few more seconds.

Because he knew the first gunman was just about to fire again . . .

Books by Marcus Galloway

No Angels for Outlaws
Dead Man's Promise
Burying the Past
The Man from Boot Hill

MARCUS GALLOWAY

THE MAN FROM BOOT HILL
NO ANGELS
FOR OUTLAWS

HARPER

An Imprint of HarperCollins*Publishers*

This is a work of fiction. Names, character, places, and incidents are products of the author's imagination or are used fictitiously and are not to be construed as real. Any resemblance to actual events, locales, organizations or persons, living or dead, is entirely coincidental.

HARPER

An Imprint of HarperCollins*Publishers*
10 East 53rd Street
New York, New York 10022-5299

Copyright © 2007 by Marcus Pelegrimas
ISBN: 978-0-06-114727-2
ISBN-10: 0-06-114727-3

First Harper paperback printing: May 2007

Printed in the United States of America

Visit Harper paperbacks on the World Wide Web at
www.harpercollins.com

10 9 8 7 6 5 4 3 2 1

THE MAN FROM BOOT HILL
NO ANGELS
FOR OUTLAWS

ONE

Ocean, California
1884

Nobody thought too much about the undertaker until it was too late.

It was a quiet yet important job that didn't draw attention—and that suited Nick Graves just fine.

The sun beat down upon Nick's shoulders as he stripped layer after layer from the side of a freshly cut plank of cedar. As slivers of wood curled up over the top of the plane, they were caught by the wind and blown back against his rough, callused knuckles. Like any other carpenter's hands, they showed the wear that accompanied his trade. The missing fingers and gnarled scars, however, weren't so typical.

It had taken a bit of effort and plenty of practice on Nick's part, but he was able to guide the plane along the wood's surface with perfect accuracy, despite his wounded hands. He moved with slow, easy motions, as if he was rocking a baby to sleep.

All the while, a satisfied grin took hold of his face.

It had been some time since he had relaxed and enjoyed his chosen profession. Nick had learned his trade when he was a boy and had been practicing it for several years, but only recently had been able to give himself over to simple physical labor while letting his mind wander among the smaller things. A man couldn't fully enjoy something like that until his face had collected a few lines around the edges.

Every now and then he let his eyes roam along the rolling hills of a field outside of town where folks were planted after serving their time on this earth. Those hills were as familiar to him as a field of corn was to a farmer. While most people felt nervous walking among the carved headstones and freshly turned piles of soil, Nick sat out there to savor the quiet or admire his handiwork.

The sounds of wood being carved, nails being driven and planks coming together were music to his ears. It had been a while since he was able to chisel designs into stone, but that was mainly because the folks in Ocean leaned more toward wooden crosses or markers with a few engraved sentiments.

That, too, suited Nick just fine.

It had been almost a year since he'd arrived in Ocean, and the locals had taken to him quicker than most. Plenty of other stragglers had found their way there after touring the California coast.

Some had stopped before ever reaching the Pacific. Very few of them offered any skills to benefit the town, and the services of a gravedigger were always needed. It also didn't hurt that Nick was accompanied by a pretty face that was anxious to smile at everyone in Ocean. Catherine did have a way of softening even the coldest of hearts. Nick was most definitely an expert on that subject.

Just thinking about her made the sun feel a bit warmer on Nick's face. The prospect of paying her a visit sooner than usual made his hands move faster while planing the edges of the planks that would soon fit together to form Eliot Pickler's casket. Eliot was the first to be brought into Nick's parlor for some time. The longevity of the Ocean locals was good for the town but bad for Nick's business. Even so, Nick knew Eliot's parents were short on funds, so he cut as many corners as he could when arranging the boy's services. Good thing Catherine's restaurant was pulling in more of a profit.

Nick sat on a small stool looking out on the wide field where Ocean's past was buried. His lean frame sat hunched over a stack of boards as his muscular arms kept peeling slivers of timber until each plank was just right. The smell of the freshly cut wood mingled with the scents of grass and dirt, making it easy for Nick to forget there was a proper town less than a mile behind him.

When he closed his eyes, the only things he saw were the backs of his eyelids. When he let out his breath, the only thing he heard was the calm rustle of the wind. The ghosts that had screamed at him for so many years were quiet for now, but he wasn't foolish enough to think they would ever truly leave him. In fact, he didn't even think he deserved that kind of peace.

As he continued to work, Nick felt the summer breeze become cooler as the sun dipped a bit lower. The buzz of insects grew louder and a few of the braver ones jumped against Nick's leg.

Suddenly, the insects stopped.

Nick picked up on the silence and felt every one of his muscles tense. His right leg shifted to make sure his gun was still in its place at his side. It wasn't.

It had been a while since anyone had taken a shot at him, but those instincts would never fade. Ever since he'd started moving about without his gun, he felt as if he'd left the house without putting on his pants. At times like these, he felt the absence of his modified Schofield even more than he felt the absence of his fingers.

After a few seconds, Nick let out the breath he'd been holding and strained his eyes to see what the insects had sensed that he hadn't. For all he knew, it could have been a coyote walking somewhere out of his sight or a bird that decided to move at the wrong time.

When he heard the rumble of horses coming his way, Nick set down his tools and started walking toward the bundle he'd brought with him from his workshop. By the sound of those hooves, it wouldn't be long before he got a look at them. As much as Nick wanted to assume that they were just passing through, he'd seen too much hell to figure everyone he came across was going to be on their best behavior.

The horsemen burst from the trees clustered at the farthest edge of the graveyard. Nick counted four of them and knew they were using a broken-down trail that led from over the Nevada border. The bundle he'd left on the ground was still a few steps away when he saw the lead horseman take notice of him and steer his ride straight toward him.

"Hey," the lead horseman shouted arrogantly. "We got a question for ya."

Nick guessed that two of those men weren't over the age of twenty-two, and all of them had a cockiness that affected everything right down to the way they sat in their saddles. Nick didn't bother checking if the riders were heeled. He knew all too well that most of that arrogance came from the weight of a firearm on a young man's hip.

Straightening up to his full height, Nick brushed some of the scraggly hair out of his face. Sweat from a hard day's work had kept his hair damp, while the last few years of his life had been responsible for numerous strands of gray.

The horsemen shifted in their saddles once they caught the brunt of Nick's stare. His cold, steely eyes bored through each one in turn before he shifted his gaze to the first rider and asked, "What's your question?"

Several years older than the other three, the lead rider had more of an experienced air about him. The dark skin of his face was smooth and unmarked by any scars. Sharp, clear eyes glared out at the world from over a hawk-beak nose. His voice had an edge to it, which gave him a good rein over the rest of the men. "Is that Ocean up ahead?"

Nick nodded.

One of the other horsemen grunted under his breath. He was a lanky kid with a sorry excuse for a mustache sprouting at odd angles from his upper lip. He wore his guns out in plain sight and rarely took his hand from the grip of his shiny new Peacemaker. "Some joke. Ain't no ocean for miles. All we seen is deserts and grass."

"Some like it that way," Nick said.

"Take it easy, mister," the lead horseman said. "All we wanted was to make certain we was headed in the right direction."

The third rider was taller than the other two and made a constant effort to keep from looking directly at Nick. So far, Nick couldn't tell whether that was because of fear or some other reason. "I told you this would be Ocean," the third man said.

"Sure, Georgie," the lanky rider said. "You also said there was a whorehouse and hot steaks in a place a few days north of here, but there wasn't anything but a stack of empty buildings and some goats."

"Shut up, Alan. I was right about everything else."

"Aw, come on, Georgie. You led us to that other town 'cause you liked them goats. I saw you sneak off that night to get behind the biggest one and—"

"You can shut the hell up, too, Bertram!" George snarled.

"Shut up, the lot of you," the lead rider snarled. "You're grousing like a bunch of little girls."

George nodded while Alan grinned and eased back into his saddle. "Sure, Dutch," he said.

By this time, Nick had moved himself closer to the bundle he'd left on the ground. Rather than stoop down to reach for it, however, he stayed within arm's reach while keeping an eye on the squabbling horsemen. "You boys can settle this in town, if you like. There's a few good saloons on Eighth Street."

"What's the matter, old man?" Bertram asked as he turned his glare toward Nick without losing any of the attitude he'd shown to George. "Are we disturbing your nap?"

"No, but a graveyard's not the place to be stomping around and tossing insults at each other like a bunch of damn kids."

Hearing that, all three of the riders started looking around wildly. When they caught sight of the rows of headstones no more than four or five paces away, they wheeled around as if they'd found themselves on a sinking ship.

"Aw, hell," Bertram grunted. "He's right. This is a damn graveyard. How come Georgie didn't know that?"

George was already riding toward town and shaking his head at the other man's complaints.

"Haven't I seen you before?" Nick asked after him.

When he glanced over his shoulder, George seemed surprised to find that Nick was talking to him. "I don't think so, mister."

Nick's eyes took on a grayish hue as he narrowed them into slits. After only a few seconds, he nodded and said, "At the Van Meter spread on the other side of town. You were one of the new boys hired on there."

The other two men stopped short. Bertram shifted to take a closer look at Nick, while Dutch glanced back and forth between all the men.

"Is that so?" Dutch asked.

George started to shake his head, but was unable to keep it up under Nick's careful gaze. "I don't know what he's talking about."

"Maybe I'm mistaken," Nick said. "You do look an awful lot like that kid, though."

"He's got a common face," Dutch said. The leader of the horsemen then tipped his hat to Nick and added, "Much obliged. I think I'll be visiting one of those saloons you mentioned."

Nick nodded and watched the men leave. Although he kept a friendly smile on his face, he stayed close to the bundle at his feet.

Sure enough, a minute later he heard more horsemen riding through the trees nearby. They circled the graveyard and then sped up to join the others farther down the trail. Nick closed his eyes but could not determine their numbers. Something in his gut told him there were too many for his liking.

Part of Nick wanted to unhitch the old horse from his wagon and find out where they were headed. But there was no badge pinned to his chest and no reason to hold a grudge against those men. He did have more than enough experience to know that curiosity damaged more than just cats.

Reminding himself of the peace he'd earned, Nick settled back onto his stool and continued putting together Eliot's casket.

TWO

———◆———

The horsemen could see the town of Ocean clearly once they had put some distance between themselves and the graveyard. The trail had opened up and the land spread out to a grassy plain. Despite the beauty of the setting sun, which cast a dark purple tint on the sky, none of the horsemen seemed very happy.

As Dutch pulled back on his reins, the second group of riders thundered up to his side. The man at the front of that group had a bulky frame and pasty white skin stretched over a crooked face. A skinny nose jutted out at a distinctly broken angle, complementing the frown etched beneath it.

"Where's the rest?" Dutch asked.

The big man with the hawk nose nodded toward the town. "They rode around to the east and should be there already. I was just about to head in there and make certain they didn't get sidetracked in some whore's bed or the like."

"Send one of the others to do that. I want you and J. D. to circle back and take care of that gravedigger. He's about my height with plenty of gray hair, and he's missing some fingers from each hand. You shouldn't miss him."

Scowling, the bigger man asked, "Why should we kill a gravedigger?"

"Don't question me, Alan. Just do what I say."

For a moment, Dutch and Alan stared daggers at each other while the rest of the men watched. Before long, the big man started to look away. Before the retreat became too obvious, he said, "All I wanted to know was why."

"Because he recognized George from the Van Meter place."

Alan's eyes narrowed to focus on George.

"I never even seen that gravedigger before!" George whined.

"That don't matter. He's seen you."

"Then maybe George should be the one to clean up the mess," Alan growled.

Dutch shook his head. "I can't risk that. We need him."

"Risk what? The guy's a fucking gravedigger!"

"For this run, George is the one man I can't do without. I don't want to risk him falling off his horse, getting hit by a shovel or any other nonsense, since Lord knows he couldn't do the simple job he had before without turning that into a pile of shit."

"I'll go clean up the runt's mess," Alan said, "just so long as Georgie pays for whatever I want at one of them saloons."

"What?" George snapped.

Waving off the two of them, Dutch quickly said, "Sounds fair to me. If George has a problem with that, he can take it up with Alan, himself. I'm already sick of hearing about this. Just make sure that gravedigger doesn't get around to telling anyone else he saw George with the rest of us."

"You can count on me," Alan said. "Come on, J. D. Let's dig us another hole in that graveyard."

J. D. appeared to be a year or two older than Alan. He also appeared to be anything but happy about following the other man to carry out the assigned task. His short-cropped black hair was stuck to his scalp with a bucket of sweat and his shirt was stuck to his back in much the same way. Both sleeves were rolled up to show lanky yet muscled arms.

Alan turned his horse around and touched his heels to the animal's sides to get it running at a quick pace. J. D. followed in his wake, both men racing toward the graveyard as the sun continued its drop in the western sky. By the time they got back among the headstones, the sky was tainted blood red and the air was as cool as the bodies under the dirt.

Nodding toward a short, narrow wagon at the edge of the graveyard, J. D. asked, "That belong to the man we're after?"

Alan's eyes were slowly shifting in their sockets, but had yet to catch a glimpse of Nick. "I guess so."

"Where's he at?"

"He was right there when we found him," Alan said, pointing to a spot currently occupied by an empty stool. "But he ain't there now."

"Yeah. I can see that. Maybe we should look for him." When he saw that Alan still wasn't moving, J. D. added, "If he gets into town, there'll be hell to pay."

"All right, then. I'll check over here and you go that way."

J. D. climbed down from his saddle so he could take a closer look at the wagon that had been left behind. The first thing he saw was the fresh droppings in the spot where the horse had stood in its hitch. He then squatted down and took a look at the ground near the wagon. A couple seconds later, he straightened up and drew his pistol.

"Did you see him?" J. D. asked.

"Nah. Looks like he skinned out of here."

"No he didn't."

"Huh?"

"That's what he wanted us to think," J. D. said, "but that's not what happened."

"How do you know?"

"There's a set of tracks next to the horse's that were put down by a pair of boots."

"So he led him a ways," Alan grunted as he got his own horse moving in the direction of Ocean. "Then he mounted up and rode into town. You're wasting time."

J. D. pointed to a narrow strip of dirt leading to the main trail. "The boot prints stop here, but the horse's go on."

"Proves my point."

Leaving his own horse behind, J. D. walked slowly around the graveyard. "Those horse tracks didn't get any deeper after the boots left. That means there wasn't any weight added."

"Now that it's getting dark, he'll be harder to find."

"Nobody got on that horse's back, you fucking idiot," J. D. hissed. "Now shut your mouth and help me find this gravedigger. He's still around here somewhere."

Whether it was due to the tone of J. D.'s voice or the sense he was talking, Alan finally did as he was told and climbed down from his saddle. He was at least right about one thing: It was getting dark awfully fast now that the sun had melted down to a warm glow in the distance.

Signaling for Alan to circle around the graveyard to the left, J. D. measured his steps carefully and circled around to the right. Since there wasn't any place for a grown man to hide among the tombstones, both of them focused their attention on the trees. When they met up at the back of the graveyard, Alan waited for his next set of orders.

"He's got to be in those trees," J. D. said.

"Either that, or he ran into town."

"If he did that, he would've already been picked

off. He's probably just hiding or running for that river we crossed on our way in here."

"You think he knows we mean to kill him?"

Raising his gun and crouching like an animal getting ready to strike, J. D. aimed at one of the misty shadows in the dank spaces between two of the bigger trees. "He does now."

Alan's eyes snapped in that direction and he reflexively tightened his grip on his gun. The tall figure in the nearby shadows had been there before, but hadn't moved enough to distinguish it from the other looming shapes. Now, J. D. knew that the man had been silently watching him from that spot the entire time.

"You the gravedigger?" Alan asked.

Nick stepped forward.

"Hold it," J. D. snapped. "What's that you're carrying?"

Nick kept his arms out to the sides. "You mean my pack?"

"Toss it."

"It's just my tools."

"I said toss it."

Nick let the bundle fall to his feet. "I don't even know you men," he said. "Why go through so much trouble to find me?"

"Never you mind," J. D. said as he sighted along the barrel of his gun. "Just kick that over toward my partner. Alan, open up that pack and see what's inside."

Nick pushed the bundle along the ground toward Alan.

J. D. watched every move Nick made. He also watched the older man's face to see if he could find any hint of weakness or fear. He found neither. Normally, folks didn't have the strength to keep their eyes fixed upon him for more than a few seconds. This gravedigger, however, showed no sign of looking away.

While rummaging through Nick's things, Alan shook his head. "All I see is tools. Hold up. I just found something else."

"What is it?" J. D. asked.

Alan answered that question by removing a battered pistol from within the bundle. The gun sat awkwardly in his hand, causing Alan to look it over with increasing disgust. The barrel was nearly as twisted as some of the roots under his feet and the trigger mechanism looked brittle enough to snap under the slightest bit of pressure.

"Well?" J. D. demanded.

"It's a gun," Alan replied. "Or at least, it used to be. Damn thing looks like it came from the bottom of a junk pile."

"Get rid of it."

Alan happily pitched the weapon into some bushes without another thought. Since he was busy digging through the rest of Nick's pack, he didn't notice the subtle, angry twitch in Nick's eye as he tried to mark where his gun had landed.

"Ain't nothing more here," Alan finally said. "Apart from digging tools and such."

"Good."

"If you're gonna shoot," Nick said, "then why not tell me what you're after?"

By now, J. D. had taken aim at Nick's chest. "Wrong place at the wrong time, mister. That's all there is to it."

Nick chuckled under his breath. "Story of my life." With that, he lifted his right leg and reached down for a slender knife that was stashed in his boot. In one, smooth motion, he drew the knife and threw it directly at the gunman.

J. D. was unprepared to feel the blade drive into the meat of his gun arm as he pulled his trigger.

Nick was already moving. The hot lead from J. D.'s wild shot whipped past him and only managed to snag a piece of his jacket along the way. His sights were already set upon Alan and he charged forward to press the momentary advantage he'd created.

Watching the turn of events with wide eyes, Alan raised his gun and fired off three quick shots that made plenty of noise without drawing any blood. Then, all Alan could do was watch Nick rush toward him like a crazed bull.

Lowering his shoulder at the last moment, Nick slammed into Alan's chest. Alan landed with a wheezing thump and both his arms splayed out to his sides. As much as Nick wanted to grab the gun from Alan's hand, Alan held onto it with every bit of strength he could dredge up. In his youth, Nick wouldn't have had any trouble with the task. Now, he was at a distinct disadvantage.

Through sheer survival instinct, Alan managed to pull his arm free from Nick's mangled fingers and roll out from under him. As he scrambled along the ground, Alan could barely decide where he wanted to go. Just as he got himself situated, he felt a powerful impact on the back of his head and the dim light of dusk turned to black.

While struggling to get his own feet beneath him, Nick balled up his fist and delivered a second punch to the base of Alan's skull. That punch landed in the same spot as the first and knocked Alan's forehead once more against the ground. Alan wasn't completely unconscious, so he managed to protect his gun by pulling that arm beneath the rest of him before curling into a defensive ball.

Nick turned around just in time to see J. D. sitting up and reaching for the knife stuck in his arm. When he spotted Nick, J. D. gritted his teeth and switched the pistol into his other hand so he could squeeze off another shot.

Pushing aside the pain in his aching muscles as well as his last vestige of common sense, Nick dug his feet into the ground and ran straight at J. D. He reached out with his right hand and just managed to slap away the other man's gun a split-second before it spat out a plume of smoke and sparks.

Nick's ears were ringing and the grit of burned gunpowder coated the back of his throat. Thanks to the close proximity of that last shot, he didn't hear J. D.'s scream when he grabbed hold of the knife still embedded in the man's arm and gave it a single, powerful twist.

The jangling in Nick's ears was slow to fade, but he instinctually glanced over to see what Alan was doing. Sure enough, Alan had flipped onto his back and was sitting up with gun in hand. There was still a confused look on his face, but Alan quickly focused in on where the fight had gone.

Nick lunged for J. D.'s gun and felt his hand close around its grip. When he got his finger on the trigger, the gun had slipped in his hand and skewed to one side. Nick was accustomed to the kind of trouble a regular gun gave him, but he cursed it all the same. Tightening his hand around the grip and taking another second to adjust for the slip, he pulled his trigger just as Alan pulled his own.

Alan's shot was panicked and rushed, which caused it to hiss through the air a few inches off-target.

Nick's measured shot carved a good-sized hole through Alan's head.

Feeling his heart pound against his ribs and the blood churn through his veins, Nick watched Alan flop over and hack up one, final gasp.

THREE

When Nick turned the gun toward J. D., he saw naked fear in the other man's eyes. J. D. tried to kick and scramble his way toward the surrounding trees while waving his hands as if he could swat away a bullet. Nick kicked J. D. onto his back while tossing away the gun. He then stood over the younger man and reached down to take hold of the knife still lodged in J. D.'s arm. Although Nick didn't twist the blade, he held onto it solidly enough to keep J. D. from moving.

"What the hell brought this on?" Nick asked. "Who are you men?"

J. D. gasped painfully. As he tried to get away again, he felt the knife staying where it was. Finally, J. D. gave up his struggle and rested on his back. "You . . . recognized George," he said, wheezing.

"George? You mean that boy from the Van Meter spread?"

J. D. nodded.

"So what if I recognized him?"

"Dutch didn't want the . . . job to be spoiled."

"What job?"

A good amount of the color had drained from J. D.'s face. His wound wasn't bleeding too badly, so Nick figured the younger man was fading due to exertion.

"Tell me," Nick growled, loudly enough to be heard through the fog in J. D.'s head. "What job?"

"Dutch . . . needed someone on the inside. To make it . . . easier."

"Make what easier? Are they going to rob Van Meter's ranch?"

Once again, J. D. nodded.

"When?" Nick asked.

"Soon. Real soon."

Nick straightened up and took his knife with him. The blade came free, allowing J. D. to finally let out the breath he'd been choking on. After wiping the blade on his shirt, Nick ran to search for his gun. Along the way, his mind raced to figure just how quickly a group of men that size could move.

If Nick knew about anything as much as he knew about his current profession, it was how a gang worked. He'd practically grown up leading one. After getting to the bushes where his gun had been tossed, Nick dropped to his knees and shoved his hands through the brush.

The sun was a memory and the dim glow in the sky was all but blotted out by the trees over his head. Since he couldn't see much of anything, he closed his eyes and let his hands continue their search on their own. In the darkness, the ghosts he thought he'd banished came rushing back to him. He saw the faces of men he'd killed, men he'd betrayed, men who were his brothers and men who'd dragged him through hell.

While trudging through those nightmares, Nick touched the familiar piece of gnarled iron. He quickly found the nub of a handle and then closed his hand around it. To the ignorant eye, the Schofield looked like a piece of cobbled-together junk. Even the handle was chipped down to a stump, but it fit Nick's hand perfectly.

Nick lifted the gun while letting out a relieved breath. The fingers clutching the weapon were just as gnarled as the gun itself. His right ring finger was nothing but a short stub and the middle finger was clipped short as well. Although his other fingers were there, the scars made his flesh look more like melted wax. His left hand was slightly better, but not by much.

Unlike J. D.'s gun, this one didn't slip. Its handle had been specifically carved to fit his hand as well as compensate for the odd balance due to his missing fingers. Every other part of the weapon was modified as well, allowing Nick to draw and fire it almost as quickly as he could in his youth.

Gun in hand, Nick hurried to where his horse was waiting. Rasa might have been way past her prime, but the horse knew better than to wander off after being freed from the wagon's hitch. While the gunshots hadn't spooked her, she was ready to put some distance between herself and that grave-yard. She took off like a shot at the first touch of Nick's heels, carrying him all the way back to the little cabin he'd built outside of Ocean.

As soon as he swung down from the saddle, Nick headed for the door and pushed it open. Catherine's face was the first thing he saw.

The brunette stood up from where she'd been sitting and rushed over to greet him. She didn't even seem to notice how close Nick's hand was to his gun as she wrapped her arms around him and held him tightly.

"Surprise!" she said.

Nick barely even knew what to think. His mind was still swimming with what had happened as well as the memories that were his constant bur-den. Finally, he managed to calm himself enough to speak in something other than an angry snarl. "What are you doing back? It's not time to close the restaurant yet."

"I left early. Something told me you'd like it if I paid you a visit. Weren't you thinking about me?"

"Yeah. Of course I was."

Catherine took a step back and held Nick at arm's length. She looked him up and down, which was more than enough to tarnish the smile that had been on her face. Her smooth skin accentuated the fine lines of her face in much the same way that the cut of her dark green dress accentuated her figure.

Long, dark hair flowed freely to the middle of her back, just the way Nick always liked it.

"What is it, Nick?" she asked. "What's wrong?"

"There was some trouble."

A look of horror flashed across Catherine's face. "Did somebody come after you? I thought that was all over."

"It is. This is something different."

"Different how? Just tell me what happened."

Nick immediately went to the small room attached to the back porch. Normally, it was a place used to store meat or other supplies. A section in one corner, however, was designated for a different purpose and was sealed off by a locked wooden panel.

"Some men rode through the graveyard while I was there," Nick explained as he unlocked the panel with a key kept in his watch pocket. "They had guns. They rode away, but some of them came back to try and gun me down."

"Oh, Jesus. Do you know them?"

"I recognized one of them, but he wasn't anyone who would want to shoot me."

"Who was it?" she asked.

Opening the panel, Nick reached inside for a handful of bullets as well as a battered leather holster that had only started to collect dust. "He was one of the boys working for Joseph Van Meter."

"The one who owns that ranch outside of town?"

"That's the one. I went there for a job a while

back and just caught sight of the kid. I didn't even say a word to him."

"Then why would he want to kill you?"

"That's what I aim to find out," Nick said as he strapped the holster around his waist and stuffed the extra bullets into his pockets.

Suddenly, Catherine took special interest in the gun at Nick's side. "Wait a second. You only kept the holster in there? When did you start carrying that gun around again?"

"I never stopped, Catherine. We may be starting a new life, but that don't mean the old one will just forget all about me."

"It won't if you keep digging it up and—"

"This doesn't have anything to do with me," Nick cut in. "It's got something to do with the rest of that gang. They intend on cleaning out the Van Meter place, and that kid I spotted must be a part of it. That's why they didn't want me to tell anyone else about it."

"You told me," she pointed out. "What am I supposed to do now?"

"Sit tight and keep the shotgun ready, but I doubt you'll need it. Those boys who came after me didn't have the first clue who I was, so they've got no reason to know about you."

Catherine took a deep breath and lowered herself onto a chair. "Are you sure they weren't just some bunch of cowboys?"

"I know killers when I see them, and these boys have taken shots at plenty more men than me. Not many more, but enough so they got a taste for it."

Catherine wanted to ask how Nick could be so certain, but she stopped short because she already knew the answer. She also knew there was nothing she could say to convince Nick to put his gun away and see a doctor about the bloody stain on his shirt. "Are you at least going to talk to the sheriff about these men?"

Nick looked up from what he was doing and was silent. The expression on his face was a mix of hesitation and bewilderment. Finally, he said, "That might be a good idea."

Catherine laughed and rubbed Nick's shoulder. "I think so. I know you're not used to working with the law, but this sort of thing is what they get paid to do."

"Fine. You get the sheriff and tell him to go out to the Van Meter ranch. I'll meet him there."

"You're still going?" she asked.

"Of course I am. I just needed to stop here to make sure I had enough ammunition."

"How much do you need?"

"More than my pockets can hold."

FOUR

———•———

Even though he'd seen the sky shift from one color to another and could feel the air growing cooler by the minute, Nick was surprised at just how quickly the light had been sucked away.

Rasa had had a busy day, and so Nick saddled up his other horse and snapped the reins. Kazys was a bit younger, but had spent the better part of two years pulling a wagon. Nick's concerns about the horse's speed were put to rest as he soon felt the wind rushing against his face.

He rode with one hand gripping the reins and the other hand upon his holstered pistol. Nick got through town without incident and quickly saw the flicker of lanterns behind windows fade away. That left the wide expanse of land beyond Ocean, which was now as black as sackcloth.

The door to the small office swung open and smacked loudly against the wall, causing the two men inside to sit bolt upright behind their desks.

When they saw Catherine storming inside, they jumped to their feet.

"Sheriff Stilson, you need to go to the Van Meter place," she said.

"What's the matter?" asked the first man to reach Catherine's side. In his mid-forties, he had a full head of light brown hair and sideburns that extended down to his chin. His features were angular. The hands he placed on Catherine's shoulders were thick and beefy.

"There's men riding out there," she said, twisting out of the man's grasp. "They shot at my husband."

Both men's eyes darted to Catherine's left hand, but neither one of them saw a ring on her finger. Suddenly, Stilson nodded. "Oh, you're the undertaker's wife."

"Yes, I am."

"He's been shot?"

"Yes!"

"What happened?"

Catherine sucked in a deep breath. From the corner of her eye, she could see Stilson's deputy studying her closely. The man was at least fifteen years younger than the sheriff and had a bushy mustache. His bulky arms were propped on his hips and his eyes were practically glued to Catherine's bosom.

Placing one hand flat against her chest to cover herself, she pretended to be out of breath as she said, "My husband's gone to help Mister Van Meter. From what he told me, you should do the same. There's a bunch of men headed out there to rob him or . . ."

"Or what?"

Catherine didn't like the tone in the lawman's voice. "I told you my husband's been shot," she said sternly. "He went off to lend a hand where it's needed and I thought he was wrong not to come here first. Maybe he wasn't so wrong after all."

"Where did he see these men?" the sheriff asked.

"At the graveyard. They rode through and then some came back to shoot him."

"And you're certain they were going to the Van Meter place?"

She nodded. "That's where he went when he should have gone to the doctor about his wound."

"I'll ride out there to see to it myself," Stilson said.

"You may need more men. Nick said there were—"

"I'll round up another deputy or two along the way," the sheriff interrupted, "but I need to leave Ben here at the office in case something else comes up."

Catherine's first impulse was not to believe what the sheriff said. Then again, she'd found it was healthier not to believe what most folks said when they started the conversation eyeing her like she was a slab of meat. "I'll come with you," she offered.

"That won't be necessary, ma'am. You should go on home and wait for your husband." Stilson didn't even try to hide his distaste. "If he comes back early, I'm sure you'll want to know about it."

"Fine." With that, she turned her back to the lawmen and headed out the door. Sheriff Stilson followed behind her, mounted his horse, and rode down the street. Catherine watched to make certain the lawman was headed in the direction of Van Meter's ranch. After that, there wasn't much else for her to do. She walked home before the deputy with the wandering eyes offered his services as an escort.

The Van Meter ranch sat five miles south of Ocean. Kazys began straining and wheezing halfway there, but Nick knew the animal could push on a little farther. If those killers figured he was dead, there was no reason for them to run their horses to death to get where they were going.

Then again, those killers also had a head start and, undoubtedly, much younger horses.

The shadows had taken over the landscape and the pale glow of the half-moon wasn't nearly enough to chase them away. Even after Nick's eyes had adjusted to the dark, he was wary of riding at a full gallop. The trail was dangerous. Anything from snakes, rocks, or rodent holes could be lying under the cover of darkness. Any one of those things could break the horse's leg or possibly snap Nick's neck in a fall.

Nick weighed what he'd learned about those gunmen and thought about the rancher they were out to meet. On the other hand, he couldn't do anyone any good if he was lying hurt or lost his horse in the middle of this open stretch of land.

Nick swore under his breath and pulled back on his reins. Kazys maintained as best he could.

FIVE

———————◆———————

"You know what the best thing is about owning land?" Joseph Van Meter said as he stretched out his legs and sank into the large porch swing.

The woman next to Joseph was curled up with her legs tucked underneath her body. Shoulder-length blonde hair fell in tight curls around her face as she tried to find the spot in the distance that had captured her husband's attention. "I give up," she said. "What is it?"

"Enjoying the quiet nights with nobody around to mess them up."

"You mean nobody except for me and the kids?"

"You three don't count."

She leaned away from him and gave Joseph a good smack on the chest with the flat of her hand. "We don't count?"

Joseph put on a grin that was almost hidden by the beard on his face. "You know what I mean. You don't count when I'm talking about other folks."

"Is that good or bad?"

Joseph snaked one arm around her waist and muscled her onto his lap. He easily positioned her so she was lying across his lap and one of his hands could work its way beneath her skirts. "That's a good thing, Anne. It means you and the kids aren't like the idiots in town or all those loud cowboys who storm through here like a pack of dogs."

"If I remember correctly," she said, squirming and trying halfheartedly to keep his hand from getting much farther, "you were one of those cowboys not too long ago. In fact, I thought you were handsome back then."

"Just back then?"

Anne took her hand away from his roaming touch and used it to brush her fingers along Joseph's chin. "You know what I mean," she said, adjusting herself so her husband could get a good feel of whatever he liked. "That's a good thing."

Running his hand along her thigh, Joseph leaned in and kissed her powerfully on the lips. Soon, they were shifting to new positions on the swing until they were a tangle of limbs and twisted clothes. Joseph was wedged in the corner of the swing with one arm pinned beneath him. Anne hung halfway off the edge with one foot on the porch to keep from falling off. After they realized how they'd wound up, both of them started to laugh.

"This was supposed to be romantic," Joseph grunted.

Anne winced and stretched her leg. "I hope you think it's romantic when we fall off of this contraption, because that's what's about to happen."

Joseph adjusted his hold around his wife and strained to set them both upright. Although the swing almost got away from them a couple of times, they somehow managed to keep from hitting the floor. When they were both sitting up properly, Joseph leaned back and let out a long breath.

"That was fun," he said. "Maybe we should move somewhere else."

Smirking and lifting one hand to the buttons of her dress, Anne was starting to lean in closer to him when she heard the squeak of the front door's hinges.

Reluctantly, Joseph took his eyes away from his wife and put on a quick smile. "Oh, hello there, Sam. What are you doing up?"

An eight-year-old boy stood in the doorway. He was small for his age, but had an intelligent glint in his eyes that was hard to miss. Actually, now that he was half asleep, it was a little easier to miss than normal. "Are we moving?" Sam asked.

"What? Oh, no," Joseph replied. "That was just talk. Why don't you go on back to bed?" Just as he got his son to turn around and head back into the house, Joseph saw his other child come right out behind him. "Laurie, you should be in bed, too," he said in a sterner tone of voice. "It's late."

Laurie was four years older than her brother.

She had her mother's features and soft hair, which was currently a mess due to her rolling out of bed. There was a toughness in her face, however, that had undeniably come from her father. "It's hard to sleep with all the noise you two are making," she said. "What are you doing out here?"

"Nothing," Anne said, after straightening her dress and checking her buttons. "Now go back to bed, the both of you."

Laurie smirked and took hold of her brother by his shoulders. "Ma and Pa want us to leave them alone. Why do you think that is?"

"Laurie!" Anne snapped.

Sam shrugged and pulled away from his sister so he could get back into the house. That left Laurie standing in place with her arms crossed and the same mischievous grin on her face. "You two were kissing, weren't you?" she asked sternly.

"So what if we were?" Joseph retorted.

"That's just . . ." After thinking about it for a second, Laurie shuddered and walked over to the swing. Without asking permission, she forced herself between them and sat with her arms folded across her chest. "I can't sleep, anyways."

"Well," Joseph said, "maybe you should try harder." It didn't take long for him to see that the girl wasn't intending on going anywhere. He could also see her head lolling back and her eyelids starting to droop. He draped his arm along the back of the swing so he could envelop his wife and daughter as they rocked back and forth.

Feeling the sway of the swing and the subtle movements of his daughter beside him, Joseph leaned his head back and let out another slow breath. Being a rancher with workers on his payroll and plenty to keep him busy, he was dead tired nearly every night. Because of that, he rarely got the chance to savor quiet moments such as these. Now, he drank in the coolness of the air as well as the sight of the blanket of stars spread out over his head. Each one glistened perfectly to form more shapes than he could ever remember. Rather than look at them as separate constellations, Joseph saw a giant work of art that changed each time he looked up. "It's a nice night," he said.

Anne looked over at him with a warm smile on her face and replied, "It sure is."

"Who's that, Pa?"

Joseph looked over at Anne first, but only got a puzzled shrug in response. "Who's . . . who?" he asked.

"Someone's coming," the girl stated. "I can hear horses."

When he looked down at his daughter, he saw the intensity on the girl's face as she listened carefully with her eyes shut tightly. Since he knew better than to second-guess her right away, Joseph closed his eyes and did his best to follow Laurie's example.

"I think I hear them, too," Anne said.

Joseph felt like he was cheating when he opened one eye to glance over at his wife. "Really?"

"I . . . think so."

"There's horses coming, Mother. I can hear them."

"Oh, well, sorry," Anne said, responding to the scolding tone in Laurie's voice. "I didn't mean to doubt you."

"It's all right."

As he sat on his porch, Joseph couldn't open his eyes all the way or even take too deep of a breath. Something in the back of his mind told him that he needed to keep listening for those horses. Laurie was known for waking up at the first chirp of a bird and hadn't told a fib since she'd gotten a scolding for it before Sam was born.

There were plenty of cattle out there, but Laurie had grown up on a ranch and would never mistake steers for horses. Besides, if there were cattle coming, it would more than likely be a stampede and would be impossible to miss. Joseph forced those things out of his mind and focused on the slow stirring of the breeze and the occasional bark of a coyote.

Finally, he heard it.

On a cloudy night, the rumble of horses' hooves might have been easily mistaken for distant thunder. His first suspicion was that some of the ranch hands were making their way back from town. But there were more horses out there than the number of hands he'd hired, and they wouldn't have been in such a hurry.

Joseph couldn't put his finger on it, but something just didn't set right with him. "You two get inside," he said.

Anne's eyes snapped open and she looked over at him. "Why?"

"Yeah, Pa. This is nice out here."

"Just, both of you do as I say and get inside!"

Both Anne and Laurie looked at Joseph with similar, shocked expressions.

Joseph forced a calmer tone into his voice. "I didn't mean to snap," he said while smiling and getting to his feet. "It's just getting cold and there might be coyotes out here."

"There's always coyotes out here," Laurie pointed out.

"There, you see? Now go inside and get to bed."

The girl moaned under her breath, but dropped down from the swing without much fuss. She stepped in front of Joseph, rose onto her tiptoes and grabbed hold of the front of his shirt. "Kiss me good night," she said, pulling her father down to her own level.

Joseph gladly obliged and even gave her a second quick kiss on the cheek as Laurie was turning toward the door.

Watching her husband and daughter, Anne couldn't help but grin at both of them. That faded a bit when she saw the grim shadow that fell over Joseph's face after Laurie went into the house. "What's the matter?" she asked.

"Those are horses and they're getting closer."

"You think it's someone from town?" Her face brightened a bit and she added, "I'll bet it's just some of the boys coming home after drinking."

"When the boys go out drinking, they sneak home like they think I'm going to scold them. Those horses sure as hell aren't sneaking."

"Then maybe they're just passing by," Anne said as she moved in closer to place her hands around the back of her husband's neck. "Why are you so worried?"

"I don't know. Please, just get inside and wait there for me to come get you. If you hear trouble, don't try to come out. Just take the kids, get the rifle and hide."

Some of the color drained from her face. "Now, you're really starting to scare me, Joseph. Do you think there could be—"

"I don't know," he interrupted. "That's what bothers me." Taking his wife by the hand, he led her to the front door and stepped inside. He grabbed one of the shotguns from the rack on the wall. He headed outside again.

Anne stopped at the threshold. "If there is . . ." Glancing back to the rooms where her children slept, she winced and then continued in a voice that she hoped her daughter couldn't hear. "If there is trouble, maybe you should fetch Sheriff Stilson."

Opening the shotgun and fitting in a few fresh shells, he said, "The sheriff's too far away."

"Then at least go to the bunkhouse. If it's empty,

you'll know it's the boys out having some fun. If it's not, at least get a few of them to come with you to check on those noises."

Joseph nodded. "That's a good idea."

Seeing the calm returning to her husband's face, Anne reached out to place her hand on his cheek. "Of course it's a good idea. It sure beats running out there with a loaded gun to spook someone else who might also be carrying a gun."

"I'll check the bunkhouse first. Now please, just stay in here and watch over those kids."

"I will." Anne leaned forward to press her lips against Joseph's. The hand that had been on his cheek slipped around to the back of his head so she could ruffle his hair while holding him close and prolonging their kiss. She opened her mouth just a bit so she could nibble on his bottom lip before easing away. "Hurry back," she whispered. "I've got plans for you."

"Me, too, darlin'."

Joseph stepped out and started to close the door. Before shutting it all the way, he stayed just long enough to see her step to the rack and reach for the second gun on the wall. Only then did he close the door tightly and put the house behind him.

The thunder of those horses was impossible to miss. Before, it had been a subtle grind in the distance, but now it had grown into a low roar. Joseph's hands reflexively tensed around his shotgun as he ran for the nearby stables. He pulled open one of the main doors and made a quick count of the animals inside. Most of them were gone. After fitting the reins around his own horse's neck, Joseph climbed onto its bare back and rode it outside.

His regular workers kept their horses in the stable, but some of the less-established ones preferred to tie them up outside the bunkhouse where they could see them. As Joseph rode up to the bunkhouse, he saw no animals there. Then he swung down and ran up to the door.

"Hey!" he shouted while knocking. "Anyone in there?"

He waited for a few more seconds before knocking again. There was no reply, so he opened the door and stepped inside.

It was empty.

According to his wife, that was a good sign. Joseph, on the other hand, wasn't so quick to be appeased. He climbed back onto his horse and rode straight toward the sound of approaching thunder.

SIX

———◆———

Joseph often said he knew his land well enough to walk it with his eyes closed. In the darkness that fell upon the ranch that night, he put that boast to the test by snapping his reins and coaxing his horse to go faster to meet the approaching horsemen. Every so often, he would veer one way or slow down somewhere else to avoid obstacles he knew were there. But he did such things without thinking. His mind was busy contemplating why his innards had twisted into a knot.

Once the sound of the horses was loud enough, Joseph pulled back on his reins and came to a stop. He stared into the shadows and was soon able to make out the shapes of the oncoming riders. He couldn't be certain, but it looked like there were at least a half dozen of them. The rancher could only guess how many more were hidden in the darkness.

Taking hold of his shotgun, Joseph felt his heart quicken in his chest as he watched them draw closer. He figured the men had spotted him by now, but not one of them was slowing down.

As they drew closer, Joseph raised his shotgun and sent a loud blast over the riders' heads. The flash from the muzzle lit up Joseph's face like a photographer's powder and a roar rolled through the air like a clap of thunder. He then brought his gun down and replaced the spent shell.

"Hold up," one of the riders shouted.

Joseph had lowered his barrel, but found himself bringing it up as he moved in a bit closer.

The rider who'd spoken raised one hand and waved it until all of the other men had slowed to match his pace. From there, they moved in a single wave toward Joseph.

Despite the uneven numbers, Joseph sat tall in the saddle and rode forward with a challenging glare in his eyes. "You men are on my property," he said while squinting to get a better look at the rider's face.

"Sorry about that. Did we wake you?"

Joseph held his ground. "Who are you?"

The man who rode forward quickly straightened up. His close-set eyes were narrowed at first, but widened as if to soak up every last detail of Joseph's face. His own face was dark and appeared sunken in the moonlight, though it wouldn't have looked any friendlier in better light.

"You're Van Meter," the man said.

"That's right. This is my land."

"You take a shot at everyone who happens to ride across your property line? I feel awfully sorry for your neighbors if'n they have dogs or little ones running about."

That elicited a chuckle from the men behind the rider, but not so much as a smirk from Joseph.

"I just wanted to get your attention," Joseph said. "Now that I got it, I can show you the quickest way onto the trail headed south or point you toward Ocean. There's plenty to do in town, if that's what you're after."

"We were in town. We didn't see no ocean."

"If it's the Pacific you're after, you'll need to ride west."

Cocking his head a bit, the rider looked to a skinny, pale-skinned man behind him and asked, "Why do you think they call that town Ocean, Bertram? Maybe our host, Mister Van Meter, knows."

The other man didn't answer. All he did was shrug and lean forward with both hands piled over his saddle horn. At the moment, Joseph realized he was the only one brandishing a weapon. The riders simply looked back at him.

"From what I hear, the town didn't have a proper name when it sprung up," Joseph said. "Then someone came along complaining about not being able to see the water and an old man wrote the word Ocean on a sign. He pointed to it and said, 'There's yer damn ocean.'"

The riders broke into laughter. A few of them even had to swipe at their eyes after a time. No one laughed more than the riders' leader, who nodded and tried to speak a few times, but couldn't get anything out.

Finally, Dutch pulled in a breath and steadied himself. "And that's how the town was named?"

"That's the story," Joseph replied.

"That's funny as hell."

As many times as he'd heard the story, Joseph still found it amusing. Hearing all the other men laugh so hard at it made it seem even funnier this time around. "So where are you men headed?" he asked.

"We're headed to your ranch," Dutch said. "From what I hear, you keep all the money and valuables in that nice, big house over yonder."

"What?"

"You heard me."

All of the humor had drained from Dutch's voice and the men around him were now staring at Joseph the way hungry dogs stare at a bit of raw meat. Joseph brought his shotgun to bear on them, which still didn't throw any of the riders off their game.

Of the seven men now gathered in front of Joseph, six of them had skinned their weapons and were taking aim. The seventh kept his head down and his hands folded in front of him.

"Get the hell off my property," Joseph snarled. "Right now!"

Dutch shook his head slowly. "That ain't no way to talk. We were just getting along so well."

"I swear to Christ, I'll shoot."

"You got two shots and you're too far to make good use of either of 'em. The best thing for you to do is just take us back to the house and hand over what you got."

"There's not enough to warrant all of this," Joseph told him. "I don't even have enough to keep a steady group of hands on my payroll."

But Dutch just kept shaking his head. "You got enough to pay almost a dozen men and you pay them real well. You also keep a stash under yer house to save for the futures of them precious little children." Leveling his gaze and narrowing his eyes, Dutch added, "If I don't get enough to make this worth the effort, I know some Mexicans who'd be more than happy to buy them pretty women of yours."

Joseph put the shotgun against his shoulder and pointed the barrel directly at Dutch's face. "You men turn around and leave right now, or I'll pull this trigger. My guess is that you don't have what it takes to see if you're right about me being out of my range."

Dutch kept his eyes fixed upon Joseph as he said, "You hear that, Bertram? The rancher thinks he's a killer."

Joseph didn't see Dutch move a muscle. All he saw was a flicker of movement followed by the crack of a single pistol shot. The bullet hit him like a sledgehammer, twisting his torso around and knocking him off the back end of his horse. Joseph pulled his trigger somewhere along the way, but knew he would have been lucky to hit anything with a pulse. When he heard the men laughing at him, Joseph knew his luck had run out.

"Nice shot, Dutch," Bertram said. "Someone go get that shotgun from him before he hurts himself."

Every inch of Joseph's body hurt from the landing he'd taken. His knees flared up when he tried to move. His ribs practically exploded when he sucked in a breath, and even his teeth seemed to have been cracked during the fall.

As the sound of footsteps drew closer, Joseph tried to reach for his shotgun, but could barely move his arm. He could feel the familiar iron against his fingertips, but couldn't get his hand to close around the grip. Before he could try again, one of the riders stepped right up to him and took the shotgun away.

When Joseph felt the cool touch of a gun barrel against the top of his head, he closed his eyes and drew in what little strength he had.

"Mind if I kill him now, Dutch?" the rider asked.

Gritting his teeth, Joseph rolled over and swung his arm out with one burst of desperate strength to knock the gun from the hand that had been holding it. The weapon landed with a heavy thump not far from Joseph's other arm and he somehow got his fingers around it.

Rather than pick out a target, Joseph pointed at the first solid thing he could see and pulled the trigger. The pistol bucked against his palm and let out a satisfyingly loud roar. Hot lead flew from the barrel, drilling a messy hole through the rider's knee and speeding out the other side amid a spray of blood and slivers of bone.

"God DAMN!" the rider howled as he dropped to the ground in an awkward heap. He fired a wild shot, which came closer to hitting Joseph's horse than the man himself.

Joseph gritted his teeth and turned to fire at the remaining horsemen. Pulling his trigger quickly, he fired a round at one of the closest men, but was quickly stopped by return fire from Dutch. At first, Joseph thought the nearby horse had clipped him. The impact felt more like a punch or wild kick. When the burning set in, Joseph felt dizzy and wavered. Even so, he still fought to keep his arm steady so he could pull his trigger one more time.

Another shot cracked through the air, followed by a sharp clang and a burst of sparks as the bullet ricocheted off the gun in Joseph's hand. When the pistol fell from Joseph's grasp, it might as well have dropped to the bottom of a ravine.

"Will you look at that?" Dutch said. "This rancher's got some real fight in him. He's putting on a hell of a show."

"I'll show you his fucking brains in a second," the horseman with the wounded knee snarled.

"Not so fast."

It took a moment for those words to register, since the fallen horseman was still lightheaded from the shot he'd taken in his knee. As he prepared to pull his trigger, he suddenly felt himself being hauled up by his hair and shaken like a rag doll.

"You heard what Dutch said," Bertram grunted, as he lifted the horseman up like he was carrying a dog by the scruff of its neck. "Not . . . so . . . fast."

The horseman hadn't seen or heard Bertram climb down from his saddle. After being shaken enough for his knee to be rattled, it was all he could do to keep from passing out. "Fine," he wheezed. "Fine."

Bertram looked over to Dutch.

Twisting in his saddle to focus on the horseman who hadn't drawn his pistol, Dutch asked, "You know exactly where to find what we're lookin' for, George?"

The silent man at the back of the row shook his head reluctantly.

"Then the rancher's coming with us. Carry him back to the house."

Despite the paltry moonlight, Joseph could make out a set of familiar features as he inspected the previously quiet man. "George?" Joseph wheezed. "What . . . what are you doing with these men?"

"Go on, George," Dutch taunted. "Go over there and tell him all about what you've been doing."

Since he knew there was no other alternative, George lowered himself from his saddle and walked over to Joseph. He could feel Dutch's eyes boring through him, waiting for him to take one misstep.

George went to Joseph's side, bent down and started taking hold of Joseph's good arm. "You need to come with us."

"You've worked for me for the better part of a year," Joseph said. "I took good care of you. My wife cooked meals for you. You . . . you played with my children!"

George only shook his head as he lifted Joseph to his feet. About halfway up, Joseph started to struggle and fight against the younger man's grasp.

"Put me down!" Joseph said. "Let me go, you son of a bitch!"

Leaning in closer, George whispered, "It's too late to do anything about this now. If you stay here, they'll kill you."

"And what if I go with them?"

George started to answer, but cut himself short and lowered his head. Pulling Joseph toward his horse became easier as Joseph lost more blood. By the time the horsemen started toward the house again, the rancher lay across the back of George's saddle, barely conscious enough to put up a fight.

SEVEN

Sheriff Stilson knocked on the front door of a small house two streets away from his office. After a few seconds of listening to the rustling inside, he knocked again. Finally, the door opened and a squat man with an unkempt beard stuck his head outside.

"What?" the short man asked.

"Come on, Miguel. Time to earn what I pay you."

Miguel glanced over his shoulder and leaned a bit farther outside. "Not now. I've got important business in here."

"Tell her to come back some other time," Stilson said. "We're riding out to the Van Meter place."

"All the way out there? Why?"

"Because someone said there was trouble, now throw on your boots and let's go."

"This is a bullshit reason to pull me out of my home at—"

"Come along now or you're fired."

Miguel froze with his mouth half open. "I'll get my boots."

A minute or so later, Stilson and Miguel were riding toward the edge of town. Miguel had the stout shape of a man who seemed very uncomfortable on top of a horse. His short legs barely reached the stirrups, and spent more time flailing to keep his balance than anything else. His face was twisted into an expression of utter concentration and was so pale, it looked as if he'd forgotten what the sun looked like.

"You always treat me worse than the other deputies," Miguel grunted.

Laughing to himself, Stilson asked, "And why's that?"

"Simple. You don't like Mexicans."

The sheriff scowled. He took a slow gander at the deputy and scowled some more. "You're Mexican?"

"Miguel ain't no white man's name."

"All right. I just changed my first name to Ping. Guess that makes me Chinese."

"Real funny. What sort of trouble is supposed to be at that ranch?"

"Some gang of robbers or something. The undertaker saw them coming through town."

"That undertaker's trouble, if you ask me." Suddenly, Miguel grimaced and looked to one side of the street. "Are you talking about the Van Meter place?"

Exasperated, Stilson said, "Yes."

"A bunch of hands from there were headed into town not too long ago."

"Really?"

Miguel nodded. "I saw 'em over on Eighth Street."

Stilson grinned and nodded. "You mean on the corner by Stormy's cathouse?"

Miguel rolled his eyes. "You see? That's the sort of disrespect I was talking about."

"Was it by Stormy's?"

". . . Yes."

"That'd be the Wheelbarrow. We can swing by there to see if those men saw anything suspicious. Good work, Miguel."

The deputy straightened up and smiled. He also knew a real good shortcut to Stormy's.

The sheriff stepped up to the front door of the Wheelbarrow Saloon. Right next to that door was the very device from which the place took its name. As always, a drunk was passed out within the wheelbarrow with his arm and leg hanging out over the side. Stilson walked inside without sparing a glance at the drunk to immediately pick out a group of young men standing at the bar.

"You boys from the Van Meter spread?" Stilson asked as he walked up to them.

One of the taller men turned around and nodded. "We are."

"Howdy, Raymond," Miguel said. "Still losing at poker?"

The ranch hand tipped his hat good-naturedly and said, "Only man in town who's worse than you."

"Looks like almost all the hired hands from Van Meter's ranch are at this bar," Stilson said.

"Damn near," Raymond replied. "Celebrating what looks to be a mighty nice salary raise. We're just waiting for a few more before everything gets started."

"A few more what?"

"George is supposed to be bringing Mister Van Meter over here so we can buy him a round of drinks. Considering how much of a raise we're getting, it's the least we can do."

"Everyone's supposed to meet here? Ain't that a long way to go for a celebration?"

Raymond shrugged. "George said we should do more than pass a bottle of whiskey around, especially considering how much Mister Van Meter's done for us. Since we don't get into town that often, I wasn't inclined to disagree."

"Makes sense to me," Miguel said.

"Was there any trouble at the ranch before you left?" Stilson asked.

The confused look on Raymond's face told more than any words could. "Trouble? What sort of trouble?"

"I got word that a bunch of armed men were headed toward that place."

Raymond shook his head. "I've been here for an

hour or so, along with most of the others. What about you, Eddie? You just got here a minute ago. You see anything on your way in?"

Eddie was a tall man with a dark beard and a narrow face. At first, he looked around as if he didn't know Raymond was talking to him. Then, he shook his head. "Nope."

"And how long ago did you make that ride?" Stilson asked.

"Like Raymond said, I just got here."

The sheriff mulled that over for a few seconds and then turned toward the door. "Thanks for your help, boys."

"Is Mister Van Meter in trouble with someone?" Raymond asked. "If he is, I wouldn't mind helping take care of it. Plenty of us wouldn't."

"Great!" Miguel chimed in. "With all that help, I can get back to—"

"We don't need any help," Stilson quickly said, "but thanks for the offer."

"So it ain't anything too serious?"

"Doesn't look like it. Looks more like someone got spooked and jumped to some conclusions. You all enjoy your party and give my best to your boss."

"Will do."

Stilson walked to the front door and Miguel was more than happy to follow. Once outside, the sheriff stopped and took a dented cigarette case from his shirt pocket.

"What a load of shit, huh?" Miguel said.

Stilson didn't respond to that. He was too busy putting a cigarette in his mouth and striking a match to light it.

Miguel nodded as if he was listening to a voice from somewhere else and looked up and down the street. "I guess you don't need backup after all."

"So long as Raymond got his story right."

"I hate that guy."

"Why's that?"

"He's an asshole."

Stilson chuckled and breathed out twin streams of smoke from his nostrils. "That undertaker's wife saw something. I believe that much. Maybe we should go out to that graveyard and have a look."

"Now? It's the middle of the night! We won't be able to see anything."

"We'll be able to see a campfire burning or a group of armed men between here and there. If there's a gang like that near my town, I don't want them riding loose and unaccounted for. I don't give a damn where they're headed."

"It doesn't sound like a job for two," Miguel grunted.

"All right, then," Stilson said as he took the cigarette between his thumb and forefinger. "You check that graveyard on your own."

Miguel froze and muttered under his breath. Still shaking his head, he climbed onto his horse. "With the both of us working on it, we shouldn't be gone for more than half an hour. If anyone's out there, we'll know. If they're camping out between here and that ranch, it'll take all night and day to search that much ground."

"You got anything better to do?" Stilson asked in a tone that made it clear he wasn't kidding around.

Miguel slowly shook his head. "Doesn't look like it."

Stilson reached out to slap his deputy on the back. "There's no need to search between here and the ranch. If there was a gang of bandits riding to the Van Meter place, one of those hands would have seen them. They ride back and forth so many times, they'd probably know if a tree was missing a few of its branches.

"And if you're worried about that lady getting bored while you're gone, just tell her the next time you see her how you got wrapped up chasing down a desperate band of killers. She might even throw you one for free."

It wasn't long before Miguel smirked and nodded. "Good idea!"

They rode to the graveyard at a quick pace and arrived in good time. The trickle of moonlight was just enough for the headstones to stand out like giant nails in an old piece of wood.

Both lawmen did a quick circle of the graveyard and stopped once they reached their starting point. Eventually, Stilson looked over to his deputy and asked, "Are you Mexican?"

"My father is. No, wait. My father's half-brother was. I'm named after him."

Stilson nodded and fished for another cigarette. As he struck it, he saw Miguel's eyes widen and his jaw drop open.

"What is it?" Stilson asked.

Raising a trembling finger, Miguel pointed to a figure crawling out from the surrounding trees and moaning softly. "Wh—what the hell is THAT?"

EIGHT

Joseph woke to the crack of a gunshot followed by shattering glass. He strained to open his eyes and was immediately rewarded for his efforts by a healthy dose of pain, which flooded through every inch of him.

Men shouted and hollered as horses thundered to and fro. There was more breaking glass, which was now joined by the crackle of flames.

When Joseph heard that crackling, his senses came back to him in a rush. He pulled in a deep breath and immediately choked on it. The acrid taste of smoke filled his nose and stuck to the back of his throat. He could hear wood splintering and more windows being broken. He could also hear a familiar voice raised in a terrified scream.

"Leave us alone!" Anne shouted.

Although he couldn't make out the words that followed, Joseph could tell they were being spoken by angry men. The night was then split apart by the blast of a rifle.

Joseph wanted to shout to his wife. He wanted

to see if she was all right or at least still alive. He wanted her to know he was nearby and would help her, but he couldn't do a damn thing. He still couldn't even see.

Another voice drifted nearby, growing clearer as a door slammed open. "Bitch shot me!" he said. "She's got a damn gun."

The reply came from much closer than Joseph had been expecting. "Then take the gun away from her," Dutch shouted. "Or is handling one woman too hard for you?"

Joseph struggled to open his eyes. Finally, he realized that his eyes had come open the first time he'd tried. The only problem was that he was laying face down over the back of a horse and was staring at the animal's flank.

Thankfully, the spots where he'd been shot had mostly gone numb. Gritting his teeth, Joseph got his arms moving and pushed himself back until he felt his weight sliding along the curve of the horse's back.

When his boots touched against the ground, Joseph expected to crumple over, but he managed to keep his balance and hold onto the horse for support. Now that he didn't have a face full of horsehair, he could take in his surroundings.

Like a nightmare, shadows clung to the sky like thick tar. The bunkhouse was on fire and the flames roared up even higher as Joseph watched. Men were going in and out of the stables, taking what horses were there and lining them up next to Dutch and one of the other riders.

Dutch sat on his horse less than ten paces from Joseph. He nodded in appreciation of the scene in front of him, but most of his attention was focused upon the main house, where several men were headed for the front door.

"The money's in there," George said, pointing to the ranch house.

"You sure about that?" Dutch asked.

"Yeah. I know it's in there somewhere! Try under the floor."

"You hear that?" Dutch shouted to the men near the house. "Look under the floor. Pull the damn thing up if you have to."

The man that had stumbled out the front door took off his hat and ran his hand through his hair before stuffing his hat back on. "That bitch with the gun's in the big bedroom."

"Then pull her outta there. If we don't get that money, this whole damn trip's for nothing!"

The man nodded and then marched back into the house.

Joseph could picture Anne and the children with their backs to a wall and one old hunting rifle separating them from the unthinkable. He balled up his fists and started to lunge forward, but was stopped suddenly by what felt like a lead weight dropped onto his shoulder. Joseph wheeled around to take a swing at whoever had stopped him. His fist made it about halfway around before it was stopped by a callused hand sporting four and a half fingers.

The weathered man who fixed his eyes upon Joseph placed a finger from his free hand up to his lips. Just the fact that this other man was crouched and hiding right along with him made Joseph trust him a bit. He felt even better when the man's face struck a chord in his memory.

"You're . . . the undertaker?" Joseph whispered. "Nicolai Graves, wasn't it?"

Nick nodded, glancing around to make sure that Joseph's question hadn't been heard through all the other noise. Seeing that the closest horsemen were still looking away, Nick turned toward an outhouse and motioned for Joseph to follow.

It pained him to move away from the house rather than toward it, but anyplace was better than the spot he'd been. Both men kept low and scurried around the outhouse. Once they were behind that small bit of cover, Joseph leaned back against the shack and took a moment to collect himself.

"How bad are you hurt?" Nick asked.

Joseph shook his head quickly as if he was just waking up. "What are you doing here? How'd you get to me so easily?"

"It wasn't easy, trust me. Do you have any weapons stashed?"

"I need to get to the house. There's other men around. Lots more." Just then, Joseph caught sight of a shape spread out on the ground a few paces from where he was standing. After squinting a bit, he saw two men piled on top of each other. Neither of them was moving.

"Did you . . . ?"

Nick interrupted Joseph's question by repeating his own. "Do you have any weapons stashed? Anything at all we can use?"

"There's an old pistol in the house. Oh, and a few more pistols behind the bunkhouse. That's where my hired hands store their guns, since I don't want them walking around my children heeled."

"Take me to those guns."

Joseph started for the bunkhouse, but Nick stopped him before he stepped out from behind the outhouse. Nick leaned past him and took a quick look around while motioning for Joseph to stay put. After a few seconds, he waved and rushed toward the burning building.

Rifle shots blasted from within the house, followed by more screams. Joseph's first impulse was to start running that way.

"No," Nick hissed. "You'll just get yourself killed. If there's more weapons to be had, we need to get them. We're already outnumbered."

"I don't even know for certain if the guns are there. My ranch hands . . . they're behind this or some might even be dead. Besides," he added, pointing toward the raging fire, "whatever guns are there are about to be melted down."

Another shout filled the air, but didn't come

from a woman or any children. It came from one
of the horsemen, who let out a piercing whistle and
tugged on a bunch of reins gathered up in his hand.
He and the horses from Joseph's stable ran away
from the circle of buildings and headed south into
the night.

"You see that?" Dutch shouted while glancing
over his shoulder. "You awake back there to see
this? If you are, you might want to do your family
a favor and . . ." Dutch's voice trailed off and was
soon followed by an eruption of obscenities ending
with, "The rancher's gone! Somebody find him,
goddamn it!"

Nick barely managed to reach out and grab hold
of Joseph's arm before the rancher bolted toward
his house.

"Let go of me," Joseph snarled. "My family
needs me!"

"You'll be captured or killed in a second if you
run out there like that. Come with me and we
might be able to turn this around."

Joseph shook his head slowly. "I can't wait any
longer. If anything happens to them . . ."

"Then at least take this," Nick said.

When Joseph looked down, he saw a small revolver in Nick's hand. He reached out to take it,
only to have it snatched away at the last possible
moment.

Having caught a bit of movement from the corner of his eye, Nick turned on the balls of his feet
toward it and gripped the pistol tightly. After a

quarter turn, he saw an armed man rushing toward him and taking aim.

In the space of a half second, Nick weighed his options and realized the element of surprise was going to be blown no matter who pulled their trigger. Nick's hand flashed to the holster buckled over his stomach and took hold of his pistol's grip. His fingers seemed to melt into the specially carved handle and the gun came out as if it had a will of its own. Pointing the weapon like an extension of his own arm, Nick took his shot, which knocked the other man off his feet.

"Take this," Nick said while tossing the other pistol to Joseph. "But don't waste your bullets."

Joseph grabbed the gun and rushed toward the main house. Nick was about to follow when he saw some more figures running toward him from another direction. The larger of the two didn't even notice the body lying on the ground. He was too busy chasing the smaller one, a four-foot bundle of flailing arms and legs.

"Get back here, you little shit," the man grunted.

Nick caught sight of the little boy's face and was drawn to a pair of wide, terrified eyes. The boy's mouth hung open in a silent scream. Since Joseph was already gone, Nick ran to help the child.

Still reaching out to try and grab the boy, the boy's pursuer glanced over to Nick and he immediately shifted to guard against him. His gun arm bent at the elbow, allowing him to fire off a quick hipshot. The bullet blazed through empty air, forcing Nick to duck rather than fire back.

As he rushed toward the boy and his attacker, Nick saw a second armed man close in on the kid from behind.

"Look behind you, boy!" Nick shouted.

The kid flinched and huddled down out of fear, rooting himself to the spot.

Nick swung his arm around to fire a shot at the second man to buy a few more seconds for the boy to escape. Just as he tightened a finger around his trigger, Nick heard the first gunman fire again. The bullet came closer than the first, but snagged Nick's coat rather than anything vital. Nick returned fire, which sent the first gunman diving for cover. Pulling his trigger again, Nick put a round into the gunman's chest before he hit the ground.

By this time, the first gunman was running straight for Nick. Before Nick could react, the gunman reached out and shoved the barrel of his pistol in Nick's face.

Nick swiped his left arm up and out to knock the man's gun away. The pistol discharged a round straight up, but remained in its owner's hand. Nick then swung his other hand in a vicious chopping motion, which ended with his gun's handle slamming down upon the other man's collarbone.

Letting out a surprised grunt, the gunman dropped to one knee. The next thing he felt was Nick's knee slamming into his face. There was a dull thump before the gunman's head snapped back. His eyes were still open, but completely vacant as he hit the ground on his back.

Nick could hear people shouting and a woman screaming. Men were swearing and shooting at each other. All of that chaos swirled amid the building roar of flames as the fire spread from the bunkhouse and made its way to the other buildings, filling Nick's senses until everything became damn near incomprehensible.

The one thing he could focus on was that boy.

The kid was scared and still running for his life.

It was only due to the raging fire that Nick had enough light to catch sight of the boy as he raced toward the open land surrounding the circle of buildings. There was a rumble of hooves in the distance, which may very well have been a stampede of spooked cattle.

Without another thought, Nick took off after the boy. He prayed Joseph could hold on until he got back.

NINE

———•———

Anne was screaming.

Through all the gunshots and men shouting back and forth, Joseph could hear his wife's panicked screams as plain as day. Those screams drove him forward, in spite of the pain that lanced through his body.

Joseph raised the gun Nick had given him and thumbed back the trigger. His eyes anxiously searched for a target.

A skinny man with a grimy face and sparse beard walked out the front door of Joseph's house dragging Laurie by the arm. His bony hand clutched her wrist, bringing a pained wince to her face with each step. The man didn't even look to his left as he came out. He was too intent on making sure he had Dutch's attention.

"Lookee here what I found!" the man said. "This sweet little thang looks real tasty, don't she? Can I keep her?"

Laurie struggled against the man's grip, but wasn't strong enough to break it. She kicked and screamed and punched, but that only served to widen the smile on her captor's face. Behind the girl, Anne's shouts were eclipsed by the sounds of breaking furniture and heavy fists landing again and again.

Just then, Laurie heard a voice cut through the chaos.

"Close your eyes, sweetie."

Laurie stopped fighting and looked in the direction of the voice. When she saw her father standing to one side with a gun in his hand, she hunkered down and did exactly as she was told.

Joseph fired at the man holding his daughter. The man's head snapped back as his face exploded amid a spray of blood. His grip loosened and he fell back into the doorway of the house.

Laurie peeked out from behind her eyelids and started to run toward her father. She was stopped by a bullet that tore through her right calf muscle and sent her, stumbling, to the ground.

"See what happens when you don't follow the plan?" Dutch asked as he rode forward with smoke still curling from the gun in his hand.

Rushing toward his daughter, Joseph didn't bother looking at anything else around him. He dropped to his knees and scooped her up with his free arm. "It's all right, Laurie. Daddy's here."

The twelve-year-old was only slightly shorter than her mother, but felt light as a feather in his arms. She winced and blinked a few times, but was more than able to wrap her arms around him and hold him tight. "Ma's still inside, they're—"

From inside the house, Anne let out another scream. The sound of it ripped a hole through Joseph's heart. When he looked into the house, all he could see was a mess of overturned shelves, splintered wood and shattered glass. He picked his daughter up and started inside.

"What the hell do you think you're gonna do?" Dutch asked, watching the scene with an amused grin as more and more of his men gathered around him. "You got lucky and killed a few of my men, but you don't think you're actually walking out of here, do you?"

Joseph was still moving. As much as he wanted to run to his wife's aid, he wasn't about to put his daughter down. The only compromise he could stomach was carrying her with him as he headed toward the dwindling sound of his wife's screams. "Where's your brother?" he asked Laurie.

Laurie was breathing in frantic gulps. Between them, she said, "He ran off when they kicked the door in. I don't know where he is."

"Watch yourself in there, boys!" Dutch shouted from outside as if he was watching a show. "You're about to get some company!"

Joseph was glad to hear the sounds of fighting from his bedroom come to a quick stop. He was even glad to see the men start drifting out to meet him. "Stay right here." He set Laurie down. "I'm coming right back."

The girl's face was pale and her leg was bloody.

The moment she was lowered onto one of the few chairs that was still standing, she pressed her hands to the fresh wound and forced herself to breathe deeply.

Without hesitation, Joseph raised his gun and took a shot. His bullet clipped one of the intruders, but wasn't enough to hold them off. The shot was immediately answered by several more from the men, who pulled their triggers as quickly as they could manage.

Joseph felt a few jolts of pain, which were like a small animal's teeth biting viciously into his flesh. He ignored them and fired again and again until one of his shots managed to drop the closest gunman. Shifting his aim to the next closest man, he shouted, "I'm coming for you, Anne! Just hold on!"

That promise could be heard even over the crackle of return gunfire and the slap of a hammer against empty bullet casings.

Once they saw that Joseph had emptied his gun, the intruders stopped firing and came out from behind the cover they'd managed to find. The men began to chuckle. One of them walked over and stood in front of Joseph, dropped his spent pistol into a double-rig holster, and drew another to replace it.

"What should we do with him?" the man shouted.

From outside, Dutch asked, "He still alive, Bertram?"

Bertram looked down at Joseph's face and studied it. The whiskers of his mustache hung just below his chin and skewed at odd angles when he smirked. "Yep."

"Bring him out!"

Joseph gathered his strength and swung his empty pistol, which smacked against Bertram's leg. Bertram answered by using his own pistol to deliver a devastating blow to the side of Joseph's neck. Laurie screamed as she watched her father drop.

"Bring them all out!" Dutch commanded.

When Joseph finally reopened his eyes, he was looking down at the ground and his own two legs bent beneath him. He tried to move his arms, but quickly realized they were each being held by a different gunman. Joseph tried to struggle, but barely had the strength to lift his head. Just then, the gunman to his left grabbed Joseph by the hair and lifted his head for him.

Dutch and two other horsemen stood a few paces away. One of the horsemen was in the middle of saying something, but Joseph's ears were roaring and he didn't catch all of it.

". . . herd into New Mexico by next week."

"Good," Dutch replied. "Do you how many head the others rounded up?"

"About twice as many as we got from the last place."

"Perfect." Finally looking over to Joseph, Dutch

said, "I was just about to lose patience with you. Did you want to see your wife?"

"An . . . Anne?" Joseph groaned through all the pain flooding through him.

"Show the man his wife, Bertram."

The hand that had been grabbing Joseph's hair wrenched to one side and twisted Joseph's face around. Joseph couldn't see much, but he could make out shreds of Anne's dress on the bloody mess of the body lying beside him.

Joseph's stomach clenched. "Jesus."

"You're the one fighting to get to her," Dutch sneered. "I could have told you not to waste your time. You might like to know that your boy got away from the house, although I'm sure he's being tended to as we speak. My guess is that you won't want to get a look at him, either."

"Wh—why? Why do this?"

"I think he's talking to you, Georgie. You want to answer the man?"

The ranch hand was on a horse, sitting quietly nearby in much the same way he'd been when Joseph had seen him earlier that night. Now, as before, the young man could only look at Joseph for a second before averting his eyes.

"I got to hand it to you, Mister Van Meter," Dutch said. "You gave us much more of a fight than we ever got on any of these jobs. Maybe after folks hear about what happened here, they won't get as worked up as you did when they see us coming."

"Laurie?"

Dutch squinted and cocked his head for a moment before finally nodding. "Oh, you mean your little girl? You want to see her too? I can arrange that if you tell me where you keep that stash of money of yours. The missus down there wasn't too helpful."

Joseph held his eyes shut as the fresh images of his wife coursed through him in an unwelcome torrent. He gnashed his teeth and clenched his fists, sapping nearly all the strength his body had left.

"She didn't know anything," Joseph snarled.

Dutch nodded and said, "I guessed as much. My boys may have had their fun, but there ain't a woman alive who would keep quiet through all of that. If you're more helpful, I might let you see that pretty little girl of yours."

"It's under the boards in my den," Joseph said quickly. "Take it and go!"

Dutch threw a quick nod to his right. "Go get it, Georgie."

As much as he wanted to pull his arms free, Joseph simply couldn't. He felt like a damp sheet hanging from a line. "You . . . didn't have to do all this."

"Maybe not," Dutch said. "But variety is the spice of life."

George came out of the house with a strongbox under his arm. "I found the money, Dutch."

"Now show me my daughter, you bastard!" Joseph shouted.

"You want to see her, Mister Van Meter?"

In the few times he'd wondered what hell was like, Joseph had never even considered anything this bad. The possibilities that raced through his mind only got worse the longer he thought about what his family had endured.

"I think he does want to see her," Dutch finally said. "Go on and show him."

This time, Joseph's head was twisted in the other direction. The sharpness of the movement sent a warm pain through his neck, which he felt as much as a raindrop was felt against the surface of an ocean.

The girl's eyes were blackened, but they were open and alive. Her entire body shook as tears streamed down her cheeks.

"You see?" Dutch said. "I'm not such a bad fellow. I waited around all this time to see if you'd wake up just to make certain you'd have something to watch." With that, Dutch looked to one of the gunmen and nodded.

The sound of a hammer being cocked back echoed through Joseph's ears. From the corner of his eye, he saw the gun. Since he didn't have the strength to fight, he savored the sight of his daughter's face one more time. Forcing the last bit of fortitude into his voice, Joseph told her, "Close your eyes, sweetie."

TEN

When Joseph's senses slowly leaked back into him, he could still smell burning wood. The scent of blood was still in his nose and his stomach was still knotted in the tight grip of panic and rage. Something touched his forehead and when he tried to bat it away, he felt practically every bone in his body cry for mercy.

"Take it easy," a voice told him. "Lie back and try to—"

But Joseph would have none of it and desperately tried to silence whoever it was that had spoken to him.

"Nick! He's awake! I need your help!"

The door to the little cabin swung open and heavy steps pounded against the floor. Soon another shape came into Joseph's view, and it was enough to get him to stop struggling for a second.

Holding Joseph's arms against the bed, Nick looked down at him and nodded. "He sure is coming around. Feels like he's got some of his strength back, to boot."

"Where am I?" Joseph snarled.

"You're in my home and I'd appreciate it if you didn't try to punch my wife."

Joseph stopped struggling so he could take a better look around. His first glimpse told him he was in a cabin. As his vision cleared, he saw the woman looking over Nick's shoulder. She was smiling warmly and had her thick black hair tied behind her head.

"Nicolai?" Joseph asked.

"I'm flattered you remember. You can call me Nick. This is my wife, Catherine."

Looking back to the brunette, Joseph said, "Sorry about that."

"Don't mention it. I'm just glad you missed."

All Joseph could manage was a shaky grin, but that only lasted for a heartbeat. He tried to sit up, but couldn't even get halfway before a flood of pain brought him down again. A gentle hand pressed down upon his chest to keep him from making another attempt.

"Not just yet," Catherine said.

"How long have I been here?"

"The better part of a week." Furrowing her brow, Catherine bit on her lower lip. "Actually it's been just over a week. It sure does feel a lot longer than that since you were brought in here. I stitched you all up, and you didn't wake up for more than a few minutes of it."

Joseph slowly brushed his fingers along the most painful spots and reached up to touch his left temple. The moment his fingertip grazed that part of his head, he thought his skull was going to crack open.

"Easy, there," Catherine said. "That wound's still a little tender."

"I . . . don't remember how this happened," Joseph muttered.

"My guess is that was the shot that was supposed to put you down for good. Seems like you had an angel looking over your shoulder who had other plans."

Gritting his teeth, Joseph lowered his hand said, "Feels like you did a good job on the stitches."

"I've had a lot of practice."

"Nick brought me here?"

She nodded.

"Why?"

"Because you were still alive and he wanted you to stay that way. He drove you here on the back of his wagon and we've been taking care of you ever since."

"What about those sons of bitches that . . ." Joseph couldn't even finish his question before the rage swelled up to fill the back of his throat.

"They're gone," Catherine said gently. Before she could say any more, the front door swung open again and Nick's voice drifted through the cabin.

"Can you help him sit up?" Nick asked.

Grudgingly, Catherine slid an arm behind Joseph's shoulders. "You're going to have to help me a bit," she said. "I'm almost as tired as you right about now."

Joseph let out a breath and strained to make her work a bit easier. Even after a pillow was slipped behind him, Joseph barely had enough willpower to open his eyes. "You should have left me where I was."

"Don't say that," Nick told him. "At least, not until you see who I've got with me."

Looking through the slits of his eyes, Joseph saw a small figure stepping around from behind Nick's tall silhouette. That was all he needed to snap his eyes fully open and nearly get him jumping off the bed. "Sam? Is that you?"

The little boy rushed to his father and hugged him desperately. Despite the pain caused by those slender arms wrapped around him, Joseph was happier than he'd ever thought he could be. Just the smell of the eight-year-old's hair was enough to make him let out a joyous sigh.

"I thought I wasn't . . . I . . . I'm so glad to see you, son."

"Me too, Daddy."

With his son's face pressed against him, Joseph looked across the room at Nick. Just as he was about to ask a question, he saw Nick shake his head and start to walk away. Joseph was more than glad to spend some time with Sam. It didn't matter much what else had come before.

Nick stepped outside and shut the door behind

him. A few paces away, Catherine leaned against the narrow wagon that carried Nick's tools when it wasn't carrying one of the caskets or headstones he'd created. A hot breeze blew stray wisps of hair into her face and she brushed them back.

"What happens to them now?" she asked.

Nick glanced over his shoulder at the cabin as if he could see right through it. It wasn't as big as some of the houses in town, but it was home and he'd put it together with his own hands. When he turned back around, he saw Catherine and the wagon outlined against the wide stretch of hills.

He shrugged and walked over to her. Placing his hands on her hips, he said, "I don't really know. To be honest, I was expecting to bury him."

"Is that why you tried to keep the boy from his bedside?"

"I guess."

"And here I thought you had some grand design in mind when you dragged him here. You seemed so certain that we didn't bring a doctor. Was that just so I could practice my sewing skills?"

"Between the two of us, we've got more than enough experience with dressing up bullet wounds. Besides, you did a fine job."

Catherine's smile lasted for all of two seconds. After that, she fixed him with a glare that was almost enough to back Nick off completely. "That man in there almost died. Could you have that on your conscience?"

"I've got a lot worse."

"What about the law? Shouldn't they know Mister Van Meter is here?"

"They knew about the men riding to his ranch," Nick snarled as he pulled himself away from her and braced both arms against the side of the wagon. "And what did they do about it? Not a goddamn thing!"

Catherine scowled and then glared toward the cabin.

Continuing in a lower voice, Nick said, "Those riders came here knowing full well what they were going to do. Those smug bastards took their sweet time in taking that place apart, which might mean they've got some of those lawmen in their pocket.

"I went to see Sheriff Stilson after the fire. He told me most of the ranch hands were at The Wheelbarrow that night. They're the ones who told him that everything was fine and that they didn't see anyone riding out to Mister Van Meter's. Even if that does rule out him being crooked, it just means he's either stupid or gullible. Either way, Stilson's as useless as tits on a bull."

"He's been asking for you, you know."

"Who has?"

"Stilson," Catherine replied. "He asked me about you yesterday and then again today."

"What's he want?"

"I don't know, Nick. Now that you've cooled off a bit, you can go see for yourself what he wants. After all we've been through, we don't need any trouble with the law. You've been working so hard lately, I hardly even get a chance to see you. "

Hearing the genuine concern in Catherine's voice cut right down to the center of Nick's soul. When he looked into her face and found her smiling hopefully at him, he wrapped an arm around her and drew her in close. After giving her a quick kiss on the cheek, he nestled his face in her hair and kept it there.

"You don't have to stay with me if you don't want to," he said. "You might even be better off somewhere else."

"So you keep telling me. But I just don't listen. Does that make me stupid or gullible?"

Nick laughed and held onto her even tighter. "It makes you the best thing that's ever happened to me."

"Then don't be so quick to invite me to leave."

"After what happened to Van Meter, I've been thinking . . ." Nick sucked in a breath. "Maybe I should make an honest woman out of you."

"Too late for that," she scoffed.

"I'm serious. We got married so quickly that it hardly seemed to happen. We should have a bigger ceremony. Maybe even throw a party."

"You've had your chance, Nicolai Graves. Besides, I may not be ready to go through all that fuss just so we can come back to the same home and live the same way we have been living." Placing her hand against his cheek, she added, "Our life is just fine. Don't think for one moment that I consider it to be otherwise. I would like to wear our rings, though."

"I know," Nick said as he winced to himself. "It's just that I'm barely able to draw any attention to myself anymore. The sort of men that have come after me would start looking for you the minute they spotted that ring on my finger. I just can't bear the thought of that happening."

"I'd risk it."

"Are you sure about that?"

"Yes," she said without hesitation. "And now that that's settled, how about getting back to my first question? What are we going to do with Mister Van Meter and that sweet little boy of his?"

"The night of that fire might have been the worst of it, but it wasn't the end. Those killers are moving along to their next job as we speak. Believe that."

"How do you know for certain?"

"In case you've forgotten, I've had some experience in these matters," Nick said.

"I haven't forgotten. Whatever you did in the past, you weren't half as bad as those men who killed Joseph's family."

Nick's face may have been pointed in Catherine's direction, but he wasn't seeing her anymore. His eyes took on a faraway look as his ears filled with the gunshots and screams from his memories. "We were killers," he said softly. "One's just as bad as another."

Blinking, Nick snapped himself back to the present. He walked around to the back of the wagon and ran his hands along its gritty floor. "We were a gang just like those killers at the Van Meter place."

"You're not like those men, Nick," Catherine said vehemently. "Not anymore."

"Maybe you don't want to think about me that way. Actually, I'd be grateful if you didn't. Still, I could tell what they were doing, Catherine, just like it was something my gang might have done back when I was a dumb-shit kid. They were there to leave their mark. It's not the first time anyone's done such a thing."

When she heard those words, Catherine rubbed his back as if she'd gotten a real good idea of what particular ghosts were haunting Nick at the moment. The muscles under his skin grew taut. "You weren't the only gang out there, you know. Not every death from those times falls on your shoulders."

He nodded but didn't look at her.

"They found what they were after and left," Catherine said. "They almost killed him with that shot to his head, so there's no reason for them to come back."

"You're right. Joseph and his boy are both damn lucky to have survived that night. After that, they should be able to pull through just about anything."

"So would you mind if I brought the doctor over here tomorrow?"

"Give it a few more days," Nick replied. "Something tells me we should wait until we know those men are long gone. I'll feel much better once I go and have a word with the sheriff. After that, I should be able to figure out if he knew about what was headed for that ranch."

"Why would Sheriff Stilson be in on a thing like that?"

Nick laughed under his breath. "You'd be surprised. I don't know how, but things could get worse if we're not careful."

"You're worrying so much," Catherine whispered into his ear. "I haven't even seen you for more than an hour or two at a stretch since you brought those two back here. Little Sammy even missed you."

That brought a grin to Nick's face. "You should have seen how he latched onto me when I found him. I thought he might tear my leg off." His grin quickly faded as his eyes narrowed into fiery slits. "I should have stopped this before that boy lost his mother and sister. Before Joseph lost his daughter and wife."

Catherine glared at him with an intensity in her eyes that brought Nick back from the dark place he was headed. "You did the best you could, Nick. You risked your life to save those two. What happened wasn't your fault, so stop griping about it. In fact, you did more than anyone else around here."

"I only hope it was enough."

ELEVEN

———◆———

Nick rode into town the next day earlier than usual. The sky was still dark, but it was so close to dawn that he could feel it in the air. After arriving at his shop, he unhitched Kazys and filled the horse's trough. From there, it was a series of little tasks that were so engrained in him that he barely even had to think to do them. That was a good thing, because there were plenty of other matters to occupy his mind.

First and foremost, he struggled with the notion of opening his parlor while wearing a gun under his long black jacket. The holster was as weathered as his own skin and moved like a part of his body with every step. And even though he'd worn that gun for the last several years, he felt its weight now more than ever.

Oddly enough, Catherine hadn't been the one to get him to stop wearing the gun during business hours. After everything they'd been through together, she took comfort from knowing he wasn't at anyone's mercy just on account of pleasing a few customers. Nick saw the move to California as a fresh start in more ways than one. Earnestly plying his trade instead of hiding behind it was just the beginning.

Nick pulled open the curtains of his front window, straightened his display and took a vase from its small stand. He placed fresh flowers in it as usual and put it back in its normal spot behind the samples of his carving and masonry work. At that moment, having the gun at his side seemed almost ridiculous.

Nick looked around the small parlor and made sure it was ready to open. There wasn't a service planned, so the chairs in the largest of the rooms were not set up and the large rectangular table at the back of the room was empty, apart from a clean white cloth.

A smaller room filled with glass-topped counters was close to the front entranceway. Nick went in there to dust off the counters and take a quick count of the merchandise inside them. Beneath the glass was a wide variety of wares ranging from picture frames and samples of invitations to small Bibles, each roughly the size of a cigarette case. Nick walked behind a counter, opened it up and removed one of them. He tucked it into an inner pocket and headed for the front door.

Nick stepped out of the parlor and locked the door behind him. A few locals were walking along the street, and one of them nodded in Nick's direction. Nick returned the gesture, while making sure his jacket didn't open far enough to reveal the holster strapped around his waist. Taking his time to soak in the morning air, he rounded the corner and kept walking until he arrived at Sheriff Stilson's office.

The bit of queasiness in Nick's belly was a reflex that had been developed in his youth and nurtured during his years of raising hell. To this day, he still felt it when he got too close to that many lawmen gathered in one place. Doing his best to look the part he was playing, Nick eased the sheriff's door open and poked his head inside.

"Ah, there you are, Mister Graves," Stilson said from inside the office. "Come on in."

Stilson was standing at a large cabinet nailed to the wall behind his desk. Several rifles and a few shotguns could be seen inside the cabinet before Stilson closed it up and locked it with a small key. Motioning to a chair in front of his desk, Stilson said, "Have a seat."

Nick removed his hat and held it in front of him to conceal his gun until he was properly situated on the chair. Just to be safe, Nick kept his hat on his lap even after he'd crossed his legs and draped his jacket over the modified Schofield.

"Graves," Stilson muttered. "That's an awfully fortuitous name for an undertaker, ain't it?"

Nick shrugged.

"Is that your proper family name?"

Once he saw that the sheriff was going to wait until he had a response, Nick sighed and told him,

"My father brought me to this country when I was a child and he couldn't speak much English. He's in my same line of work and was trying to get a job the moment we got off the boat. Someone heard him mention graves, so it was marked as our name."

"That's a nice story. So, what's your real family name?"

"My wife told me you wanted talk to me," Nick said. "I do have a business to run, so I'd appreciate it if we could get this done as quickly as possible."

Sheriff Stilson nodded and drummed his fingers on top of his desk. "That was a hell of a thing that happened at the Van Meter ranch," he finally said.

"Yeah. I believe my wife tried to get you over there before it was too late."

"She did come over to tell us something about some men you saw at the graveyard."

"And what did you do about it?" Nick asked.

"I did my job." This time, it was the sheriff who found himself looking at an unyielding face that would not be satisfied by the short answer. "I found a bunch of men who work at Van Meter's place at the Wheelbarrow and had a word with them. Not one of them knew something like this was going to happen."

"Are you sure about that?"

"I'd stake my badge on it."

"Maybe you should do just that," Nick muttered under his breath.

Stilson slapped both hands against the edge of his desk and leaned forward as if he meant to bite Nick's head clean off his shoulders. "Excuse me? Could you repeat that a little louder?"

Looking at Stilson's face, Nick was quickly reminded of why he'd never gotten along well with most lawmen. "I was just wondering why you happened to end your investigation at a saloon while a man was getting shot to pieces and his family was being killed in front of him."

Stilson's face remained impassive for a moment before he shifted his eyes away. Leaning back into his chair, the lawman rubbed his eye with the heel of his hand before shifting his hat a bit further back upon his head. "Actually, that brings me to the reason why I asked to have a word with you."

"I'm here," Nick said. "Say your piece."

"My deputy and I didn't while the night away at that saloon. In fact, we spent a good portion of time following up on what your . . . wife told us."

The snide tone in the sheriff's voice was hard to miss. Nick also picked up on how Stilson's eyes flicked down to the empty spot on Nick's left ring finger. He didn't care for the lawman's judgmental tone, but it wasn't uncommon from those who didn't know any better.

"Do you have something to say about my wife?" Nick asked.

And, just like that, the subject was closed.

"I'd rather talk about what we found when we went to that graveyard," Stilson said.

Nick blinked in surprise and paused to make sure he couldn't have heard something else. "Did you say you went to the graveyard?"

Stilson nodded.

"Why would you do that?"

"Because," the sheriff said, "that's where you supposedly saw these riders."

"They were headed to the Van Meter place. Catherine must have told you."

"And we had reliable witnesses say they didn't see anyone anywhere near that ranch that didn't belong there. Your wife was the one who told us you'd spotted some of those gunmen riding through the graveyard, so my deputy and I went there to see if they'd come back. You want to know what we found?"

Nick rubbed his eyes, but that didn't do a bit of good against the ache that had settled in behind them. "Why don't you tell me, so I can get on with my work?"

"I found a man that had damn near bled out in the trees."

When he heard that, Nick felt as if he'd been jabbed in the gut. He looked up slowly to find the sheriff staring back at him expectantly. Without giving the sheriff anything in the form of a reaction, Nick asked, "Who was this man?"

"You know damn well who he was, Graves. Or, you at least know how he was wounded. Ain't that so?" Leaning forward, Stilson asked, "You want to say hello?"

"Is that why you asked me to come over here?"

"Don't you want to see him? He's right over there," the sheriff said while pointing toward the back of the office.

"Was he armed?"

"Yes."

"So, you went looking for a gunman around that graveyard. You found one. Now, you think I had something to do with it? Who do you think told my wife to come get you in the first place?"

"I doubt she would have wanted me anywhere near this fella if she knew what kinds of things he had to say."

"It's too early in the morning for word games," Nick said.

"All right, then. I'll just cut right down to it. When I found that man, he was hanging on by a thread. Someone had cut him up pretty badly. He says it was the gravedigger and the last time I checked, you were the only gravedigger who works in this town."

"Didn't my wife tell you that I was attacked?"

"Yes and you seem to be making a good recovery. For your information, that's also why he's resting up in a jail cell as opposed to a bed in much more comfortable surroundings. The reason I asked you down here was so you could take a look at him and see if he's one of the men you saw before."

Nick could tell there was more to it than that. He could feel the sheriff's eyes studying him and, so far, Nick figured he'd done fairly well under the lawman's scrutiny.

"And what if he is?" Nick asked.

"Let's just cross that bridge when we come to it."

Getting up, Nick was careful to keep his jacket closed and his hat in front of him to make certain his gun remained out of sight. "Should I go back there and have a look?"

Gesturing toward the back of the office with a sweeping gesture, Stilson said, "Be my guest. Try not to get too close to the bars. I'll be right here if you need anything."

Nick walked to the small room at the back of the sheriff's office where rows of bars sectioned off four small cages separated by a wide but short aisle. The only occupied cell was in the right corner. Sitting there with his back to the wall was the man who'd been on the receiving end of Nick's knife not too long ago. Judging by the frightened look in his wide eyes, the prisoner had no trouble recognizing Nick.

"You stay the hell away from me," J. D. said.

Lowering his voice to a quick whisper, Nick hissed, "I could finish the job I started real quickly, so just pretend like you never saw me and I'll be on my way."

Seeing the disbelief in J. D.'s eyes, Nick opened his jacket just enough for J. D. to get a look at the gun at his side. The prisoner's jaw dropped and he pulled in a breath. Before he could say anything, Nick cut him off.

"We both play dumb and we'll both walk out of here without any charges against us. Sound good?"

"I'm not sure if . . ."

"Everything all right over there?" Stilson asked from his desk in the other room.

"Don't answer him," Nick snarled. "Answer me and be quick about it."

"You won't keep your end up," J. D. said defiantly. "If I'm gonna rot in here, then so are you, asshole."

Heavy steps thumped from the next room and drew closer to the cells. Nick lowered his hand to his gun and stoked the fire in his glare when he said, "If I wanted this done, you would have been dead then, just like you could be dead right now. Believe that."

Just then, the sheriff stepped into the doorway and looked between the two men. "What'd you say, Graves?"

"I said I believe that I've seen what I needed to see."

"Is he the man who attacked you?"

Nick sighed and furrowed his brow. "I can't really say for certain. There were so many men coming through there. All I know is that I took a shot at the one who took a shot at me. I can't really say this is him."

"What about you?" Stilson asked J. D. "Is this the fellow who knifed you?"

J. D. looked back and forth between Nick and the sheriff as if he didn't know what the hell to say.

Eventually, he caught the scent of freedom and took the olive branch that Nick had offered. "I . . . can't really say for certain."

"Honestly, Sheriff," Nick said as he wiped his brow in a way to be certain the lawman could see his mangled hand and missing fingers, "it's been a while since I've been any good with a knife."

"Oh, for Christ's sake. You mean to tell me all this bullshit was for nothing?" As the sheriff looked at the two men for his answer, all he got was a few reluctant shrugs. "Get the hell out of my sight," Stilson growled as he pulled a ring of keys from his belt. "Both of you!"

TWELVE

J. D. stepped out of the sheriff's office with a smile on his face and steam in his stride. After a cautious look down either side of the street, he turned and walked to the corner. Every step of the way, he thought about the saloon he'd spotted when he'd been dragged into his cell. Already, he could taste the whiskey he meant to order and the woman he meant to buy. Those thoughts alone were more than enough to widen the grin on his face.

Stepping down from the boardwalk, he hurried across the street and headed for the nearest corner. There weren't many folks near the saloons at this early hour, so nobody was there to see J. D. get pulled into an alley by the collar.

"What in the hell?" J. D. shouted as he was dragged off the street. He kicked as much as he could while trying to maintain his balance. He even balled up his fists and swung behind him, but only managed to land a few glancing blows.

"Hello," Nick said casually as he slammed J. D.

against a wall halfway down the alley. "Long time, no see."

"Son of a bitch! I knew you wouldn't hold up yer end of the deal."

Nick frowned and pulled in a shocked breath. "What a horrible thing to say. I did just what I promised. You're out and so am I."

J. D. glared at Nick, swatting at the hand that was still holding him by the collar. Following up with a harder swing, J. D. still couldn't get Nick to let him go.

Grinning, Nick opened his hand and clamped it over J. D.'s mouth. "It'd be better all around if you kept your voice down."

Once Nick lowered his hand, J. D. said, "I don't have to do a damn thing you tell me."

The next thing J. D. felt was the barrel of Nick's modified Schofield digging into his stomach.

"Then I'll have to set an example by being real quiet, myself," Nick said. "I'll bet if I pull my trigger right now, no one will hear much of anything."

J. D. swallowed hard and nodded. "All right," he said in the calmest voice he could muster. "Fine. Have it your way."

Although Nick eased back a bit, he didn't holster the gun so J. D. was still reminded of its presence. "I want to know who raided Van Meter's ranch."

"Who's Van Meter?"

Nick's eyes narrowed into fiery slits and he

shoved his gun even deeper into J. D.'s stomach. "Van Meter's the man who lost his family and home thanks to those fucking animals you ride with. Disgrace those folks once more by acting dumb and I'll hollow you out right now. I'm sure Mister Van Meter would be happy to see your carcass in the back of my wagon."

"Oh, oh! Van Meter! I thought you said—" J. D. was cut short by a cautionary tilt of Nick's head. "Yeah. I know who you're talking about."

"Who were you riding with?" Nick asked.

"There's a couple dozen in all. We've been riding together for a little while."

"A couple dozen?"

J. D. nodded. "Give or take. Some join up and tag along for a job or two, while others drop out and lay low for a while. The law don't know who they're looking for that way," he added with a smirk.

"Real good system you got there."

"It works pretty damn well."

"How about you smile a little wider so I can knock all your teeth out with one punch instead of two?"

Receiving Nick's point good and clear, J. D. took the smug grin off his face and settled back against the wall. "There were about two dozen or so of us on this job."

"Bullshit. I heard maybe a dozen and that's being generous."

"Half passed by that graveyard," J. D. explained.

"The other half was circling around to approach that ranch from the southeast, since that's where most of the herd was grazing."

"They got the herd, too?"

J. D. looked as if he thought Nick was kidding. "That was the plan," he said finally. "Half the boys were to round up them cattle after taking out whatever was left of the hands."

"How many of Van Meter's workers did your friends kill?"

"Not as many as we could've killed. That's because Dutch made sure to get one or two of the workers working for us instead of for the rancher. That's another system that's been working real good." This time, J. D. didn't have to be warned to keep from gloating too much. "We had two workers from this place on our side. They told us the layout of the place and got the rest of the hired hands out of there when it came time for us to ride in."

"How'd you get those workers cleared out of there?"

J. D. shrugged. "I don't know. I don't even care. However those men we pay off do it is fine by us. Prevents a whole lot of killing that way."

Nick tightened his grip on J. D.'s shirt and leaned on his gun a bit more. "You and your friends are real concerned about sparing lives? Where was all that concern when it came time to kill that rancher's family?"

"I wasn't even there," J. D. replied. "I was bleeding in the dirt, remember?"

"And if you had been there, everything would've turned out so much better?"

J. D. started to say something to that but knew better than to make a sound. Nick looked too close to pulling his trigger for him to risk it.

"The leader of that gang turned that ranch into a slaughterhouse for a reason. Either him and his men are bloodthirsty animals or they were out to leave a mark of where they were."

"We heard about a stash of money that rancher was keeping. Georgie told us about it. That's what we were after from the start. If anyone got hurt, then they must have gotten stupid and tried to get in Dutch's way."

Nick gritted his teeth and felt his finger tighten around his trigger. "That family barely put up a fight," he said.

As much as he wanted to rein in his temper before blasting a hole through J. D., Nick simply couldn't come up with a good reason of why he should. J. D. wasn't the least bit sorry about what his gang had done. It might have been a lifetime ago, but Nick remembered how that felt.

"Who's this Dutch?" Nick asked in a voice that strained like a bowstring on the verge of snapping.

"Dutch Groves. Ask around about that name and you'll know he's not the sort of man you want to fool with."

"Who else rides with him?"

"Bertram Dorsett is another. The rest come and

go. I couldn't tell you all their names if I wanted to. Now, are you gonna let me go or are you gonna shoot me?"

Nick nodded and let out a single, humorless laugh at the other man's pluck. He glanced up and down the alley to find that there was nobody else in sight. The few locals who'd walked by since Nick had snagged J. D. hadn't even bothered to glance in their direction.

Nick raised the gun so it was wedged up under J. D.'s chin. "If you put it that way . . ."

J. D. immediately started to tremble and his eyes bulged out, straining to get a look at the gun. When he heard the metallic click of the hammer being thumbed back, J. D.'s legs wobbled until Nick's other hand was the only thing holding him up.

"I didn't mean that," J. D. moaned. "I swear I didn't!"

"Where are those riders headed to next?" Nick asked calmly.

"I don't know. I've been locked up. They . . . they don't plan a second job out until they're done with the first one."

Nick shook his head slowly. "If they've got these things planned out so well, they've also got their next couple of stops all lined up."

"No! They . . . they'll take the cattle to be sold and then . . . then that's when they'll figure out where they're headed."

After a few moments, Nick shrugged. "All right."

Seeing the sincerity in Nick's eyes, J. D. let out the breath that had been trapped in his throat and let his shoulders come down from around his ears.

"Since you proved to be completely fucking useless," Nick said, "I might as well blow your brains onto this wall and bury you in my field. I've got a few spare caskets anyway, so . . ."

"New Mexico!" J. D. shouted. Wincing, he dropped his voice down to a stage whisper. "New Mexico. That's where they're headed."

"Where in New Mexico?"

"If I tell you . . . will you let me go?"

"Only if you swear to get the hell out of here and never come back."

J. D. nodded vigorously. "I swear. I swear."

After a few silent moments, Nick asked, "Where in New Mexico?"

"Oh. Right. Some place called Dos Rios. It's a ranch called the Busted Wheel."

"When's that job lined up?"

"Not for a little while. Dutch was just getting his hooks into one of the men working out there. He'll ride down first and the rest of the men will gather up some more help to replace the ones who parted ways here. That's the way it always goes, I swear!"

The words had come from J. D. so quickly that there wasn't enough time for him to put together a convincing lie unless he was reciting one from memory. Considering how much J. D. was trembling with fear in front of Nick's gun, it was doubtful he could have even recited his own name from memory.

Nodding slowly, Nick let go of J. D.'s shirt and backed up a step. He lowered his gun, eased it into his holster and kept his palm on the grip.

"Can I go now?" J. D. asked.

"Sure."

J. D. took a few tentative steps toward the mouth of the alley. He must have glanced back at Nick twenty times before stepping into the open. Once he'd gathered enough courage, he bolted down the street and out of Nick's sight. Even so, Nick could hear J. D. trip and fall at least twice on the board-walk.

THIRTEEN

———•———

It was two days before Joseph felt well enough to walk. His wounds were scattered over most of his body and they took their toll now more than when he'd received them. Fortunately, there wasn't much for the doctor to do when he finally paid him a visit. In keeping with the doctor's orders, Joseph stayed with Nick and Catherine while he rested up.

Sam was more than happy with the arrangement, since he had a new field in which to play and plenty of new sights to take in. During the day, the boy watched Nick carve or helped load and unload the wagon when he went into town. Even the boy could tell Nick was uncomfortable getting so much attention. Whenever he asked why, all he got was a shrug and a tentative pat on the head.

After a particularly long day in his workshop, Nick climbed down from his wagon and started unhitching Rasa from her bridle. There were only tools in the back, so Kazys wasn't needed to pull the load. When he glanced toward the house, he found Joseph waiting there instead of his son.

"Up and around, I see," Nick said.

Joseph nodded and winced as he began taking some steps. For a moment, it looked as if he needed help staying upright. Rather than try to prop himself up with the arm he extended, he offered his hand to Nick. "I never properly thanked you for all you did."

Shaking Joseph's hand, Nick replied, "There's no need to thank me."

"You saved my boy's life. That's a hell of a lot to thank you for."

"You're welcome."

Looking at the back of Nick's wagon, Joseph pulled in a breath and let it out slowly. Finally, he said, "I . . . want to see my wife and daughter."

Nick's body froze, but his eyes darkened as if he'd been dreading the arrival of those words. "When you're feeling better, I can take you to—"

"No. I want to see them now. If I don't, I'll lose whatever's left of my mind."

Chuckling under his breath, Nick said, "There's still plenty left in there."

Joseph lifted a hand to his left temple and brushed his fingers along the one wound he didn't remember getting. It was a nasty gash that felt gruesome even after it had been stitched shut. The wound started at the front of his head just over his eye and continued in a straight gouge that ended above his ear. "They're all I can think about, Nick. Please."

Patting Joseph's shoulder as he walked by, Nick stuck his head into the cabin and let Catherine know where they were going. He received a quick kiss on his cheek and then walked back to the wagon. Knowing Joseph would want to climb onto the passenger's seat on his own, Nick watched him closely while fixing Rasa back into her rig.

Joseph stumbled a bit, but made it onto the wagon just fine. Once there, he breathed deeply and kept himself steady by gripping the seat with both hands.

"You sure you're ready for this?" Nick asked.

"Yeah. Just be ready to collect me if I fall out of this seat."

Nick snapped the reins and got the wagon moving at an easy pace. The road from his cabin was fairly smooth and sloped downward to hook up with the main trail. Rather than turn right toward Ocean, Nick steered the wagon left toward a much more open stretch of land.

"Where are you going?" Joseph asked. "Isn't your parlor in town?"

"It is, but they're not in my parlor."

Looking ahead to see where they were going, Joseph let out a frustrated breath and asked, "You buried them? I never gave permission for that."

"I know."

"But, I wanted to see them! I wanted to see their faces one more time before they were put into the ground!"

Nick met Joseph's gaze and said, "I know what

you're saying, but ... you didn't want to see them."

Somehow, those words didn't sound ominous coming from Nick. They settled into Joseph's mind like weights that slowly bowed his head. He didn't say another word during the short ride to the graveyard. In fact, he was so lost in his memories that Joseph felt as if he'd only looked down for a second before the wagon rattled to a halt. When he looked up again, the graveyard was spread out in front of him.

Nick climbed down from the wagon and ran his hand along Rasa's coat as he moved around the animal. "You need some help climbing down?"

Joseph shook his head and gritted his teeth with determination. The pain from most of his wounds barely even registered, but the gash on his temple forced him to pause when his boots touched the ground. Once the dizziness faded, Joseph straightened up and walked to where Nick was waiting.

The graveyard was surrounded on three sides by trees with one well-tended trail leading straight into it. Thanks to Nick's constant attention, the place felt more like a park than a graveyard. None of the wilderness from the open field made it onto the hallowed ground. The grass was free of weeds and every last tombstone was properly cared for and in good repair.

"This way," Nick said.

Steeling himself for the walk, Joseph made his way down the path until he'd caught up to Nick.

It was early in the summer evening and the sun was low in the sky. It still cast a warm glow, but the trees to the west blotted out most of its light. The shadows cast by the tombstones and grave markers were long, but not particularly thick. Instead, they seemed more like smears of dark pain along the ground. As the wind blew, it brought the smell of fresh grass and damp soil to both men's noses.

"I get the impression that you haven't done this work your whole life," Joseph said.

"Is that a knock against how I maintain this place?"

"No, not at all. I was thinking more about how you handled a gun. You don't normally see that sort of grit in an undertaker."

"Actually, my father groomed me for this line of work since I was a kid," Nick said. "The rest . . . came a bit later."

"My father ran cattle from Kansas to Texas. He taught me an awful lot about my work as well. Mostly, he showed me the benefits of planting roots and starting up a ranch rather than riding from town to town with the herd."

"Smart man. Is he still around?" Nick asked.

"Nah. He died not too much before . . . before Laurie was born." Those words stung Joseph, but he choked back the pain and sucked in a breath. "What about yours?"

"My father's still about," Nick said. "He came with us to California, in fact."

"Where is he?"

"He started up a small cabinet shop along the Coast, not far from San Francisco. Also does some masonry work when he can. I'm just glad I convinced him to stop digging holes for a living. At least this way, he won't break his back before I'm able to pay him another visit."

"Sounds like you two get along pretty well," Joseph said. "Me and my father were always squabbling about something."

"Actually, we fought about plenty. It wasn't until recently that we didn't come to blows damn near every time I came within a few paces of him."

"That why he lives so far away?"

Nick put his hands in his pockets and shrugged. "He wanted to be near the ocean and I just wanted to visit it. Besides, riding with him all the way here from Nebraska was more than enough for both of us to appreciate being apart."

Both men shared a bit of laughter and kept walking slowly among the burial plots. Joseph looked up at the orange-tinted sky and pulled in a lungful of fragrant air. He could feel the sunlight brushing against his face like a warm breath. When he looked down again, he saw Nick standing at a pair of freshly turned piles of earth.

"Here they are," Nick said.

The uncertainty in Joseph's steps turned quickly into another bout of dizziness. He knew the feeling didn't come from any wound. At least, not from a wound that could be seen by the naked eye. As he

walked closer, he kept his eye on the ground between the two graves or the grass around them.
Even when he got directly in front of them, he
wasn't able to lift his head right away.

Placing a hand on Joseph's shoulder, Nick said,
"If you don't want to do this right now, I can always bring you back later."

The dizziness subsided enough for Joseph to
shake his head. Slowly, he raised his chin and
brought his eyes up to the graves. They were just
piles of dirt of roughly the same size. Although
there wasn't anything particularly distinctive about
the dirt, he knew he would remember the position
of every last groove in the soil as well as every indi-
vidual pebble.

But the sight wasn't nearly as jarring as Joseph
had expected. That was due to what he saw when
he moved his eyes a bit past the graves and slightly
up. At the head of the first grave was a stone marker
with Anne's name carved in elegant letters into an
image of a scroll that went from the stone's top to
its bottom. Laurie's marker was carved in a similar
fashion, but what distinguished them from each
other were the figures that had been carved into
the sides of the stones. They were obviously not
quite finished, but were far enough along to be ap-
preciated.

Anne's bore the image of an ethereal woman in a
wispy dress, gazing down toward the next stone. On
Laurie's marker, there was a carving of a younger

figure dressed in a shorter dress made from the same wispy material. The younger figure looked up and directly into the eyes of the mother on the stone to her left.

"My God," Joseph breathed. "They're beautiful. Did you make those?"

"Yes. I left room for more on an inscription if you wanted one. Also, I didn't know their birthdays. I can add all that on if you like."

"And the carving? The pictures?"

"I thought it would be nice."

"But . . . when did you have the time for this?"

"I started the day after I brought you into my home," Nick said.

Reaching out to run his hand along the carved stone, Joseph said, "But you couldn't have gotten these done so quickly. You would've had to work night and day."

"Pretty much."

"This is more that I could have asked for. I don't even know when I can pay you."

"You don't owe me a penny," Nick said.

Joseph kept his hand on the face of the rock, moving only so he could alternate between his wife's and his daughter's stones. Keeping his fingers on top of Laurie's marker, he looked over to Nick and found the tall man standing quietly with his hands clasped in front of him. "Isn't it customary to take photographs of the dead before they're buried?"

Nick reflexively winced at the sound of that, but

managed to keep it all but hidden from sight. "Yes. It is."

"I want to see those photographs."

"Joseph, you need to remember your family the way they were. I did my best to clean them up and make them presentable, but . . ."

"I want to see their faces."

Nick looked into Joseph's eyes and stared all the way down to the burning embers of rage at the other man's core. Even in the face of all that hatred, Nick kept his own face calm and his voice steady when he told him, "I didn't take any pictures of your wife and daughter."

"What?"

"You heard me."

"But that's part of your job."

"I know what my job is and most of it pertains to the folks left behind. You must remember how they looked before I got to them. Trust me when I tell you that's the way you'll want to remember them."

Now it was Joseph's turn to wince, but he kept pulling in haggard breaths while forcing himself to stare directly at Nick.

"You can't tell me," Nick went on to say, "that you or your boy would get anything good from having pictures like those around. I did you a service by making certain they wouldn't even exist. I had to grow up with one of those damn pictures and all it ever gave me was nightmares. Remember how Anne and Laurie were on their best day, not their last one."

"I don't need any help in remembering their best days," Joseph snarled. "I want to make sure their dead faces are in my head the next time I see the bastards that put those two angels in the ground. Thanks to this," he said while stabbing a finger toward the wound on his temple, "that night's already starting to fade."

"Consider that a blessing," Nick replied. "I've got memories of my own that I wish could fade."

"I'll hold onto this pain until I can visit it upon those fucking killers who took my girls from me. It may take a while to find them, so I want to make sure the fire's still burning inside me just like it was that night."

"It'll always burn," Nick told him. "In the meantime, though, maybe this will give you something else to think about." With that, Nick dug into his pocket and fished out the small book he'd taken from his shop earlier that day.

Joseph accepted the book and opened it. "A Bible?"

"A mourner's Bible. It just has passages meant to ease your mind at a time like this. Try to live with the way things turned out. That's the only choice you've got. Nothing you can do will put it out of your mind and nothing you can do will make it any better. You hear me? Nothing."

Joseph's face twisted into an expression of bitter

anger. Kneeling in the fresh dirt and lowering his
head, he said, "I'll just have to see about that."

Nick took a few steps back and left the other
man with his wife and daughter. There would be
time for talking later.

FOURTEEN

———◆———

Catherine woke up the next morning to a gentle yet insistent tugging on her arm. She stirred just enough to open her eyes and see less light drifting in through the bedroom window than usual. Figuring that she had at least another half hour or so before needing to climb out of bed, she started to roll on her side and get back to sleep.

The tugging continued.

When she opened her eyes again and rolled back over to find someone staring at her, she nearly cleared the bed.

"I'm hungry," Sam said.

"Good Lord," Catherine gasped. She sat up and did her best to pull her nightgown over the proper spots so she could safely remove her covers in front of the child. "You scared me, Sammy."

"Sorry. I'm hungry."

"All right. Let's see what we can do about that."

Nick was still in bed, which told her it was even earlier than she'd thought. He began to stir, but was appeased by a few little pats on his back from Catherine.

The floor seemed especially cold that early in the morning. In fact, the whole cabin felt different. It was almost as if the place itself was still sleeping and she had to sneak so as not to wake it all up. She found herself whispering to the little boy even though it would have taken cannon fire to rouse Nick.

"How about some eggs?" she asked. "Would you like that?"

Sam nodded and situated himself on one of the two benches at the dining table.

Without even thinking about it, Catherine poured a cup of milk and set it in front of Sam before tending to the food. She glanced over to the bed they'd set up for Joseph and his son in a corner of the room and saw a figure huddled under the blanket.

"You're up early," she said to Sam. "Didn't you sleep well?"

"I had bad dreams," Sam replied after drinking noisily from his cup. "About my sister."

"Well, those won't last long. When they're gone, all you'll remember is the happy times you had with her. Your mother, too. That's the way they'd prefer it."

"Really?"

She nodded over her shoulder at him and shifted her attention back to fixing breakfast. It took a bit more concentration than normal to keep from spilling anything as her tired hands fumbled to light the stove.

After finishing off his milk, Sam asked, "Will you take care of me?"

"What do you need, Sammy?"

"When Pa left, he said you'd take care of me."

Catherine was still cracking an egg when those words finally sank in. Her hand was frozen in place as she looked back over to Joseph's bed. Egg white oozed over her fingers as she squinted into the shadows. The shape under the blankets wasn't moving or making the slightest bit of noise.

Letting the egg drop, Catherine rushed over to the bed and reached out to tap the figure lying there. She instantly realized that the shape under the covers actually was formed of the blankets themselves, which had been mussed and piled up in one spot. Out of sheer disbelief, she lifted them and looked at the bed.

"Where's your father?" she asked.

Sam was sitting in his spot, swinging his legs from the bench. "I don't know. He said he'd be back, but maybe not for a long time. Kind of like when he rode away and left me at home with Laurie."

"Back from where?"

After thinking it over for a second or two, Sam shrugged his shoulders and tipped the cup all the way back for the last drop of milk. "Are you still making eggs?"

Catherine bolted into her bedroom, grabbed

Nick's shoulder and shook him vigorously.

"What the . . . ?" Nick grunted as he slowly emerged from his sleep.

"You've got to wake up, Nick. Wake up right now!"

The urgent tone in Catherine's voice snapped Nick's eyes open and got his arm flashing toward the gun under his bed. The revolver was smaller than his modified Schofield, but his hand clasped around it tightly enough for him to thumb back the hammer without too much difficulty.

"What's wrong?" he asked.

"Joseph's gone," she told him.

"What?"

"Joseph's gone."

"What about the boy?"

"Sam's at the table," Catherine explained. "But Joseph's not here. Sam said that he left."

Nick pulled in a few breaths and gathered his thoughts. Since there wasn't a fire or someone kicking in his door, his brain needed a moment to hit its stride.

"Put that gun down," Catherine said.

"Huh?"

She reached out to push his hand down and ease the gun from his fingers.

"What's on your hands?" he asked.

"Breakfast. I'll finish cooking it while you find that boy's father."

Nick swung his legs over the side of the bed and

struggled to clear his thoughts. "Maybe he just went into town."

"No," Catherine said emphatically. "He left. I can just tell. He even told Sam he might not be back for a long time."

"Or at all."

"What did you say?"

Nick's eyes had cleared and he was more awake than if he'd been splashed with cold water. He burst into motion and started pulling on his clothes and boots as though the cabin had caught fire.

Catherine rushed to get in front of him before Nick bolted out the door. "What did you mean by that?" she asked. "Answer me."

Rather than answer her right away, Nick left the bedroom and headed straight toward Sam. Since the boy was watching both of them, Catherine restrained herself from saying what she'd meant to say.

"Where did your father go?" Nick asked as he knelt down to the boy's level.

"He didn't tell me."

"What did he tell you?"

Sam looked up as if the answer he needed was written on the ceiling. "He said he loved me and that I should stay here where I'll be cared for. He also said I could go to Uncle Ken's house if you didn't want me to stay here. I like Uncle Ken I guess, but are you going to take care of me?"

Gently holding onto the boy by both arms, Nick

made sure Sam was paying attention before asking, "What else did he say?"

"That he might not be back for a long time and that he loved me very much and was leaving to do something for Ma and Laurie."

Nick let go of the boy and straightened up again. "Jesus Christ," he muttered as he ran back into the bedroom. Before Catherine could ask another question, he stormed out of the bedroom, buckling his holster around his waist.

"What are you doing, Nick?" she shouted.

That wasn't enough to get Nick to stop, so she followed him out the front door.

"Wait! Damn it, Nick just wait a second and tell me what the hell is going on!"

Her tone caught Nick's attention and caused him to pause while lifting the saddle onto Kazys's back.

"Do you even know where you're going?" she asked, placing herself between her husband and his horse.

"I've got a hunch."

"Then why not tell me? First Joseph disappears and now you want to follow. If you're going to be my husband, then you should act like it, for God's sake!"

After cinching up the saddle, Nick asked, "Did Joseph go anywhere recently?"

"Yes. He went into town the other night."

"Why didn't you tell me that before?" Nick

grumbled as he craned his neck to look in every direction leading away from the cabin. "Why'd he go alone in his condition?"

"He's doing well enough to ride with you to the graveyard," she replied. "He's doing well enough to help around here when you're not around. He's doing well enough to play with Sam. Since when did I have to tell you every little step he took? Now, will you please explain what you're doing? Do you know where Joseph went?"

"I just might."

With that, Nick started to climb into his saddle. Catherine pulled him back down again. When he dropped back to the ground and looked at her, Nick saw a defiant gleam in her eyes that told him she wasn't about to let him leave things the way they were.

"After all we've been through," Catherine said, "why won't you trust me?"

"Trust doesn't have anything to do with it. Time is a factor here. Joseph might have taken off to do something very stupid. Just step back and let me go check on something, Catherine. I swear I'll be back before too long, whether I find out anything or not."

Reluctantly, Catherine nodded and stepped back. It took every bit of willpower she had to keep from grabbing hold of Kazys's bridle or even chasing after the horse once her husband rode away. Instead, she stood there and watched Nick leave. After he rode out of her sight, she turned and went back into the cabin, where Sam was waiting patiently.

The little boy looked at her and asked, "Are the eggs almost ready?"

FIFTEEN

⬧━◆━⬧

Nick swung down from the saddle and stepped into the sheriff's office. Stilson's desk was empty, but the deputy named Miguel sat at one of the smaller ones. Since Miguel had been half-drunk the last time Nick had spoken to him, he doubted the lawman even recalled the instance.

Miguel dropped the book he was reading and covered it with an old newspaper before he even got a look at who was coming in. His round face was flushed and he jumped to his feet while shoving the pile of reading material behind him. "The sheriff's not here," he said.

"I just wanted to ask about the prisoner you had in here the other day," Nick said. "The man that was found at the graveyard."

Miguel's eyes narrowed and he studied Nick closely. Cocking his head slightly, he wagged his finger at Nick and said, eyes wide, "I know you. You're the gravedigger!"

"I am. I just wanted to know—"

"Sheriff Stilson won't want to talk to you. He
. . . uh . . . mentioned that before he left."

"That's fine. You could probably answer my
questions. All I want to know is if anyone else has
come in asking about the man who was locked up
here."

"You're lucky you're not in that cell," Miguel
said as he stepped around his desk and folded the
corner of the newspaper up to check underneath it.
"The sheriff thought for sure he'd have you in there
right alongside that other one. You should've heard
the things he said about having to let the both of
you go."

Nick nodded and fought to maintain his temper.

"What's with the gun?"

When he heard that question, Nick put on a
slightly embarrassed expression that had gotten
plenty of use over the years. "It's not much of a
gun, really," he said, opening his coat so the deputy could see.

Miguel looked for a second and shrugged. "It
sure isn't. I heard some things about you. Something about you running with a bad crowd some
years ago."

"Haven't we all?"

"Hell yes," Miguel replied, even though he
looked like he'd run afoul of more baked goods
than anything else. "Mister Van Meter came in
here. Hell of a thing that happened to his family."

"It was. What did he want?"

Settling into his chair, Miguel tossed the newspaper to one side and picked up the bawdy novel he'd been hiding. Now that he knew whom he was dealing with, he didn't seem to mind flipping through the book. "He was asking about that fella we let go. Not you. The other one."

"What did you tell him?"

"Why do you want to know?"

"He's still hurt," Nick said matter-of-factly. "The doctor's charged me with looking after him. Since he still hasn't showed up yet, I need to know where he might have gone."

"Like I said, he asked about that prisoner we let go." Gazing over the top of his book, Miguel added, "I don't know why he wanted the information, but he paid a good amount for it."

"How much?" Nick asked.

The deputy shrugged and flipped a page of his book. "Ten dollars?"

Digging into his pockets, Nick fished out some money, counted it up and set it on the desk. "How about five?"

"Close enough," Miguel said as he swiped the money from the desk and pocketed it. "The prisoner was after a horse. He asked where he could find a stable that had some for sale right before he left."

"Is that it?"

"That's all I know. He had an outstanding balance with the doctor, but I don't know if he went there or not."

"And when did you tell Joseph the man was headed

for the stable?" Seeing the puzzled look on the deputy's face, Nick added, "Joseph Van Meter."

"Oh, Mister Van Meter left about half an hour ago. Maybe less."

Calmly tipping his hat, Nick left the office. Once the door was shut and he'd put some distance between himself and the law, he jumped onto Kazys's back and bolted for the stables. A few minutes later, he was riding down the street again amid a thunderous flurry of hooves.

Nick didn't ease up until he arrived back at his cabin. Before both of his boots had touched the ground, he saw Catherine come through the front door to greet him. The anger that had been on her face when he'd left was replaced with relief.

"Did you find him?" she asked.

Glancing around, Nick asked, "Where's Sam?"

"Inside, finishing up his breakfast. What about Joseph?"

"I didn't exactly catch up to him, but I have a real good idea of where he went."

"Where?"

Nick pulled in a deep breath and let it out like a gust of steam coming from a train's engine. "I think he went off to find the men that burned his ranch."

"Oh dear Lord," Catherine sighed. "Are you certain?"

"Pretty much. He paid a visit to the sheriff's office and talked to one of the deputies about where that prisoner went after he was let go. Joseph found out where that man was headed after he was freed and then followed. Both of them went to the stables and left town from there. Hank was working at the stables when I checked in there myself and said he told Joseph that the prisoner took the southerly trail out of town."

"Is that enough for Joseph to track someone down?"

"It could be. So long as a man's got the determination, he can find a way to do damn well anything. Besides, that gang leaves a pretty big set of tracks behind them, and Joseph's not short on determination."

Catherine shook her head slowly and crossed her arms. "What could he be thinking?"

"The same thing I'd be thinking if anyone did to you what they did to Missus Van Meter. I tell you, Catherine, when I saw what was left of that woman and that little girl, I wanted to gut those bastards myself."

"He'd be a fool to do something like that. I don't think he even has a gun. He's going to get himself killed."

"I know. That's why I intend on going after him."

"What?" she asked

Nick pulled open each of the bags hanging from Kazys's saddle and checked inside. "You said it yourself. He's going to get himself killed and I can't allow that. Not after I went through the trouble of getting him and that boy away from that ranch."

"Don't talk about this like it's some sort of whim, Nicolai."

It was one of the few times he'd heard her call him by his full name and it caught Nick's attention. Most of the time, he didn't like the way folks often shortened his name without asking for the privilege. From her, however, the shorter version of his given name had always struck a sweeter chord.

"I know how rough it's been for Mister Van Meter and that precious little boy in there," she said, now that she had his undivided attention. "But things get hard for everyone, and folks deal with what comes their way. They get stronger for it. If not, they don't survive. That's just the way the world works."

"You don't have to preach to me on that subject."

"Then why are you about to ride off, leave me behind and risk your neck after everything's been so good for us?"

"Because this is a terrible mistake that Joseph's about to make," Nick said. "I need to fix it now, before you take Sam to see three graves instead of two."

"Or four," Catherine said quietly.

After thinking about it for a few seconds, Nick nodded and replied, "Two's more than enough for that boy to look at."

Catherine stepped up to him and held his face in her hands. She moved her fingers just enough to caress his cheeks and then slip them through his coarse, dark hair. "You've done more than enough already. You've saved Joseph's life and his son's. I'm so proud of you, but maybe I'm also a little selfish. Seeing what happened to Joseph made me think how terrible it would be if I lost you. I just don't think I could live through it."

"You're not going to lose me," Nick assured her.

Tightening her hold on him just enough to keep him from looking away, she asked, "And what happens when you cross paths with those killers again? Joseph's going after them, so that means going after Joseph will put you in the same spot."

"Not if I catch up to him fast enough. If you let me gather the things I need, I might be able to round him up before the day's out. He's still hurt, which means he'll either need to rest more than that prisoner or will keel over somewhere along the way. Both of those things makes my job easier, just so long as I don't waste too much time in getting there."

"That's just it, Nick. This isn't your job."

Nick didn't look away from her. Instead, an old darkness crept into his eyes as he said, "Then maybe I just know a bit more about what Joseph is thinking than most anyone else around here."

"And what's he thinking about?"

"Revenge."

Slowly, Catherine took her hands away and shifted her eyes from him. She became still and let out a measured breath. It now seemed she was several miles away from him. As Nick walked around her to collect the things he would need, she stayed in her spot with her arms folded.

After stuffing the things he'd collected into the saddlebags, Nick walked in front of her and wrapped his arms around Catherine's waist. She resisted at first, but then hugged him and nestled her chin against the base of his neck.

"I'll come back to you," he whispered.

"You'd better."

Nick brushed his lips against her shoulder, using his finger to gently ease down the edge of her blouse so he could touch her bare skin. As much as he wanted to follow through on that line of thought, he only kissed her neck before moving back up to nibble on her ear.

"This reminds me of something my father once told me," he said.

"Nick, if this reminds you of your father . . ."

"No," he chuckled. "Not like that. I told him once that I felt like someone was looking over me. He said there were no angels for outlaws." Leaning back so he could see her face, Nick said, "I had to fight for years to prove him wrong. I wouldn't subject any other man to that test."

Catherine nodded and pressed her face against Nick's shoulder one more time before he left. There was no way for her to talk him out of going, so she savored the last couple moments he was there.

SIXTEEN

———•———

As he rode away, Nick fell into thought. So far, he had been concerned more with what Joseph ultimately intended on doing rather than what how the rancher would actually do it. Nick was all too used to simply throwing his things into a bag and riding away. Most folks weren't so transient, however, and in Joseph's case, the man didn't have much more than the clothes on his back. No matter how distraught he was, Joseph would know he'd need more than that if he was to ride off after anyone.

That meant returning to his ranch.

Nick touched his heels to Kazys's sides, which got the horse moving at a full gallop. The dark stallion might have been old, but years of pulling a wagon had made him hunger for the thrill of tearing over a trail without anything dragging behind him. Kazys was gasping for breath by the time he arrived at the Van Meter ranch, but didn't let up until Nick pulled back on the reins.

As soon as he saw Rasa tethered to a splintered

hitching post, Nick knew he'd gone to the right spot. He tied Kazys next to the other horse, patted both animals on their noses and started walking toward the ruins of the main house. Before he could get within five paces of the front door, Nick saw someone moving inside. The figure stopped just short of the doorway, with both arms filled to brimming with scavenged items.

"Nick?" came Joseph's voice from inside the house. "Is that you?"

"Yeah, it's me. If you wanted to collect some of your things, you should have mentioned it. I would have let you borrow my wagon."

"You've done plenty," Joseph said as he emerged from the house.

Nick looked at the items Joseph was carrying. There were a few articles of clothing, which were used more for wrapping up a shotgun than anything else. Its barrel poked out of an old shirt.

"What've you got there?" Nick asked.

"Just some things I'll be needing. Sorry about taking your horse, but I figured on returning her as soon as I rounded up one of my own. There's got to be a few still wandering around here. If not, I'll have to buy one."

"What about Sam? Were you just going to leave him?"

"Catherine has been doing a fine job of taking care of the boy. Better than I could manage for now. I told him to go to his uncle's if you two looked like you had your hands full."

"Isn't that a big decision to put on a boy's head?" Nick asked.

Joseph squinted as if contemplating that was giving him a headache. Finally he waved off the question and muttered, "I can't think about that right now. He's taken care of himself before and he knows how to get to his uncle's just fine."

"You're not thinking straight, Joseph."

Joseph was quiet for a few moments, but when he looked at Nick, there was the glimmer of a smirk on his face. "Catherine sent you out here, didn't she?"

"Not at all. She's concerned, but I'm the one that's got a better notion of how you're feeling right now."

"Have you seen your family slaughtered in front of you?"

Before he could prepare himself for their arrival, the ghosts swarmed back into his head, filling it with visions of lynch mobs and friends dangling from nooses. He could smell the potent mix of burned gunpowder and freshly spilled blood. Echoes of screams rolled behind his ears.

"I've seen plenty," Nick said. "Maybe not the same things as you, but more than enough to know what it's like when all you can think about is paying someone back for the wrongs they did to you."

"So what?" Joseph grumbled. "Are you going to try and tell me how I should just forget about everything that happened, take Sam to another place and try to be happy?"

That was more or less what Nick was going to say. Unfortunately, he didn't know exactly what to tell Joseph next. As he took a moment to think of something, Nick realized that there wasn't much of anything he could say to make the man feel any better. The wounds were too fresh. Many of Nick's own wounds were several years old, and they still caused him no end of pain.

"What if I can help you?" Nick finally asked.

Joseph studied him carefully, as if he was waiting for the second boot to drop. "If you want to bury those murdering bastards when I'm done with them, you're welcome to it. Otherwise, I don't see how you'd be much help."

"You plan on hunting that gang down by yourself? There's at least a couple dozen of them. By now, they might have already replenished the ones they lost the night they took your ranch."

Joseph shifted on his feet and gazed around as if he was seeing it all for the first time. There were burned-out shells where there had once been buildings. Scorched dirt covered spots where his children used to play. Dried blood stained the ground where his wife and daughter had made their last stand.

Watching him take in the sight of it all, Nick swore he could hear the other man's ghosts settling in and making themselves at home.

"I've got to do this," Joseph said. "I won't be able to look at myself in the mirror again if I don't. Already, I can barely stand to see Sam smile at me.

He looks at me like I'm something special, and I couldn't even keep his mother and sister alive."

"He'll always look at you like that. I'm sure he'd rather see you sad for a while than dead."

Joseph pondered that, but his eyes were drawn back to the ranch. "I've been standing here for a while. I thought I'd collect what I needed and get moving, but then I realized I hadn't been back here since everything happened."

"I thought about taking you here when you mentioned it the first few times, but that was only a day or so after you were hurt. You may not even recall saying anything."

"I don't."

"It may have been better for you to not come back here at all."

"Why's that?" Joseph asked with a hint of venom in his tone. "So I would forget?"

"You'll never forget. That night will be like a scar, but it don't mean there's a reason to tear it open on purpose."

"If I didn't know any better, I would have pegged you as a preacher rather than a gravedigger."

"This is something I know about. Things would have been a lot different if someone had tried to talk some sense into me when I was at the start of taking on more than I could handle."

"Yeah, but would you have listened to them?"

Joseph's question hung in the air. After enough time had passed, Joseph nodded and started walking to the house. "I need to get one more thing.

That is, if it's still there. Whatever I decide on doing, I'll need it."

Nick followed Joseph into the ranch house. The
place looked even worse on the inside than it did on
the outside. Walls were charred black and nothing
was in its proper place. The stench of smoke was
thick in the air and Joseph kept his hand over his
mouth to keep from breathing too much of it in.

After stepping into a large room toward the back
of the house and across from the kitchen, Joseph
lowered himself to one knee and placed both hands
upon the cracked floor. His head hung low and his
fingertips pressed between two chipped boards as
if he meant to pull it up.

Recognizing that posture from folks mourning
at a fresh grave, Nick took a few steps back and
left him to his grief. Then Joseph straightened his
back and lifted the two planks from the floor. They
came up halfway before catching on one of the
shattered boards next to them. After a few more
pulls, however, the boards came free and Joseph
tossed them aside.

Nick stepped forward and craned his neck to
look over Joseph's shoulder. "What's that?"

A gunshot blasted through the room, accompanied by the sound of shattering glass. Joseph
dropped to the floor and rolled away from the rectangular hole he'd uncovered. Nick flipped his coat
open so he could draw his pistol. Both men looked
in the direction of the shot and found a skinny
man leaning out from behind a cabinet that had

been propped in a corner. The man's face was as filthy as the rest of the room, and his wild eyes stared from behind the filth like it was a mask. Ashes and splinters were tangled in his hair. He peeked through one of the cabinet's doors, which dangled open on one set of hinges. The gun in his hand was still smoking. "Dutch knew there'd be more!" he shouted.

Nick closed his hand around the nub of his pistol grip and brought the weapon up. The grooved contours of the gun's barrel fit within the matching ridges inside his holster to shift the pistol into the palm of Nick's hand, compensating for his missing fingers. Although he drew the weapon fairly smoothly and quicker than a man in his condition should have, he wasn't fast enough to fire a shot before the gunman behind the cabinet took another of his own.

Firing several times in quick succession, the gunman squirmed out from behind the cabinet until he was able to pull free of it. He flinched as a few shots from Nick's pistol chipped away at the wooden frame in front of him, but managed to get in a lucky shot that was close enough to move Nick back a distance.

"Get away from that money!" the gunman shouted.

Just as Nick settled his aim, he saw the gunman lower his empty pistol and make a hasty grab for another one wedged under his belt.

"Dutch said you'd be back to collect the rest of

that money, and he sure as hell was right!"

Nick pulled his trigger and blasted a hole through the gunman's hip. He started moving toward the gunman, but had to stop as the other man's empty pistol was thrown directly at him.

Despite the blood flowing from his hip, the gunman staggered forward and fired a shot in Joseph's direction. He snarled through gritted teeth, but couldn't manage to form any words.

After the empty gun bounced off his forearm, Nick stepped forward and fired another shot at the gunman. He was aiming for the man's other leg but took too much time in doing it. As he was pulling his trigger, he saw the gunman twist around to fire two quick shots at him.

One bullet blazed past Nick's torso and the other clipped a bit of flesh from under his arm. Being hit in such an awkward spot threw Nick off balance as pain coursed through his shoulder. Even so, he kept his wits about him and took the shot he'd been lining up.

"Son of a bitch!" the gunman moaned as his legs crumpled beneath him and he dropped like a sack of rocks.

Nick walked over to him and stepped on the gunman's wrist, pinning his weapon to the floor. Staring down at him over the barrel of his modified Schofield, he asked, "How long you been waiting there?"

"I been here for days," the gunman wheezed. "You . . . didn't even see me."

Reaching into the hole in the floor, Joseph pulled out a small strongbox and held it out. "Is this what you were after?"

The gunman's jaw clenched as he eyed the strongbox. The sight of it made his legs squirm and his arm struggle beneath Nick's boot. "We knew you had a bunch of cash stored. Plenty more than what we found. George told us it was in this room. We just couldn't find where you squirreled it away."

"Now you know," Joseph said.

"So you just waited here until someone came back?" Nick asked.

The gunman nodded. "Dutch said you'd be back. He said any man would want to check on that much money on the chance that it survived the fire. Looks like he was right." Sucking in a series of quick breaths, the gunman shifted his eyes to Nick and said, "You let me go and I can tell Dutch the money burned up."

"I suppose you'd expect a percentage of what's in that box in return for that kind of service, huh?" Nick asked.

"That'd only be fair."

"Tell me where Dutch is headed," Nick offered. "Then we'll see about payment."

"They're splitting up. Some are rounding up some more boys and the rest are taking the Silver Gorge trail."

"I've never even heard of the Silver Gorge trail. You're making it up. And where will they be looking for men?" Joseph asked as he walked up to the gunman with the strongbox tucked under his arm.

The gunman's eyes fixed upon the strongbox as he licked his lips expectantly. "One of the places is called San Trisha or something. There's some other town along the way, but I can't remember the name. I'll tell you where they're all meeting up once I get a taste of that money. After that, we can part company."

Nick leaned down until his gun barrel was less than an inch from the gunman's face. "You wouldn't be lying to me, would you?"

"No, no! I swear."

"Why the hell should we believe you?"

"Because it don't matter if you know where they're at or not. Dutch's got everything covered against anything that can go wrong. He's also got ten times more guns than you and anyone else you know put together. Besides, I was done with them after this job, anyways. I need all the money I can scrounge up."

"You're not afraid of Dutch finding out how we came by this information?"

The gunman winced and sweat poked out of his brow for the first time. "Why bother telling him? We're working together, ain't we? I don't even expect much money in return. Just let me go and tack on . . . say . . . five hundred dollars and we'll call it even."

"How about you just fuck yourself instead?"

Joseph said as he raised the gun in his other hand and pulled the trigger.

The single shot sounded louder than the gunfire that had come before. It exploded inside the room and sent an icy chill through Nick's body.

Joseph looked down the barrel of his gun as smoke curled out and drifted up. He focused on the gunman's open, lifeless eye before shifting his gaze to the bloody hole where the man's other eye had been. "That was one of the men who dragged my wife out of her room," he said.

Nick holstered his gun and watched the man's face. "He was also the man who could have told us where those killers meant to group up."

Finally, Joseph let out the breath he'd been holding and lowered his gun. "I would have told him about this money," he said more to himself than to Nick. "I was going to tell them about all of it, but I didn't get the chance. Those sons of bitches didn't give me the chance."

Joseph didn't say another word. Instead, he tucked his gun away and carried the strongbox outside.

SEVENTEEN

Nick followed Joseph from the house and away from the surrounding buildings. There was a horse inside the remains of the stable, which Nick guessed had belonged to the gunman. Joseph emptied the saddlebags and filled them with things he'd collected from the house. After that, he climbed into the saddle and set the strongbox on his lap. Without looking the gift horse in the mouth, he snapped the reins and got moving.

A good portion of the grass and nearby field were burned as well, but the charred blackness spread out for less than a quarter mile before eventually giving way to the greens and browns of life. The ride was as quiet as a tomb. Nick kept a watchful eye on Joseph the entire time. All he saw from the other man was an occasional shake of his head as they moved slowly across his property.

They made it all the way to the fence line before Joseph stopped and turned around. "They're gone," he said as Nick came up alongside him.

"All of them are gone. The whole herd, the horses, even the goddamn hands who swore up and down they'd look after this place like it was their own."

Looking over to Nick, he added, "I didn't expect that kind of loyalty from all of them, but a few of them . . ."

"They were tricked," Nick said. "Whoever this Dutch is, he got a few men working for him on the inside and they got the others into town at the right time."

"How?"

"By saying they were having a party for you." Nick let out a sigh and said, "I had a word with one of the members of that gang. One of them was in jail. He told me how the gang got it to work."

"You . . . weren't going to tell me?"

"What good would it have done?"

"I could have done something about it," Joseph said without a trace of emotion in his voice.

"And I thought I could steer you away from this before more blood was spilled."

"Too late for that."

"Yeah," Nick said. "I guess so."

"What else did he tell you?"

"I'm not going to say."

Joseph's eyes narrowed and his hand drifted to his gun. Before he could think twice about it, the pistol was in his hand and being brought up to aim at Nick.

To Nick, the movement seemed slower than molasses in the summertime. Oddly enough, when he found himself staring down the barrel, he wasn't completely surprised.

"Tell me what was said," Joseph demanded.

Nick didn't twitch.

He didn't blink.

And he didn't make a sound no matter how vehemently Joseph demanded.

Finally, Joseph blinked and lowered his gun as if he was just now waking up. "Sorry. I . . . don't know what I was thinking."

"I do. That's why I came to try and talk some sense into you."

"I just don't know how I could change my mind. Not after I . . ."

Nick let that sentence drift off without being finished. He knew what Joseph meant to say, just as he knew all too well how hard the first kill was. For some, it was like making love to a woman the first time and got easier and better with practice. For others, it was like breaking through a rock wall. After that, the thought of breaking through another didn't seem as bad.

With all the thinking he'd done on the subject, Nick couldn't decide if either one was truly worse than the other. Both roads led to the same spot. Despite everything Nick had said and done to avoid it, they were standing in that spot right now.

"They're riding into New Mexico," Nick said.

Joseph looked over to him and blinked. "What about the Silver Gorge trail?"

Nick didn't meet the man's stare, but looked out onto the stretch of barren land in front of him. "It's an old route used by smugglers and bandits. It's a hard ride over some rough country, but it's fast and not a lot of lawmen know about it. At least, not the sort of lawmen that we should be concerned about."

"We?"

Nodding, Nick said, "I'm coming with you."

"Why would you do something like that?"

"Because you have no idea what kind of hell you're riding into. Since you're not about to change your mind on going, I figure the least I can do is go along to see that you don't get killed."

"That still doesn't tell me why."

Shifting in his saddle, Nick looked toward Joseph, but not directly at him. "You can change your mind and decide to go home at any time up to a certain point. With me along, you stand a better chance of getting home before crossing that line."

Joseph chuckled to himself. It was a tired sound that ended with him seeming to have lost all his breath. "You don't think the line's already been crossed?"

Nick's eyes subtly shifted in their sockets. "Like I said, you don't have the first notion of what kind of hell is in front of you."

Joseph reflected on Nick's words for the first time since they'd left the graveyard. Despite that brief glimmer of hope, Nick quickly realized that it wasn't going to last long.

"I have to go after those bastards," Joseph said. "Anything less would disgrace the memory of my Anne and Laurie."

"What about your Sam?"

"This is for him, too."

"All right, then. If you want to ride into a meat grinder, than you'll be leading me there, too."

"I'm not asking you to come," Joseph told him. "So don't try to appeal to my sense of guilt. Where this matter is concerned, I don't have any guilt left in me." With that, he put his ranch behind him and snapped the reins.

After riding a few paces, Joseph stopped and turned back around.

Nick was surprised to see the sudden bout of remorse in the man's face. He was even more surprised to see the gun in his hand.

"I have a feeling you could outdraw me," Joseph said. "But I should be able to pull my trigger before you make a move."

"What the hell is this about?" Nick asked.

"You don't want to come along with me, but you don't think you have a choice. I appreciate the trouble, Nick, but I'll take this choice out of your hands. Whatever you think you've seen or done, it doesn't hold a candle to what happened to my family. Go take care of Sam for me until I get back. If I don't come back, at least he'll know his father died trying to set things straight."

Nick let out a discouraged breath and shook his head. The muscles in his arm were twitching to draw his gun, but he kept his arm still.

"Toss the gun and get off that horse," Joseph demanded.

Holding his gun in a loose grip, Nick tossed it a couple yards away. He then climbed down from his saddle and stood next to Kazys.

"Sorry, Nick, but I need to do this." With that, Joseph sighted along the top of his barrel and pulled his trigger.

The gun in Joseph's hand barked. Joseph's horse hopped off his front legs at the sound and shifted nervously from one hoof to another as Joseph struggled to keep control. Even as the bullet kicked up a mound of dirt a few inches from where Kazys was standing, that horse didn't even flinch.

Nick had yet to change his expression.

Scowling, Joseph thumbed back the hammer and aimed again. Because his horse was still fretting beneath him, he couldn't level his arm before Nick could collect his Schofield and walk right up to him.

Nick stopped a few inches shy of butting into Joseph's barrel. "You know what the problem is?"

Joseph cursed under his breath while calming his horse and trying to steady his pistol.

Nick's hand flashed up and around in a quick arc. The back of his left hand smacked against the side of Joseph's gun, knocking it to one side. The gun went off as Joseph's finger awkwardly hit the trigger, propelling its second round into the ground well away from the two men and their horses.

Even though his eyes didn't leave Nick, Joseph
didn't see him raise his modified Schofield until it
was pointed directly at his face.

"The problem," Nick said calmly, "is that my
horse has seen more gunfights than you have."

Looking over toward Kazys, Joseph saw the animal calmly nibbling at a patch of grass while his
own horse was still shaking its head and wriggling
nervously.

"You're a good man," Nick said. "I know you've
been through a lot. I'd like to help you. But don't
ever point a gun at me again. You understand?"

"I just wanted to spook your horse so—"

"Do . . . you . . . under . . . stand?"

Feeling like a kid that was being scolded after
breaking a window, Joseph swallowed his pride
and nodded.

"Good," Nick replied as he holstered his gun.
"What you're feeling right now is the sting of being outclassed in a fight. Consider yourself lucky
because, for most men, it's the last thing they feel
before getting their brains blown out the back of
their skull. The men you want to hunt down will
kill you without blinking, and they'll take pleasure
in doing it."

"I know that," Joseph said coldly.

"If I know you like I think I do, you're also feeling a cold knot in the bottom of your stomach after shooting that man back at your house. That
knot's gonna be there forever." Nick nodded sol-

emnly. "I went through all this trouble to try and spare you them demons, but it's too late now. The demons will come, and the more you kill, the louder their voices will get.

"But that's not the only thing you started here by firing that shot. Whoever this Dutch is, he'll know the man you killed is missing. Some of those others may have been replaceable, but that man was meant to bring back the strongbox you're carrying, which means he's got a whole gang anxiously awaiting his return. When he doesn't come home, that whole gang will have one hell of a burr under their saddle."

Joseph paused to let that sink in. After pulling in a breath, he lifted his gun and wedged it under his waistband. "They're not the only ones who are upset about a few things."

Nick walked over to Kazys and climbed into the saddle.

"If you think this is a fool's mission, maybe you shouldn't come along," Joseph added.

"In case you forgot, my wife is looking after your son. When those men find out who killed their friend . . . and they will find out sooner or later . . . they'll come after your boy and anyone who's there with him when they arrive. They'll do it out of principle, no matter what we decide to do from here on out."

"How can you be so certain?"

"Because," Nick said calmly, "it's what I would have done."

EIGHTEEN

Virginia City, Montana
1866

Nick was in his early twenties and barely more than a kid. He'd tried to make amends for the hell he'd raised, but found himself with a group of vigilantes who were worse than any gang Nick had ever joined.

One of those men stood over him after beating Nick within an inch of his life. His name was Red Parks and he'd just finished slicing off several pieces from Nick's hands. The smile on his face was just as wide now as it had been when he'd done the cutting.

"Your days as a bad man are over, all right. I promise you that," Red told him.

The next thing Nick heard was a quick series of pops.

Each pop was a shot from Red's gun.

Each bullet blew off the mutilated remains of

Nick's middle and ring fingers like bottles being shot off a fence.

Once those shots died away, the men who'd called themselves the Vigilance Committee watched Nick squirm until he finally passed out. Their eyes were still glaring down at the young man when a sound from outside the old barn caught their attention.

"Someone's coming," said one of the men.

Red reached behind him to find a burlap sack that had been tucked under his belt at the small of his back. Pulling the sack over his head, he adjusted it until two holes cut in the rough material lined up with his eyes. The rest of the men in the barn followed suit.

"Let's go," Red told his men. "We've done plenty for one night."

Most of the hooded men nodded and filed out the door like a parade of scarecrows. Two of them lingered over the bloody kid curled up on the floor. Their eyes glared down at Nick through the holes in those burlap sacks and seemed unable to look anywhere else.

"What about him?" one of the masked men asked.

Red looked over as if to admire his handiwork one more time. "Leave him. He'll probably never even wake up."

"And what if he does?"

"Then he'll serve as a warning, just like I said before. He'll show all his murderous friends what happens to their kind if they come near Virginia City." Red walked out of the barn to address the locals who'd gathered outside.

The one man left behind stared down at Nick with his gun in hand. Since he wore a long brown coat, heavy boots and gloves along with the mask, his eyes were the only part of him that was exposed. Those eyes stared down at Nick the way they'd stare down at a wolf caught in a trap. He started to lift his gun and aim at Nick's temple, but hesitated. If anyone else but Red had set that trap, he wouldn't have hesitated to put the boy out of his misery. The hooded man knew all too well he might be the next one in such a predicament if he went against Red's orders.

Reluctantly, he holstered his gun and left the barn.

Outside, Red had already convinced the locals that there wasn't anything in the barn for them to see. Some of the locals took Red at his word. The rest knew how unhealthy it was to question him.

Nick woke up with the stench of blood filling his nostrils. He tried to straighten up, but that sent a wave of pain through him that nearly dropped him right back into unconsciousness. As he started to keel over, he caught himself with his hands against the floor. For a moment, he thought he'd slapped both hands against a red-hot grill.

A scream worked its way up from the back of his throat, but was muffled when it reached his tightly shut mouth. Nick's jaw tightened reflexively and he flopped over so he wouldn't have to use his hands again. As he lay there on his back, the memories of what had happened rushed back to him.

He couldn't stay in that barn.

Red couldn't find out he was alive.

He had to get out.

Nick started to crawl toward the barn's rear door when he heard voices coming from outside. The surge of blood from his panicked heart was like a fresh load of coal shoveled into a steam engine. He got to his feet and charged toward the back door without a moment's hesitation.

When he got to the door, he tucked his hands against his body and slammed his shoulder against it. The door had been latched shut, but gave way easily under the young man's attack. Nick bolted into the night and kept running until Virginia City was behind him.

Along the way, he spotted a few shocked faces trying to get a glimpse at him, but none of them was covered in burlap. Nick's lips curled into a feral snarl as he used the pain churning inside of him to fuel his steps. He ran into the darkness before he stopped to think about where he was headed.

After a few seconds of squinting and filling his lungs with air, he guessed he was headed toward the mountains. Anything more than that was beyond his ability to grasp, so he kept on running until his legs felt close to collapsing under his weight. Even then, he managed to run for a few hours more.

* * *

Feeling something warm on the back of his neck,
Nick jerked awake and pulled in a mouthful of
dirt. His legs were pumping as if still running, and
he reached out to turn himself over. His mangled
hands still hurt, but the pain had become Nick's
only companion. He pushed through it and forced
himself up.

Nick was crawling on the ground with trees surrounding him on all sides. His eyes darted back
and forth, searching for anything to let him know
which direction he should go in when he managed
to stand up and start running again. All he had to
go on was the direction his head was already pointing. Guessing that was the way he'd landed when
he was running the night before, Nick pulled himself up and kept moving.

The sunlight hurt his eyes when he tried to look
over his shoulder. Once his brain cleared a bit, he
figured he was running south or southwest. After a
while, his legs started to cramp and every breath
was almost too much of a labor for him to accomplish. Cursing his own body for being so weak,
Nick dropped to one knee and pressed the back of
one hand against his mouth.

He didn't know how long he stayed in that
spot.

It seemed like his feet were rooted there for
hours.

When he tried to move again, Nick felt as if he'd
only rested for half a second.

The sounds of feet crunching against fallen leaves and twigs made Nick's next breath catch in his throat. His could only see two blurry figures moving toward him. One of the figures was bigger than the other, so that was the one he chose when he attacked.

Nick lunged off of both legs with his hands held in front of him. Working off of pure animal instinct, he tried to grab the bigger of the two's throat to show that he wasn't weak. His bloody hand made it to the man's neck, but the pain from his mangled fingers was too much to bear.

Blackness flooded through Nick's head and his legs turned into straw, crumpling him to the ground as his hand snagged upon the other man's collar. Using his last bit of strength, he reached up with his other hand to try and finish off the job he'd started.

The man in front of Nick was slightly shorter than him and at least thirty pounds lighter. His short, brushy hair was a subtle mix of light brown and some red. A neatly trimmed mustache covered his upper lip and a pair of small, round spectacles sat on his short, rounded nose. The eyes behind those spectacles were wide with shock and fear.

The second of the two figures was a woman. She was slightly shorter than the man and slender in build. Her long brown hair came almost down to her waist and was tied into a single thick braid. She rushed over to the man, but stopped short of getting within Nick's arm's reach.

"Don't come any closer," the man said. "He's a wild one."

"I can see that, Doug! He might hurt you!"

Doug waved to her and slowly eased his other hand around Nick's wrist. He was able to peel Nick's grip from his collar without much effort. "He's hurt. Pretty badly by the looks of it."

The woman stepped closer. She moved tentatively at first, but then relaxed when she saw Nick was practically hanging off of Doug's arm. "Oh, my God," she gasped. "Look at his hands."

"I know. There's plenty of other wounds as well. We'd better get him back to the house."

"What?"

"We can't just leave him here, Sue. He'll die."

"You don't know that."

"These wounds are fresh, but they can become worse if they're not tended to. Now help me carry him to the house."

Sue was less than a few feet from Nick, but she eyed the boy as if he was a distant curiosity. The harshness in her face melted, but only when she turned again to her husband.

"Please," Doug said. "I'm not about to drop this boy here and walk away like I never saw him."

"Fine." She sighed and went to Nick's other side, sliding in under Nick's other arm. "But if he takes a swing at me, I'll drop him like a hot rock."

"Fair enough."

NINETEEN

———◆———

When Nick woke up for the second time that day, it was one of the most disconcerting moments of his life. The memories of what had been done to him by the Vigilance Committee were still fresh in his mind, as was his flight into the woods. The sight of a normal room and the feel of a normal bed were complete oddities.

A face looked down at him and smiled warmly, which put Nick even further off his guard.

"What the hell's going on?" Nick snarled as he sat bolt upright and pushed his back against the wall. "Who the fuck are you?"

"My name's Douglas and that woman behind me is my wife, Sue."

With a bit of effort, Nick focused his eyes enough to see the woman standing at the opposite end of the room. She was pretty, but very nervous. She was also holding a shotgun aimed at Nick's bed.

"You assholes working for Red?"

Doug squinted and shook his head. "I don't know a Red."

"Red Parks," Nick growled as if the name was an obscenity. "I know I didn't run far enough away for you to not know him."

"Oh, you mean the man who leads those vigilantes in Virginia City?"

"That's the one."

"I don't know much more than his reputation, but I can tell you that men like him were why we moved out of town to live here."

"How far did I make it?" Nick asked.

"Did you come from Virginia City?"

"Yeah."

"Then you made it just over seven miles," Doug told him.

Nick felt the weight of those miles drop onto his shoulders. The aches in his muscles flared and he barely had enough strength to keep his head up.

When he looked around again, the quaint little room felt much less like a fever dream. The window was open and decorated with frilly curtains. The furniture looked new and was all freshly dusted. In fact, Nick felt more like a guest in a nice hotel than a bloody fugitive stretched out on a stranger's bed.

Looking back to Sue, Nick asked, "Why's she got a gun?"

"Well," Doug told him, "you haven't been very easy to manage."

"God damn, did I give you them bruises?"

Doug winced as if he could feel the dark spots

on his cheek and jaw with renewed intensity. "Yep. You sure did."

"Sorry about that."

Doug smiled right away and shook his head. "Don't even worry about it. I'm more concerned with what happened to you."

When Doug reached out to pat Nick's hand, Nick reflexively pulled his arm in against himself. A good amount of the blood had been cleaned away, but the bandages had also soaked up more than their share.

"If you don't want to say anything now, that's fine," Doug said. "But at least let us get you a doctor. With you being so . . . rambunctious before, we didn't want to start in on stitches until you had a chance to wake up."

"Did you clean me up?" Nick asked.

"No. My wife did that. I had to hold you down."

Nick ignored the shotgun in Sue's hands and looked into her eyes instead. "Thank you, ma'am."

Her face lost some of its hardness as a timid smile began to shine through. When it did, she looked even prettier than before. "You're welcome."

"Will you agree to see a doctor about those hands?" Doug asked. The moment he saw Nick nod, he stood up and let out a relieved breath. "Great. Our neighbor was an army medic. I'll bring him over and he can do what he needs to do. Sue, I think you can put that shotgun down now."

Sue looked as if she'd been asked to undress in front of the young stranger. "What?"

"The shotgun. We don't need it anymore. This young man was just out of sorts. There's no need to—"

"It's all right," Nick said. "Actually, I don't blame you if you want to keep it. I must look like some kind of animal right about now."

Although Sue softened up a bit more, she didn't deny Nick's statement. She also didn't put down the shotgun. She did, however, lower it so he wasn't forced to look down its barrel.

"Since we're all situated here," Doug said to his wife, "I'll take over guard duty and you can send the girls to fetch Bill Mather before making something to eat for our friend here."

Sue nodded, but didn't leave until Doug came over to her and took the shotgun. She whispered something in his ear and then nodded to Nick. "Sit tight," she said. "Bill will be here before you know it."

After Sue had left the room, Doug pulled up a chair and sat down. He was just about to say something when Sue poked her head in again and fixed him with an intense glare. Flinching as if he'd been knocked in the head, Doug held the shotgun in his hands rather than setting it to one side, as he'd just been about to do.

"Things around here have been a little . . . rough," Doug said. He shrugged down at the shotgun and explained, "We moved far enough away so we wouldn't have to watch those vigilantes ride down the streets, but that also means we need to protect ourselves."

"I understand," Nick said. "A lot worse than you have pointed a gun at me."

"I don't believe I got your name."

Before he answered that, Nick paused to wonder how far his own name might have spread. Since he was too tired to think that much, he simply replied, "Nicolai Graves."

"That's a name you don't hear too often. I'll bet most folks call you Nick."

"Yes sir, they do."

"How long have you lived in Virginia City?"

Since the genial smile was still on Doug's face, Nick figured he wasn't a known member of the Committee outside of Virginia City. "A few years now," he said, to answer the question.

Reflexively, Doug's eyes went to Nick's hands and the bloody cloths that were loosely wrapped around them. Although another question obviously gnawed at Doug's brain, he kept from speaking it out loud.

Nick leaned back and savored the silence, no matter how awkward it was.

Over the next twenty minutes or so, Doug seemed perfectly happy with sitting quietly and letting Nick rest his eyes. A bit later, the front door swung open and several sets of footsteps echoed through the house.

"Sounds like the girls are home," Doug said.

Sure enough, two little girls with blonde hair poked their faces into the room before being pulled out once more. As soon as they cleared the path, a skinny old man wearing a brown suit came into the bedroom. His egg-shaped head was bald on top with a ring of gray hair around the back.

"Bill Mather, this is Nick Graves," Doug said in his normal, friendly tone.

Mather squinted down at Nick and said, "Let's see what the problem is." After pulling a stool next to the bed, Mather sat down and peeled away the bloody cloths. "Jesus Christ," he squawked. "What happened to your hands, boy?"

"They were shot," Nick said through clenched teeth. Just looking at the wounds was enough to re-ignite the rage inside him.

"He's got other wounds, too, but his hands are the worst," Doug said.

"Well, we'll just see about that."

Mather systematically examined Nick from top to bottom. The only sounds he made were the occasional grunts and mutters to himself. His hands worked quickly and without much concern for Nick's comfort. It reminded him of stories he'd heard from men who'd fought in the War Between the States. They'd told Nick that the doctors in those field hospitals were sometimes worse than the assholes who'd put the bullet in you.

As much pain as Nick felt, he made less noise than Mather. He moved when he was pushed or pulled in one direction or another and he gritted his teeth through the rest. When he saw the needles come out to stitch him up, Nick picked a spot on the wall and stared at it.

"This is going to hurt," Mather said. "You want a drink or something to bite down on?"

Nick glanced at the old medic and then shifted his eyes back to the spot he'd picked on the wall. He shook his head and swallowed hard, knowing that Red would love nothing more than to see him squirm right about now. That was all it took for Nick to steel himself.

It took hours for Mather to do what he needed to do. In that time, Nick didn't make a sound.

It was early evening when Doug walked out of the bedroom. Sue fixed him with an upset look and asked, "Shouldn't one of us be in there?"

Doug propped the shotgun in a corner and shook his head warily. "That poor young man's barely able to sit up straight. If he's strong enough to take a swing at Bill, I think that's a good sign."

"Did he try anything like that?"

"No. He just stared at the wall."

Doug and Sue did the same thing until the bedroom door swung open again. Mather stepped out, wiping his brow, and then took the spectacles from his nose so he could clean them.

"How is he?" Doug asked.

"I'd say the bigger question is *who* is he," Mather grumbled. "Did either of you find that out before taking him into your home like a stray?"

Ignoring the look he got from his wife, Doug said, "He was bleeding and lying on the ground. What was I supposed to do? Just let him lie there and die?"

"If he was some killer on the run from the Vigilance Committee, then yes. That'd be the smartest thing to do."

Sue covered her mouth with her hand. "Oh, my God. Is he a killer?"

"I don't know, but I do know those wounds are mostly from gunshots. Some of the others looked like the bayonet wounds I saw in the war, but they could have come from a knife. Either way, that young man was in a serious fight. The last time someone was tore up that bad and on the run out of Virginia City, it was from that Committee. Has anyone been looking for him?"

"No," Doug said. Turning to his wife, he asked, "Did anyone ask about him while you were out?"

Sue shook her head. "No."

"Then maybe he got clear of whoever shot him up," Mather offered. "Considering the condition he's in, they probably think the young man's dead."

"His name is Nick Graves," Doug told him.

"I don't care if his name is Ulysses Grant. If he's a killer with other killers after him, it'd be wise for you to be rid of him. Especially since you've got the girls to worry about."

"Thanks, Bill, but we can make that decision."

"Suit yourself. I cleaned and dressed the wounds as best I could. He needs plenty of rest, but he might just make it. Judging by how he took the stitches and everything else, I'd say it's nothing but bullheadedness that's kept him alive this long."

"What about his hands?" Sue asked with a wince.

"You saw 'em for yourself. They're shot to hell, and there isn't a damn thing I can do about that. Still, they're not fatal wounds. By the looks of it, whoever shot him up was either trying to rip him apart or was just one hell of a bad shot. Since there was a knife involved, I'd put my money on the former."

"What's a knife got to do with it?" Doug asked.

"You have to get up close for it to work," Mather replied warily. "Takes a bit more resolve."

Doug nodded as if he was learning a foreign language. "Right. Of course."

"So," Mather said as he headed for the front door, "you want me to ask the marshal about your guest in there?"

Doug looked to his wife, but didn't get much more than an uncertain shrug in return. Taking a deep breath and letting it out decisively, Doug said, "No. We'll keep an eye on him until he's feeling a little better."

"That should give you until tomorrow at least,"

Mather said. "He passed out when I was filing
down the bone of one of his fingers. Anyone else,
I'd say they would be laid up for a while, but that
one in there will probably be trying to get up in the
morning."

Although he tried not to squirm at the casual
way Mather tossed out those last few sentences,
Doug wasn't able to hide the fact that his face was
now white as a sheet. "All right, then. What do I
owe you for this?"

"We'll work something out. Right now, I just
want to get some sleep. Talk to you both later."
With that, Mather threw a wave over his shoulder
and left.

Both Doug and Sue jumped at the sound of the
slamming door.

"What in God's name do we do now?" Sue asked
in a frightened whisper. "That man may be a gun-
fighter or an outlaw."

"He doesn't have a gun on him," Doug said as if
to comfort himself along with his wife. "And he's
in no shape to harm anyone, even if he . . ." Suddenly realizing he couldn't comfort anyone by going along that line of thought, Doug stopped
himself. Unfortunately, he wasn't able to think of
anything better to say before one of his little girls
came running into the room.

The girl wore a cute little blue dress, but was
small enough that a potato sack could have covered her just as well. "Does the scary man want
my blanket?" she asked.

"No, princess," Doug said. "He's sleeping just fine."

Without another word, she nodded and ran off.

"You'll keep an eye on him," Sue said to her husband. "And you'll have that gun close by when you do it. I'll fix a plate for him in case he gets hungry during the night."

And, just like that, the decision was made.

TWENTY

———◆———

Every time Nick opened his eyes, he didn't bother
checking if it was night or day. Sometimes there
was light streaming through his window and sometimes there wasn't. The biggest problem was that
he couldn't get himself to care about where the sun
happened to be. Most of the time, he wondered if
he would be better off if he simply didn't wake up
at all.

Nick had never been given to self-pity, and he
sure as hell hadn't picked up anything like that
from his father. In fact, Stasys's voice passed
through Nick's mind more often than any other.
He felt as though his father was constantly scolding him for the mess his life had become.

The smell of freshly baked bread drifted through
the house, causing Nick to stir. No matter what
else had happened or what was going through his
mind, Nick was always glad to see the Hemphill
family. Doug was quick with a joke and kept them
coming even though Nick wasn't in the mood to
laugh. Sue always made him feel better, even by

doing something as simple as dabbing his face with a wet cloth or rubbing his arm before she left. The children were heard more than seen, but their laughter would drown out the other echoes that drifted through Nick's mind.

He never realized just how much attention he'd been paying to the sounds inside that house until a new one entered the mix. First, there was the creaking of the front door. Then, there was a rough voice from outside, which grew louder the longer it talked.

"I don't think the question was too hard, Hemphill. All I asked was—"

"I know what you asked," Doug cut in.

Nick winced at the angry tone in Doug's voice. Although most folks sounded angry every now and then, Doug hadn't raised his voice in such a way the entire time Nick had been there. In fact, it was difficult for Nick to picture what Doug might have looked like if he was angry.

When Doug continued, some of the edge was already missing from his voice. "I wish I could help you, but I just haven't seen any strangers pass through here. It's rare we even get to see you."

"You can bullshit me all you want," the first voice said, "but there've been reports of a man around here fitting this description. He's wounded and he's dangerous, so it ain't a very good combination."

Nick eased to the edge of the bed and then slowly got to his feet. It was an effort to stand up, but that was only because he'd been content to lie on his back and count the boards in the ceiling until now. He made it across the room and pressed his ear against the door.

"If I see anyone, I'll let you know. That's going to have to do for now, Marshal."

Nick heard the hinges creak, but that sound was interrupted by a solid thump.

"Move your foot, Marshal," Doug said.

There was a silence and then a lower, growling voice. Nick pressed his ear even harder against the door until he was able to pick out more of the marshal's words.

". . . friends that're very interested about this fella. If I have to tell them you wouldn't let me have a look inside, I'll just have to let them come see for themselves."

"Then tell them to come back on Sunday," Doug said cheerily. "Sue's making a cake."

Nick waited to hear the marshal's response, but all he heard was a shuffle and the creak of the door shutting. He opened the bedroom door to take a look out and saw Doug turning around to face him.

"Nick, you're up!"

"Who was that?" Nick asked.

Doug looked back at the door and shrugged. "Just a neighbor."

"I heard some of what he said. He said he was looking for a man and he wanted to search this house."

"Someone must have seen you that day and gotten the wrong impression. Like I said before, you were out of sorts."

Although he hadn't meant to, Nick put a vicious snarl in his voice when he asked, "What was his name?"

"Marshal Bagley. Do you know him?"

After a moment, Nick recalled hearing that name once or twice from Red. "He's the law in a few little towns around here."

"That's right. It's just some bad luck he's around here right now. Don't worry, though. He's just making the rounds."

"Who were the friends he mentioned?"

Doug chuckled and asked, "Did you have a glass against the wall?" When he saw Nick wasn't laughing, he added, "Marshal Bagley says he's on good terms with the Virginia City Vigilance Committee. Most folks around here think that's just hot air to frighten the troublemakers."

"God dammit," Nick growled. "I need a gun."

"What? There's no need for that."

Responding to Doug's raised voice, Sue stuck her head in the door. "Is the marshal still here? What is Nick doing out of bed?"

"I need a gun," Nick said to both of them. "Any gun you've got."

"Nick thinks Marshal Bagley intends on doing him some harm," Doug called over his shoulder to his wife.

"Does the marshal have a reason to do you some harm?" Sue asked.

The way she was staring him down, Nick knew better than to try and lie. "Maybe."

"You see?" Doug said quickly. "There's no . . . what? Maybe? What do you mean, maybe?"

"If that marshal of yours keeps in touch with the Committee," Nick explained, "there may be a chance that he's out to put me down."

"Why?"

Before Nick could answer, Sue interjected, "That damn Committee doesn't need a reason. They never have. That's why we left Virginia City, remember?"

"I know plenty about the Committee," Doug said with some of the anger that Nick had heard in his voice a little while ago. "But I also know they go after some deserving targets as well. Which one are you, Nick? Be honest with me and I'll stick by you as much as I can."

Nick found the shotgun propped against a wall and snatched it up before Doug could do a thing about it. Checking to make sure it was loaded, he said, "Neither of you knows a damn thing about me. You don't know the half of what the Committee is capable of, either."

"Then tell us what we need to know," Doug insisted.

"For one, I need to make sure that marshal don't send word to Virginia City. Once Red hears about someone giving shelter to a wounded man, the Committee will come here looking for me. You don't want that. Did you tell anyone my name?"

Doug recalled mentioning Nick's name to his

neighbor and cursed under his breath. "Damn it, let me go talk to the marshal. I can tell him you ran away."

Nick looked at Doug and saw genuine concern in a face that he barely even knew. Although Sue was busy with the girls in another room, she had looked just as concerned when she looked through the doorway at Nick. It should have been easy for him to pick up his things and leave.

It should have been easy for Nick to take the Hemphills' money as well as a fresh horse and start riding in any direction other than toward Virginia City. A few short months ago, Nick would have done all of those things. Hell, a few days ago he had been entertaining that very notion.

"How many deputies does that marshal have?" Nick asked.

"Don't worry about that," Doug said.

Sue came to her husband's side. When she spoke, there was no uncertainty in her voice. "Three. There may be more, but I've only seen three men riding with Marshal Bagley."

"Were any of them with him today?"

Finally Doug nodded. "Just one."

Nick tucked the shotgun under his arm and walked into the kitchen. When he came back out, he was buttoning one of Doug's jackets over him and patting the gun into place. "Hope you don't mind if I borrow this," he said.

Doug forced a smile onto his face and said, "Only if you bring it back."

"You might not see me again," Nick replied without returning even a fraction of Doug's smile. "I'll try to stop by again, but I can't make any promises."

"Where are you going?" Sue asked.

By this time, Nick had made it to the front door and was peeking outside. "I'm going to make sure that marshal doesn't report back to Red in Virginia City. After that, I've got some business of my own to finish."

Doug reached out to grab hold of Nick's arm. "You're in no condition to ride anywhere. You shouldn't even think about it."

Nick got the man to release his grip with nothing more than a warning glare. Once Doug stepped back, Nick said, "You've done enough already. Whatever happens after this, it's best that you don't know about it. Whatever you think you know . . . forget it. And forget me, too, while you're at it. It'll be better all around that way."

Doug was standing halfway between his wife and the door. His arm was still extended from grabbing Nick's elbow and he extended it once more with his hand open. Nick paused for a second, and then reached out with one of his bandaged hands. Closing his fingers tentatively, Doug slowly shook Nick's hand as if he was trying not to break an expensive piece of china.

"If you need to go," Doug said earnestly, "just go. Take whatever you need. Take the shotgun, but don't use it on our account. I'll do my best to make certain news doesn't spread from here about you."

"I appreciate the thought," Nick said, "but I'd be asking way too much."

Doug smirked, but it was less humorous and more conspiratorial. "Not as much as you think. I work at the telegraph office a mile from here and we get plenty of news before Virginia City does. We also get plenty of notices posted there by the law. Knowing that Committee, they'll be posting one there, themselves, before long. It'll be burnt as soon as they leave."

Knowing it wouldn't do any good to refuse the man's help, Nick nodded and shook Doug's hand in earnest. Although he felt the familiar burning pain shoot through his hand, his grip was stronger than it had been even earlier that same day. "I won't ever forget you folks," he said.

"Take care of yourself," Doug told him.

Sue rushed forward and wrapped her arms around Nick. "Just run," she whispered into his ear. "That's all you need to do. Everything else will sort itself out whether you fight for it or not."

Nick didn't say anything. He just savored the warmth of her hug and stopped asking himself why the hell these people would do so much for an outlaw they'd scraped off the ground a matter of days ago.

When he stepped outside and helped himself to one of the Hemphills' horses, Nick vowed that

those folks wouldn't suffer because of their gener-
osity.

Nick didn't have much doubt as to where he
should go next. The only thing that concerned him
was getting there in time.

TWENTY-ONE

—————————◆—————————

The deputy's fist slammed into Mather's face, sending a spray of blood into the air. Marshal Bagley stood nearby with his thumbs hooked in his belt, watching as if he was getting bored of the sight.

"What's the meaning of this?" Mather grunted.

Marshal Bagley shook his head impatiently. "You know damn well. The man we're after was wounded. Wounded real bad. We know he came this way, so that only leaves three choices. If he was dead," Bagley said while ticking off one finger, "we would'a found a body by now."

Ticking off another finger, Bagley said, "He might've gotten away, but he would'a had to steal a horse or walk faster than any man could, or we would'a spotted him. And three, he got patched up somewhere. Let me tell you, there are men in Virginia City who don't like that third one very much at all."

"I don't know who you're talking about," Mather said.

Leaning down to snarl in the old medic's face,

the deputy asked, "Then how come I seen you coming back in here carrying that case a while back?"

"I treat a lot of folks around here."

"But none of them *needed* treatment," Bagley pointed out. "I asked." When he saw the old man wasn't about to say anything, the marshal nodded to his deputy, who then delivered another punch to Mather's face.

"They're good people," Mather said as he spat out a wad of blood.

"Who are?" Bagley asked. "All we want is the fugitive. We get him and we'll forgive the rest."

Mather reflexively glanced to the right-hand window of his front room. "None of the folks around here deserve any trouble," he said.

"And they won't get it from me, just so long as I have something to pass along."

Hanging his head low, Mather said, "I heard mention of a name. It may be the man you're looking for."

"What was the name?"

"Nick Graves."

"That's better," Bagley said with a smile. "Now, just tell me where you heard that name." Seeing the old man turn to look the other way, Bagley glanced to his deputy and told him, "Make this old buzzard spit out who was hiding that fugitive. Remember, he don't need his teeth to say it."

Grinning like a kid that had been given the keys to a candy store, the deputy grabbed Mather by the shirt collar and hauled him over to the dining room. Weathering more than a few blows from the medic, the deputy threw the older man into a straight-backed chair and started pounding his fist into Mather's face again and again.

Bagley remained in the living room and sat on the padded arm of the medic's sofa. As he lit a cigarette, Bagley heard a horse racing toward the front of the house. Without disturbing his deputy, Bagley moved to a window and pulled the curtain to one side. He spotted the horse and recognized it as one of the animals that had been tied to the front of the Hemphill place.

The man climbing down from the horse wore a jacket that was just a bit too small for him and a hat that looked as if it had been trampled by an entire team of mules. His hands were bandaged and the ferocity in his eyes could have been seen from a mile away.

Walking to the front door, Bagley pulled it open and stepped outside. He clenched his cigarette between his teeth and rested his hand upon the grip of his holstered .45. He couldn't see much more than the young rider's face as he walked around his horse. "What can I do for you, boy?"

"You're Marshal Bagley?"

"That's me."

"I'm Nick Graves. I hear you're looking for me."

Bagley's eyes widened and the cigarette dropped from his mouth as he quickly drew his pistol.

Unfortunately for Nick, the years of throwing

hot lead for a living overpowered what had happened in the last few days. His instinct to shoot first won out and he brought up the shotgun that had been wedged under his arm. Although Nick managed to get his left hand under the barrel, his right hand fumbled at the trigger guard. He knew he would have trouble working the trigger, but he had no way of knowing how badly his aim would be compromised. In fact, Nick was barely able to hold onto the shotgun when it roared and bucked in his grasp. The fresh blood that had soaked through his bandages and smeared along the surface of the weapon didn't help matters either.

Marshal Bagley dropped to one knee and hunkered down as the shotgun went off.

Nick moved forward and forced himself to aim the shotgun one more time. He got his left hand back into place and then situated his right as well. For a moment, he swore he could feel his missing fingers gripping the weapon tightly. The subtle motions of aiming weren't right, however. He could feel that the moment he tried to sight along the barrel.

Bagley fired a quick shot at Nick, which only missed by an inch or two. "Get out here!" he hollered to his deputy. "Right now, goddammit!!"

Seeing the uncertainty flicker through Nick's eyes, the marshal dove to one side and swung his .45 toward the younger man.

Nick dropped to the ground just as the marshal's shot blazed over his head.

The front door swung open to reveal a surprised

man with bloodstained fists. "Jesus!" the deputy said as he lifted the gun that was already in his hand. "You all right, Marshal?"

Sweat poured from Nick's brow. It was the most rattled he'd ever been in a gunfight since the first time he'd fired at another man. His hands felt as if he was being forced, arms first, into a vat of melted iron. The panic in his heart mixed with the pain to fill his entire body.

Nick saw the deputy, but also saw Marshal Bagley in his line of fire. All but choking on his next breath, Nick fought through the pain and aimed the shotgun. The moment he pulled the trigger, he could feel the gun sliding through his hands. Without a firm grip on the stock or barrel, the shotgun tilted downward just before the hammer dropped.

The thunder of the shotgun blended in with the gut-wrenching scream from the marshal as a load of buckshot ripped through his leg just above the knee. Bagley dropped and pulled his trigger as quickly as he could until the .45 was empty.

Amid the flurry of return fire, Nick ran for the first piece of hard cover he saw. He dove behind the corner of Mather's front porch and scooted down as far as he could. The porch was only about a foot and a half high, but Nick was able to get most of himself behind it while frantically digging for the extra shells he'd stuffed into his pocket.

Still firing at the porch, the deputy dragged Marshal Bagley toward his horse.

"Holy shit," the deputy gasped. "Your fucking leg—"

"Just kill that son of a bitch," Bagley snarled.

The deputy straightened up and took another shot at the edge of the porch. He then climbed up onto the porch and strained his neck to get a look along the other side of it. "I think he's gone. Probably went back to them Hemphills. They're the ones that patched him up before."

"That squirrelly little prick," Bagley snarled as he grabbed hold of his wounded leg. The moment he felt half of his leg hanging by a thick, meaty strand, he pulled in a hissing breath and took his hands away. "Go get that kid and kill anyone that stands in your way."

"What about you, Marshal?"

"Just go!"

More than happy to look away from the gruesome sight of Bagley's leg, the deputy mounted his horse and dug his heels into its sides. The animal let out a whinny and launched into a full gallop. Riding toward the Hemphills' property, the deputy spotted Nick, headed in that direction.

Nick had been reluctant to leave, which was why he wasn't that far ahead. When he heard the sound of someone following him, he brought his horse around. He'd already reloaded the shotgun, so he took it in his right hand and rested the barrel along the top of his left arm. Even though his finger was still a little shaky upon the trigger, it was a bit easier to steady his aim while only using one damaged hand.

The deputy spurred his horse straight toward him and fired a shot, which hissed a few feet from Nick's head.

Once the other horse was close enough, Nick pulled both of the shotgun's triggers and unleashed its two barrels. The gun bucked up off of Nick's arm and gave a thunderous roar that rolled through the air in all directions.

The deputy's horse reared and kicked its front legs out while letting out a terrible scream, which was already fading by the time the horse keeled over. Although the animal caught most of Nick's buckshot, the deputy in the saddle had gotten his share as well. He tossed himself wildly from the saddle, but wasn't quick enough to keep from being caught underneath.

Nick walked over to the deputy while reloading the shotgun. "Who'd you tell about me?" he shouted.

"Don't worry, asshole," came the hurried reply. "Red's gonna know soon enough where to find you! If I was you, I'd start riding for Mexico right now!"

"He's gonna know? That means he doesn't know yet."

The deputy felt his stomach knot. He also felt his legs start to gain some leverage as he continued to wriggle out from beneath his dead horse. "If

you hurt me, them folks that took you in will pay
for it."

"What did you say?" Nick asked.

The deputy sensed he'd gained some ground and
nodded. "Marshal Bagley gave the order, his self. I
told him you were holed up with them folks and
he'll bring hell down on them if you hurt his men.
Ride off now, and—"

A blast from both barrels of the shotgun cut the
deputy off in mid-sentence, while also nearly separating his head from his shoulders.

Nick looked down at the bloody mess and said,
"Nobody's gonna know I was here and they're not
gonna know who took me in."

He fumbled through the motions of opening the
shotgun and digging in his pocket for fresh shells,
but his bandaged fingers didn't find any. Nick tossed
the shotgun and picked up the gun from the deputy's hand. He tried to fish a few rounds from the
dead man's gun belt, but his fingers weren't up to
the task. Swearing under his breath, Nick kept at it
until he'd gotten one bullet free of its leather loop.
That brought the gun's cylinder up to half capacity.

It would just have to be good enough.

Nick rode back to Mather's house and discov-
ered Marshal Bagley was still there. The lawman
had pulled himself to his horse and was just starting his painful climb into the saddle when Nick
arrived. The moment he saw who was coming toward him, Bagley looped one arm over the horse's
back so he could reach for his gun.

Nick knew better than to try and shoot at him from where he was. Although he knew he could hit the marshal on any other day, his fumbling with the shotgun had put him in his place. He climbed down from his saddle, carefully wrapped his hand around the pistol he'd taken from the deputy, and walked over to Bagley.

"I know who patched you up," Bagley said. "You put that gun down or those folks will get a visit from Red's Committee."

There was no emotion in Nick's face as he walked up to within five feet of the marshal. His hands may have been bloody and his fingers mangled, but his aim was good enough to keep Marshal Bagley from moving his gun arm one more inch.

"You fucking bastard," Bagley spat. "No wonder them vigilantes are looking for you."

"How long have you been taking orders from them?"

"Long enough to know it don't pay to go against them. Besides, most of the assholes they string up got it coming, anyway."

"Most? What about the Hemphills? What do you think will happen to them if you manage to tell Red they helped me?"

"You know . . . just as well as I do," Bagley wheezed as his vision started to fade and his grip upon the side of his saddle loosened. "Red likes making . . . examples of folks like that."

Nick flexed his mangled hands and muttered. "An example just like me."

"Let me go . . ." Bagley pleaded. "I need a doctor. Let me . . . get to one and I'll see what I can do about Red."

Shaking his head solemnly, Nick said, "There's only one thing to do about Red and I'm the one to do it. You're just another crooked lawman who shits on the folks he's supposed to protect."

The marshal froze in his spot as he stared down the barrel of Nick's gun. The color was already gone from his face after losing so much blood. Even now, it was getting harder to maintain his grip on his saddle. "The rest of my . . . men will come. They . . . must have . . . heard the shots."

"Here's one more for them to go by," Nick said before pulling his trigger.

TWENTY-TWO

***

Arizona Territory
1884

A cheerful whistle drifted through the air. The man doing the whistling had gathered up an armful of dry wood and was stacking it in a ring of rocks to make a healthy campfire. Since he hadn't wanted to mark his position until he was far enough away from anyone who might see him, this would be the first night that he could have something other than cold beans and jerked beef for supper.

The food was stacked up and ready to be prepared. A freshly killed rabbit lay nearby and he was ready to make a pot of coffee. As the sun eased its way down past the western horizon, the man settled into a spot beside his crackling fire and kept whistling.

He was mistaken about one thing, however.

He wasn't too far for anyone to see him.

The two men who crept up to his campsite just didn't make any noise.

J. D. drifted from one tune into another while his hands busied themselves cleaning the rabbit and placing the meat over the flames. When he turned around to get the bag of coffee beans he'd left in his saddlebag, he saw one of the men crouched not too far away.

"Who the hell?" J. D. snapped as he went for the gun at his side. Behind him, he could hear the subtle brush of iron against leather as the second man drew a pistol and put it against the back of his head.

"Such a nice night," Nick whispered. "No need to ruin it with gunshots."

Letting out an aggravated sigh, J. D. let his gun slide from his hand and into his holster. "If you want to rob me, you're not gonna find much."

"I know. You did just get out of jail, after all."

J. D.'s eyes widened as he started to turn around. The man behind him backed up a bit, but kept his weapon drawn. When he saw Nick's face, J. D.'s knees buckled and he landed with his backside in the dirt.

"You let me go and I left," J. D. said quickly. "I answered your questions! What the hell else do you want from me?"

Nick sat down as Joseph moved up behind J. D. When Joseph took the pistol from J. D.'s holster, he got no resistance. Nick lowered his gun.

"I came up with a few more questions. We'd like to know where you're going," Nick said.

"I thought I might go into Old Mexico. Seems to be a lot safer down there."

"Is that where your friends are headed?"

"I'm alone."

"You know why that is?" Nick asked. "Because the only people who use this trail are either lost or on the wrong side of the law. You're riding to catch up with some of your friends."

"Look around! I'm alone!"

"For now," Joseph grunted.

J. D. shifted to get a better look at Joseph now that he was closer to the fire. When he saw Joseph's face, he scowled and shook his head. "Goddamn gravedigger needs to hire on some help just to keep me from eating my dinner."

Joseph's free hand snapped forward and knocked the hat off of J. D.'s head. Grabbing a handful of J. D.'s hair, Joseph nearly wrenched the man's head off as he forced J. D. to look at him again. "I'm not a hired gun. I'm the man that your friends tried to kill. Those same friends of yours killed my family."

"As you can see," Nick said, "my partner here is a little upset. He'd like nothing more than for me to walk away and let him find some creative ways to put different parts of you into that fire."

J. D.'s muscles slackened and his voice rose to a high-pitched whine. The more he talked, the closer he sounded to breaking into tears. "I already told

you about Dutch and where they were headed.
What more do you want from me?"

"We heard the rest of your gang were using this
trail," Nick said. "So that means there was more you
could have told me before. I want the rest of it."

"Like what?"

"Like the names of the places where the rest of
the gang is going to pick up your new members."

J. D.'s mouth moved, but no words came out.
Judging by the look on his face, even he was im-
pressed as to how much Nick had learned. When
he felt Joseph's grip tighten on his hair, J. D. sputtered, "Pe—Perro Negro!"

"Where's that?" Nick asked.

"A day or two ride east of here, farther into Arizona."

"Where are they headed from there? You might
as well lay it all out for us, because if we need to
track you down again . . ."

"San Trista, and then they'll hit a ranch called
the Busted Wheel."

"Is that the place near Dos Rios?" Nick asked.

"Jesus Christ, who told—"

Joseph shook J. D.'s head as if he was trying to
shake something loose from his ears. "Is it?" he
shouted.

"Yes! Yes!" J. D. squealed. "The man who owns
that place is supposed to have a stash of gold hidden away. It's left over from the strike that let him
buy up so much land."

"Dutch found himself another source of information, huh?" Joseph snarled. "Is that it?"

"Yeah. Something like that."

"And killing the folks there is just a means to an
end? That's how you assholes work, isn't it?"

J. D. squirmed as he tried to think of an answer
that wouldn't buy him a close-up look at his campfire. Unable to find one, he merely clenched his
eyes shut and let out a whimper. When the gun
barrel touched his head once more, the next thing
J. D. felt was the warm flow of urine down the inside of his leg.

"Looks like you made a little mess there," Nick
said through a smirk. Glancing up to Joseph, however, took that smirk right away from his face. "All
right, Joseph. Ease up and let the man talk. He still
needs to tell us the quickest way to find his
friends."

"Anything," J. D. sniveled. "I'll tell you anything
you want. Please . . ."

Nick's eyes narrowed as he studied Joseph's face.
There was fiery rage in the man's expression that
was all too familiar. "You hear me, Joseph? I said
ease up."

Joseph stared intently down at J. D. The anger
that had flared up in his eyes was receding once
more to give way to a coldness, which concerned
Nick more than anything else.

"Hey!" Nick shouted. The sound of his voice
was enough to make both of the other men jump.

J. D. clenched his eyes shut even tighter and whimpered to himself.

Joseph, on the other hand, looked as if he'd been revived with a splash of water. He looked back down at J. D., but without the intensity that had been in him only moments ago. Twitching out of frustration, he shoved J. D. away and stormed from the fire.

"There now," Nick said as he let out a breath. "See how easy that was?"

"That asshole's crazy," J. D. said. He was still letting out the last bit of those words when Nick's fist cracked into his jaw. After J. D. was knocked to one side, he stayed put as if playing 'possum was the only option left.

"That man lost his family, and your friends took them," Nick growled. "You should be praising the Lord above you don't have a bullet in your head right now."

J. D. sputtered and made a weak hissing noise. At first it sounded as if he was trying to spit out the tune he'd been whistling before, but then it sounded as if Nick had knocked a tooth loose.

After a few seconds of that, Nick sighed and said, "Stop it. If I wanted you dead, you'd be dead already."

J. D. kept making the noise. Now he sounded like a whistling teakettle that was moving back and forth from the flame.

"Pull yourself together."

"I can't . . . can't do it," J. D. cried.

"Just take a breath and—"

"It's two short, one long and one short."

Nick stopped and sorted through what he thought he'd just heard. Even after a few seconds, he was still coming up short. "What?"

"The signal," J. D. whined. He started making the noise again, but only wound up with his face buried in the dirt out of frustration and exhaustion.

Nick let out a series of crisp whistles: two short, one long and one short.

"That's it," J. D. said as he lifted his head and nodded. "That's the signal to get in close to Dutch and the rest of the boys. Otherwise, they'll shoot you off your horses before you get within a hundred yards. But you probably already knew that."

Keeping his best poker face intact, Nick said, "Yeah, I knew that. All I needed was the signal."

"Now you have it, just please don't let that other one near me. He's gonna kill me, I can see it in his eyes."

"Stay here," Nick said.

"Oh, God."

"Better yet, just leave."

"Are . . . are you sure?"

"Yeah," Nick said with an annoyed wave. "Just as soon as you give me those directions. And if I smell a lie on you, I'll stick you in that fire, myself."

J. D. rattled off a string of directions to the places his partners would be going. After he was done, he looked to Nick expectantly.

"Get the hell out of here," Nick told him.

"You've got a good heart," J. D. said as he scurried toward his horse. "I don't know about that other one, but . . . I mean . . . never mind."

Nick was headed to where Joseph was standing, but paused long enough to see what J. D. was doing. "Leave the horse," he said.

J. D. stopped with one foot in the stirrup and one hand on the saddle horn. "What?"

"Leave the horse," Nick repeated. "You can go, but you've got to run."

"There ain't much of anything around here."

"Run," Nick growled.

J. D. eased his hand away from the saddle and took his foot out of the stirrup. "All right. I guess I'll be going." With that, he sauntered away from the camp. As soon as he put some distance between himself and Nick, J. D. broke into a run and quickly disappeared.

Taking the rifle from J. D.'s saddle, Nick slung the weapon over his shoulder and walked to where Joseph was standing. "That's a hell of a way to get the most out of someone."

It took a few seconds before Joseph even acknowledged Nick's presence. When he did, it was only with an off-handed, "Huh?"

"The founder of this feast here was holding out on us, but he spilled his guts after that little display of yours."

"I wanted to kill him, Nick."

"Really?" Nick said sarcastically. "I couldn't tell."

Joseph looked back toward the campfire. "Where is he?"

"With the speed he was running, probably getting close to Old Mexico right about now."

"Running?"

"I wasn't about to give him a horse so he could catch up to his friends before we did."

Chuckling under his breath, Joseph said, "You should have just let me kill him rather than leave him stranded out here."

"He's got a better chance than you think," Nick said. "Outlaw trails like this one have all kinds of surprises. There's always a few cabins or caves or something like that for them to use if they get lost or followed."

"You know an awful lot about that."

"Yeah."

Turning away from the fire, Joseph looked back out toward the wide-open stretch of rugged land to the north. "You know an awful lot about a lot of things."

It wasn't a coincidence that there was no better-known trail established through there. The land was a harsh mix of jagged rocks, a few clusters of trees and uneven slopes. In the subdued light of dusk, however, those edges were hidden and the wildness of the land could be seen in a less threatening way.

"Who did you lose, Nick?"

"What?"

Joseph glanced over to him and then looked

back to the landscape. "You talk about things you've seen, but you've never said what happened, exactly."

"There's not enough time to say it all," Nick replied. "Even if there was, I wouldn't want to dredge it all up again."

"I want to stop thinking about my wife and my daughter," Joseph said quietly. "I know that sounds terrible, but I just wish I could put them out of my head. Just for a few minutes so I can rest."

"Now's the time to rest. Once you do, those memories will . . ." Nick winced and then corrected himself. "Actually, they won't ever fade, but they'll be easier to bear. Carrying out what you want to do when those wounds are fresh won't end in anything good."

Although he could tell that Joseph wasn't ready to turn around and go back to his son, Nick could at least tell that the other man was listening.

"You see this?" Nick asked as he held out what remained of the fingers of one hand. "This, and a lot worse, was done by a vicious bastard I used to know. He led a group of killers who called themselves the Vigilance Committee. They're the ones who cut me up and shot pieces of me like I was target practice."

Nick needed to steel himself before continuing. "There were some folks that were kind enough to take me in after I was left for dead. I knew those folks would be in trouble if it got out that they'd helped me. Well, word did get out, and they were in trouble from a group of lawmen who took orders from the Committee.

"The woman who cared for me . . . her name was Sue. I can still see her face every now and then. At the time, she was the prettiest thing in my world. She said that everything would sort itself out whether I fought for it or not. Of course I didn't listen. In fact, I took off and killed enough lawmen to put a price on my head that I'll never shake. All I wanted was to get my hands on those bastards or anyone connected to them in any way. All I wanted was to make them hurt, spill their blood, kill them or anyone they loved, just to pay them back for what they done. Sound familiar?"

Joseph nodded slowly. "Sounds to me like they had it coming."

"When it was all said and done, I rode off to visit the Committee directly and figured those good folks who cared for me were better off if they never saw me again.

"I checked in on them some time later and they were gone."

"Where'd they go?" Joseph asked.

Nick slowly shook his head. "I don't know. Nobody knew. Their house was cleaned out. Their things were gone. The man and his wife . . . their children . . . they were all gone. I'd like to think they headed to greener pastures, but I don't know if that was the case. I do know that I didn't make one damn bit of difference. The Committee came anyhow and took over just like they did in Virginia

City. They rode in like some kind of goddamn army. That family I wanted to protect was driven out . . . or worse. They might have been killed, or maybe Red made an example of them to discourage anyone else from taking in a wanted man."

Nick's eyes drifted toward the empty land. Rather than linger on the muted edges of rock or the trees huddling together to survive, he looked up to the stars that glittered overhead. "I was one of Red's examples. Thinking about those good folks and their daughters going through half of what I did tears me up worse than any blade."

When he looked at Joseph again, the steely resolve was back in Nick's eyes. His face looked as if it had been carved from a slab of granite. "There's plenty of folks out there who deserve plenty of punishment, but all the blood you spill stays on your hands. It doesn't help tip any scales. Just remember that, no matter how bad things are right now, they could be worse. You're alive. So's your boy. Things will work themselves out whether we fight for it or not. Don't fight to make them worse."

Joseph nodded and said, "I just want to make certain they work out the way they should."

"We'll just have to see about that."

TWENTY-THREE

———— ◆ ————

J. D. had built one hell of a campfire. It burned hot enough to cook Nick and Joseph's supper and kept burning through the rest of the night. As the first rays of the sun broke through the next morning, both men were up and saddling their horses. When he saw Nick standing for a little too long at Kazys's side, Joseph walked closer and spotted the bottle in Nick's hand.

Nick turned and held the bottle out. "You want a sip? It takes the chill out of your bones."

Taking the bottle, Joseph shook it back and forth to watch the clear liquid swirl inside. He assumed it wasn't water and took a sniff from the top just to be certain. His suspicions were correct and the liquor's scent scorched the back of his nostrils. "What the hell is that?"

"Vodka. It's a taste I picked up from my father. Try some."

Reluctantly, Joseph put the bottle to his lips and tilted it back. At first, the liquid was cold and even refreshing. Then, the fire hit him as though someone had flipped a match down his throat. The heat traced a path all they way down to his stomach and forced a wheezing breath up from the bottom of Joseph's lungs.

Nick watched with a grin and took the bottle back. He kept right on smiling as he took another healthy sip for himself.

"You drink that?" Joseph huffed. "Seems like it'd be put to better use cleaning out a gun barrel."

"I never thought of that."

"Just keep it away from me."

Nick replaced the cork in the top of the bottle, wrapped it in a towel and carefully set it in his saddlebag. "You just don't know any better. This stuff is hard to find. Most folks would rather drink whiskey that tastes more like kerosene or beer that was brewed in some saloon owner's outhouse."

"Do you have any kerosene?" Joseph asked. "I could use it to wash this taste out of my mouth."

While climbing into the saddle, Nick shook his head and muttered a few words under his breath. Although Joseph couldn't make out most of them, he did catch *vaikeli* somewhere toward the end.

"You see?" Joseph said as he stuffed his bedroll beneath a strap at the back of his saddle. "That firewater made you forget English."

"It's my native language. Something else I picked up from my father. Basically it means . . ." Nick struggled with the translation in his head. "It's like calling someone a tenderfoot."

"Just because I don't like drinking that poison?

Sounds to me like your father didn't think of a tenderfoot the same way everyone else does."

"Actually . . . what I said was closer to 'whiny little kid.' "

Settling into his saddle, Joseph shrugged and said, "Beats drinking kerosene for breakfast." With that, he snapped his reins and started riding.

Nick gave the other horse a small lead before flicking his own reins. Kazys took a few seconds to warm up his muscles, but the horse quickly fell into stride and got moving fast enough to overtake Joseph's horse with ease.

The two of them thundered over the rugged terrain, heading east to meet up with the more well traveled trail that led to Perro Negro. It wasn't a straight route by any means. Every so often, Nick had to turn north or even double back until he was able to find a spot to cross a river or cross a particularly deep gorge.

As he rode, Nick couldn't help but think back to Doug and Sue Hemphill. He thought back to the last time he'd been to their house when there was still life and laughter within those walls. The more he thought about his younger self, the more he wished he could reach back and shake some sense into his arrogant head.

As always, that train of thought led him to the memory of when he'd revisited that house a year or so later. It had been just as he'd described it to Joseph. Actually, it had been worse.

Talking about how bad the silence was when

compared to the laughter of those little girls
wouldn't have helped matters. It would have only
rekindled the fire in Joseph's belly. That fire was
for Nick alone. He hadn't told Catherine or anyone else about the Hemphills. It was almost as if he
was just as afraid of putting them in danger now as
he'd been back then.

Some of the vodka's burn still lingered in Nick's
mouth, but it wasn't nearly enough to wash away
the bloody memories that had revisited him. All
Nick could do was try and move along.

Things would work themselves out.

Letting those words flow through his mind, Nick
could almost hear Sue's voice. Her tone was gen-
tler now—more comforting.

Perro Negro wasn't as much of a town as it was an
overgrown mining camp. Ruts in the ground from
the carts led into a wall of rock to the southeast.
Old storefronts lined the streets and were marked
with faded signs advertising supplies that were no
longer needed. The town and that rock formation
were now very much alike: battered husks popu-
lated by vultures that were too lazy to fly away.

As Nick and Joseph rode through town, the sun
was throwing down an orange glow, but it would
be night soon. The locals went about their un-
seemly business as if they had the full protection of
the dark. One man knifed another in one of the
abandoned storefronts. Whores pulled down the
fronts of their dresses to anyone who looked in

their direction. Drunks puked on the warped remains of a boardwalk and then collapsed in their own mess.

"What are we doing in this dung heap?" Joseph asked. "Looking for an outlaw here is like looking for a needle in a haystack."

"More like one particular piece of hay in a haystack," Nick corrected.

Joseph shook his head and looked around once more. "Those killers could be anywhere around here. I doubt there's any law to point us in the right direction."

Nick laughed and leaned over so he could speak in a whisper. "I wouldn't even mention law around here. Besides, the men we're after aren't here. They would've moved on a while ago."

"Then why are we wasting time?"

"There could still be something around that can help us. We needed to water the horses, anyway, so we'll just do that here and look around."

"Any suggestions on where to start?"

Nick rubbed his chin and shifted in his saddle. "I'm not sure. Do you see anyone that looks suspicious?"

Joseph was clearly not amused. "I think you've been drinking too much of your father's liquor."

"Looks like there's only two main streets," Nick said. "You poke around at the saloons on this one and I'll take the saloons on the other. Say you're looking for work and ask if anyone is hiring."

"What kind of work?"

"You were a rancher," Nick pointed out. "The men we're after stole your herd and are probably out to sell it. What kind of workers do you think they'd be looking for?"

"Probably brand artists, most likely," Joseph replied without much hesitation.

"Brand artists?"

"Yeah. They cover up another ranch's brand or find some way to change it around. It's easy enough to spot if you know what you're looking for. Anyway, that's the sort of talent someone would need if they're dealing with all those stolen cattle."

Nick nodded and said, "Learn something new every day."

"That's not the answer you were expecting?"

"I wasn't expecting anything. You're the rancher, not me. At least now I know what to ask for at those saloons. See what we can accomplish when you're not stomping around with your dander up?"

"Yeah, sure. What kind of information are we asking about?"

"First of all, it would be good to have a better idea of how many men we're up against. I could guess, but that won't get us anywhere. That gang came through here looking to replenish their numbers, so we should try to find out how many took them up on their offer. If there wasn't many takers, we might be able to ride in on them a bit faster. Also, have you ever heard of San Trista?"

Joseph thought about that for a moment and shook his head. "Never heard of it."

"It'd be good to know what kind of law they have there, how big the place is, if there's been any trouble. Some better directions would be nice."

"Asking that asshole back at his camp would have been a good idea."

Nick laughed. "That fellow may have been scared, but there's no way I'd go by any directions he gave. He could barely spit the name out. If he had any sense at all, he would have told us just enough to get us good and far away from him before turning back."

"I do have a notion as to where the Busted Wheel Ranch is. Some of my men used to talk about it."

"Can you get us there?"

Joseph started to nod and stopped short. "It could take a while."

"Then we could use any information on that as well."

"Not asking for too much, huh?"

Nick shrugged and said, "Keep your ears open about any of it. If we find a few things on one of those subjects, we're better off than when we started."

"Got it."

After checking the battered watch in his pocket, Nick said, "Let's meet back here in two hours whether we're done or not."

"Good. Hopefully we'll be ready to get the hell out of this hole," Joseph said distastefully.

"Maybe. This town actually brings back a lot of old memories."

"Remind me to never ask you about them."

With that, the men parted ways. Joseph rode toward the closest end of the street and Nick rounded the corner.

When Joseph tied his horse to the post outside the first saloon, he doubted he'd ever see the animal again. He stepped through the swinging doors that were rotting on their hinges and thought he'd pass out from a stench that hit him like a slap in the face.

The place was as much of a saloon as Perro Negro was a town. Fewer than a dozen bottles were kept on a shelf behind a bar tended by one Indian with greasy hair. The bar, itself, was just a pair of long tables set end to end. One of the tables was raised up so it came up to the Indian's waist. A few small round tables were scattered about, outnumbering the chairs two to one.

The people drinking in there were loud and leaning against one another, since there was nowhere to sit. Joseph walked through them, doing his best not to touch anyone unless there was no other choice. He could see the Indian behind the bar glaring at him well before he made it to the taller of the two tables.

"I was hoping you could tell me—"

"What do you want?" the Indian interrupted.

"I need to know—"

"What to drink?"

"Nothing right now."

"Then get out."

Joseph recoiled as if he wasn't certain he'd heard the Indian correctly.

"Drink or get out," the Indian told him. "It's not hard."

"I'll have some water."

The Indian took an empty jar from under the table and then turned around. He held the jar below his waist, fidgeted with his pants, straightened up and let out a slow breath. Soon, the sound of something pouring into the jar could be heard. It was followed by a sharp, bitter smell.

The Indian fidgeted with his pants some more and then turned back around. Wearing a broad, obscene smile, he set the jar on the table and said, "Drink up."

Joseph looked down at the jar and its pale yellow, slightly foaming, contents. Although he wanted nothing more than to knock that jar of piss straight back at the one who'd made it, he took a second to think. The Indian looked ready to fight. In fact, he looked as if he was already planning on where to dump Joseph's body.

"I'll have a whiskey," Joseph said as he pushed the warm jar away. "And if you put any water in that, I'll make you drink it."

For a moment, the Indian was quiet. Then, his smile returned and he laughed loudly. "I wouldn't ruin whiskey that way," he declared, taking the jar away and dumping it on the floor.

Joseph watched the Indian like a hawk, but didn't see anything besides whiskey go into the glass he was given. After taking a sip, he set the glass down. The Indian stood directly in front of him.

"What else did you want to ask?" the Indian said.

"I want . . . a job."

"I don't need any help."

"Not here," Joseph added. "I'm a brand artist."

The Indian nodded. "You're too late. Someone came around hiring cowboys a few days ago."

"Did they get any takers?"

"A few. Some gun hands went along. Sons of bitches still owed me money."

Since he didn't know what else to say, Joseph looked down at his whiskey and then took another sip. The burn of the liquor didn't do much to ease the frustration filling his gut.

"I don't know how to catch up to them," the Indian continued without missing a beat, "but Schultz might."

"Schultz?"

"Fat man with hair that looks like a bird's nest. He owes me money, too."

"Tell me where he's at and I can see about collecting that debt."

The Indian grinned as if Joseph were a child who'd decided to stand up to him. "That's asking for a lot of trouble. Too much trouble to be worth eighteen and a half dollars. He drinks and sleeps at the Six-Forty, down the street. One of his brothers rode off with those cowboys."

"You sure?"

"Shultz was bragging about how his brother gave him some of the advance pay he got when he was hired on. Like I said," the Indian added with a deadly glint in his eye, "that son of a bitch owes me. Waving money around without paying doesn't sit right. If you see him, punch him in his fat stomach for me."

Digging in his pocket, Joseph took out a carefully measured wad of money and set it on the table. "There's twenty dollars," he said. "I made the offer, so I'll back it up."

"What about the rest of it?"

"I'll try to punch him at least once."

Joseph could hear the Indian laughing even after he'd walked out of the saloon.

TWENTY-FOUR

Joseph realized he should have asked for better directions. He assumed "Six-Forty" was the name of the place, but half the saloons he saw didn't have any signs on their fronts. One of them, however, had an old clock dangling precariously from a copper arm. Sure enough, the hands on that clock were stuck at six-forty. Joseph stepped into that place and wasn't as affected by the pungent aroma that hit him in the nose. This saloon was a bit bigger than the first one and even had a real bar. Looking around, he spotted a couple of card games going on in the back.

The sound of knuckles cracking against flesh and bone rattled through the stale air, followed by a torrent of raucous laughter as something heavy hit the floor. Two skinny drunks with half a set of teeth between them were fighting. Sitting close to the fracas was a fat man, wearing a gray shirt, who seemed to fit the Indian's description.

Joseph walked up to the fat man and tapped him on the shoulder.

"Uh?" the fat man grunted as he strained to look up and around at Joseph.

"Are you Schultz?"

"What the fuck do you care?"

"Is that a yes?"

"Sure it is, now go fuck your mother."

Joseph balled up his fist and slammed it into Schultz's mouth. The sound brought another wave of cheers from the surrounding drunks, along with two men who stood up and marched toward Joseph with fire in their eyes.

Seeing those other men close in around him, Joseph turned and said the first thing that came to mind. "Stay out of this. I'm collecting money for the Indian."

One of the other men was a stout fellow wearing at least four different pelts buckled around different parts of his body. He squinted through a pair of light brown eyes and asked, "What Indian?"

"The one behind the bar at the saloon down the street. Which one did you think?"

The men looked at one another, studied Joseph and then looked at the fat man with the fat lip. Sniffing once, like a dog examining a table scrap, the man with the furs said, "Sorry, Shultzie. You're on your own."

Joseph did his best to keep the confident look on his face as the other men slowly drifted away. At the very least, he managed to keep himself from looking too surprised when they left him and Schultz alone at the table. By that time, the rest of the saloon had already found other things to worry about.

"Look here," Schultz said as he squirmed around to the other side of the table. "I got the Indian's money. I just don't got it with me."

"Then tell me about the men who came through town looking to hire cow hands."

Shultz squinted and sputtered, "What?"

"You need to be more helpful, or I'm supposed to start taking scalps."

The moment he said that, Joseph thought he might have pushed just a little too far. Judging by the horrified look on Schultz's face, however, the Indian barkeep must have been known for worse things than just serving piss to his customers.

"This ain't a cow town," Schultz quickly said. "There's no work for cow hands."

"Don't give me that bullshit. You know what kind of work I mean."

"Then you already know they was looking for branders and anyone who would get their hands dirty for pay. They also needed scouts."

"Scouts?"

"Yeah. Riders with fast horses who could cover a lot of ground. My brother weren't one of them, but one of his friends fit that bill just fine. Anyone looking to work was supposed to meet someone in San Trista."

"Where is that?"

"A few days' ride south of here. It's just a hacienda with a general store that serves drinks. Ride south until you hit a dried up riverbed. Follow that until it hooks east and turn west, instead. You'll hit San Trista before long. I don't know who'll be there, though. They said not to bother if it took too long to make up their minds."

"I'll just have to take my chances."

"You like taking chances, don't ya boy?"

"Pardon me?"

Schultz spread the corners of his mouth apart in a wide, filthy grin. He snorted and wheezed with the effort of leaning forward until he was close enough for Joseph to smell the rotten meat stuck in the fat man's teeth.

"You ain't asked for the money I owe that Indian," Schultz grunted. "I bet you can't even tell me how much it is."

"Eighteen and a half dollars," Joseph recited.

"You still seem to have forgot all about it so you could ask about them men that came along to give my brother a job. You the law, boy?"

Every time Schultz called him boy, Joseph felt his teeth grind together. The fat man seemed to have picked up on that right away and now put extra emphasis on the word.

"I asked you a question, boy. You the law or are you just trying to stick yer nose into my brother's affairs?"

Before Joseph could answer that, he heard boots scraping against the floor behind him. A few quick glances over his shoulders told him that those men who'd been scared off before were now closing in

on him again. As the men got closer, Joseph wondered if he could draw his gun before they made
their move. In the time it took to ponder that question, he knew he was already too late.

"We don't take to the law 'round here, boy,"
Schultz grunted. "Fact is, we like to slice law dogs
open and pin their badges to the fucking wall behind you. That's why I prefer this here place over
that Indian's saloon. What do ya say, Stein? You
think this asshole's got another badge to pin to the
wall?"

The tallest of the men standing behind Joseph
laughed under his breath and dropped a hand on
Joseph's shoulder than felt more like an anvil. "If
he don't, I'm sure his balls'll do just fine."

As the men closed in behind him, Joseph could
hear them all laughing to each other. They were
looking at him as easy pickings and that, alone,
sparked a fire inside his gut.

Balling up his fist, Joseph turned and swung his
arm around like a whip. The side of his fist cracked
against a man's head, making him stagger back and
to the side. Pain flared in Joseph's hand, so he swung
his other one with the same amount of fury.

"Get 'im Stein!" Schultz hollered.

The man who responded to that was taller than
Joseph and outweighed him by at least fifty pounds.
His blond hair was cropped so short that it looked
like bristles on a brush. He grabbed hold of Joseph's shoulder and shoved him hard enough to
spin him like a top.

Joseph's first reaction was to take a swing and Stein stood there to let him do it. His fist made solid contact, but thumped uselessly against a wall of pure muscle. He swung again, but only got a pain in his knuckles for the effort.

Stein grabbed the top of Joseph's head in an iron grip. He pulled back his left fist and smashed it into Joseph's face.

For a moment, Joseph thought that Stein was the only thing holding him up. His legs turned to pudding and he couldn't feel the floor beneath him. He only realized he was falling a split-second before his backside hit the floor. When he dropped, all the air was forced from his lungs.

It took a second for Joseph's vision to clear. He was sitting on the ground with his legs splayed out in front of him, leaning back on his arms for support. Above him, Stein was trading jokes with Schultz as the fat man pulled himself out of his chair to get a better look.

Joseph couldn't see everyone else in the saloon, but he could hear them shouting and cheering as if they were watching a stage show. When Stein looked down at him with a cruel purpose in his eyes, Joseph knew he had to make a move before he was knocked out for good. Frantically grabbing for the gun tucked under his belt, Joseph fumbled a few times before finally managing to pull the weapon free.

"Lawman's got a gun," Stein growled. "But he don't got the sand to use it."

Holding the pistol in hand, Joseph placed his thumb on the hammer and immediately thought back to the man he'd killed with that same gun. The longer Joseph waited, the wider Stein's smile grew.

"Maybe he ain't no law dog," Shultz said.

Stein slowly drew a gun from his own belt. In the big man's hands, the weapon looked like a toy. "Maybe, but he sure as hell won't be walking out of here."

Joseph couldn't hold his gun up. It weighed his arm down to the point that the end of the barrel tapped against the floor. When he heard that sound, Joseph snapped his eyes up as well as his arm. The pistol made a satisfying thump as he slammed it straight up into Stein's groin.

Stein's knees bent and his body slumped forward. He dropped the gun so he could move his hand between his legs. For a second or two, Stein didn't make a sound. He then let out a strained moan and lowered himself to one knee.

Joseph collected the gun that Stein had dropped and jumped to his feet. Holding a pistol in each hand and keeping the rest of the saloon at bay felt good enough to make him forget about the throbbing pain in his face. "Anyone else interested in trying their luck?" Joseph asked.

There were no takers.

Swinging one of his guns to aim at Schultz, Joseph said, "Put any weapons you got on the table."

The fat man complied, producing a gun from his holster and a knife from his boot.

"How many men came through here looking for hired guns?" Joseph asked.

The fat man sputtered for a bit and then spat out, "Five or six."

"And how many took them up on the offer?"

"Maybe another five or six. I don't know for certain."

Joseph glared over the barrel of that gun as he tried to think of anything else he should ask. Unable to come up with anything, he nodded and backed toward the door. "All right, then," he said. "Anyone who wants to push their luck can follow me out this door."

The rest of the men that had been fighting on Shultz's behalf lowered their heads and backed away. Everyone else in the saloon was just waiting to make sure the show was over.

Once he was on the street, hardly anyone bothered to look at Joseph. The fact that he still had a gun in each hand didn't seem to carry much weight. Joseph tucked his gun back into its regular spot and then found another space under his belt for the one he'd taken from Stein.

Passing by the next saloon, Joseph went straight to the one at the end of the street simply because it was far away from the rest. He went inside, ordered a drink and downed it in one swig. The next drink went down just as fast.

TWENTY-FIVE

———◆———

"So," Nick said as he walked up to Joseph a while later, "you get into any trouble?"

Although the question was meant as a joke, Nick could tell Joseph was rattled by it. His eyes quickly picked up on something else, as well.

"Where'd you get the second gun?" he asked.

When Joseph let out his breath, it was thick with the stench of cheap whiskey. "Let's just get the hell out of here."

As they were riding out of Perro Negro, Joseph told Nick about what had happened during his tour of the saloons. Nick listened and nodded, every so often checking Joseph's face to see if he could spot any hint of a lie. When he didn't see one, he let out a low whistle.

"Jesus," Nick said. "All I got was a belly full of bad beer and a few stories about men riding through there looking for cowhands. Sounds like this was your lucky day."

"Lucky?" Joseph muttered. "I damn near got killed."

"But you didn't," Nick pointed out. "Very lucky."

It was pitch black, but they kept riding until Perro Negro was well behind them. Nick made a small fire while Joseph threw together a quick meal of beans and coffee. While they ate, both men compared what they were able to gather during their expedition through town.

"I feel like I was the lazy one," Nick said. "You waded into that mud hole and came out with damn near everything we needed."

"Cost me twenty dollars, but it was well spent."

"From what I've seen, you've got plenty to spare."

Joseph instinctively looked over to his horse. The strongbox was no longer hanging from his saddle, since the money inside of it had been secreted away between himself, his horse and Nick. "If it costs me all I got to see this through," Joseph said as he shifted to face the fire, "it'll be worth it."

"Well, I might not have had as much excitement, but I did learn a thing or two while I was away," Nick said.

"Really? What's that?"

"One of the men I found was planning on heading down to San Trista to meet up with the fellow offering those jobs."

"So we're not too late?"

"We're cutting it close, but we should make it."

Joseph nodded. "That is good news."

"Here's some even better news." Nick grinned

and leaned forward as if he was afraid one of the
rabbits in the shadows near the camp would over-
hear him. "This same fellow's already gotten word
from San Trista that there's only one or two men
waiting there to round up whatever men answer
the call."

"Then we might as well head straight for that
ranch, since that's where folks are going to be in
real danger."

"On the contrary, I think we should get to San
Trista as soon as we possibly can."

Joseph looked at Nick's face, but still could not
figure out what was causing the excitement on it.
"All right, I give up. Why should we go there just
for one or two of that gang and a few locals?"

"Because those locals are the gang's backup. If
we can swing in there and take out at least those
two that are waiting for them, the rest will be cut
loose altogether. Remember that signal our friend
on the Silver Gorge trail told us about?"

"Yeah."

"I'd bet everything I've got that those two men
waiting at San Trista won't tell the others about
that signal until it's absolutely necessary. Hell, they
might not even tell them about it when they get
there. What're a few whistles if you don't know
any better?"

Suddenly, Joseph's eyes widened as a look of un-
derstanding flashed across his face. "This would
be like cutting off a supply line."

Nick nodded and leaned back again. "Exactly!"

"That's actually pretty smart. It's a good thing you're here. I think I'm starting to lose my nerve."

"Why do you think that?" Nick asked. "Because you didn't leave a pile of bodies in that saloon?"

"No. Well . . . maybe not a pile of them."

"But a few would have been nice?"

Joseph shook his head and looked away, but it was clear that Nick had hit close to the mark. "I guess those just weren't the men I wanted to see."

"Well, don't worry about that. It sounds like we'll be meeting up with them soon enough."

With Joseph leading the way, the short ride to San Trista soon became a race between their two horses. Although he'd started out in the lead, Joseph eventually found Kazys nipping at his heels. The older horse had built up a head of steam and ran past Joseph so quickly that his horse shied away.

It took Nick a few miles to rein in Kazys and slow Joseph down as well. By the time the small settlement known as San Trista came into view, both animals were chomping at the bit to keep the race going. They weren't the only anxious ones.

"What's the matter?" Joseph asked as Nick slowed to a stop a fair distance from the shacks in front of them. "That looks like the place up ahead."

"And it won't be going anywhere," Nick assured him. "Unlike the men who could bolt from there at a moment's notice if they don't like the way we're riding up on them."

"There's only two or three buildings over there. You think there's a way we can sneak up on them? Hell, they probably already saw us coming."

"Which is why we shouldn't look like we're out to stampede over them. Think for a second."

Although he wasn't too happy about it, Joseph finally had to nod. "I guess I see your point."

"Good."

"So what are we going to do?"

Nick leaned forward in his saddle toward the small cluster of shacks. Squinting at the crooked buildings, he said, "I can only see a few horses there. Could be the men from Perro Negro, or it could be the ones waiting for stragglers."

"I say we ride up like we're looking for work, just like we did at those saloons."

"Now you're thinking. This time, though, let me do the talking."

The town was made up of a run-down general store and a pair of shacks, which were probably home to whoever owned the store. The two men were only thirty or forty yards away from the store when someone came outside, looked in their direction and went back in.

"I don't like the looks of this," Nick said.

"Why? What happened?"

"I think he recognized us."

Narrowing his eyes to angry slits, Joseph checked the guns under his belt and said, "Let's get moving."

Before Nick could say anything for or against the plan, Joseph was carrying it out. Nick kept alongside Joseph, watching for any hint of movement around the store.

By the time Nick and Joseph rode up to the storefront, its inhabitants were noisily pushing open its rattling doors. Boots stomped against the ground as men rushed outside.

When Joseph saw George among the men coming out to meet him, the color drained from his face and his voice dropped to a barely audible tone. "I'll be damned," he said.

George was with two other men and all three of them were armed. In fact, all three of them had their guns up before Joseph's surprised statement was out of his mouth. However, it was Nick's modified Schofield that sent the initial clap of thunder through the air.

The man to George's left had a wiry frame and a quick gun hand. He was so quick that his trigger was halfway pulled when Nick's round caught him in the upper chest. The impact of the bullet took the wiry gunman off his feet as his finger jerked around the trigger. His shot went straight into the ground.

The gunman standing to George's right was barrel-chested and a bit longer in the tooth. He took his time in drawing and firing a shot. If Nick hadn't already started swinging down from his saddle, he might very well have caught the incoming round. As it was, the bullet hissed over his head and barely caused Kazys to twitch an ear.

Even though George had drawn his gun, he had

yet to pull the trigger. It seemed that the frightened young man wasn't even thinking about firing when he caught the brunt of his former employer's vicious stare.

"Where the hell are you going?" Joseph snarled as George backed away. He nearly stumbled over the planking in front of the general store in his haste to get back inside. The barrel-chested gunman took a quick glance, but he had a full plate already, since Nick was still intent on using his Schofield.

As Nick moved forward, he took in the scene as if he was admiring it from afar. His eyes calmly darted from one spot to another, watching for any additional threats while keeping track of the ones already in front of him. His arm remained extended and he stopped firing once he saw his target drop behind a stack of old crates piled up near the store.

"Joseph, watch out!" Nick shouted when he spotted Joseph headed straight for the store.

But Joseph did not seem to care that he was heading toward the other gunman. Joseph's only concern was George inside.

Although he couldn't see the barrel-chested gunman, Nick had no trouble figuring out the man's intentions. As Joseph was about to pass the crates where the gunman was hiding, Nick shot his last two rounds through the dirty wooden boxes. Dust exploded from the splintering wood and Joseph stormed through it on his way to the door.

Nick kept his eyes on those crates as he went through the well-practiced motions of reloading his gun. Holding the pistol in his left hand, he plucked spare bullets from his gun belt using his right little finger and flipped them into his palm. He slid each round slid into the cylinder, transferred the pistol to his right hand and shut it with a snap of his wrist.

Before Nick could do anything else, the crates were knocked over as the barrel-chested gunman stormed toward him. He still was too busy reloading to take a shot. After snapping the cylinder shut, the stocky man balled up his fist and drove it into Nick's midsection.

"I hear you're the one that killed J. D.," the gunman snarled as Nick doubled over and let out a pained grunt. "Fucking gravedigger shot him in the back. J. D. was my friend."

Nick struggled to straighten up, but wasn't even able to draw a breath. He was surprised to find that he still had his gun in his hand.

The bigger man seized him by the throat and pressed his gun barrel against the top of Nick's head. As soon as the iron touched his skull, Nick's instincts took over. He flattened his left hand and shot it straight up, catching the gunman's wrist and forcing his pistol into the air. The gunman's finger snagged against the trigger, sending a shot above their heads, as Nick fired a bullet of his own into the gunman's foot.

It was the only shot that Nick could take that

had no chance of missing. Hot lead drilled through the top of the gunman's boot and foot, and dug several inches into the ground beneath it. The instant he saw the man's wounded leg jerk up reflexively, Nick leaned forward and knocked the him on his ass.

The man landed with a heavy thump and let out a surprised grunt. His wounded foot stayed in the same spot, while his gun arm splayed out over his head. His eyes focused on Nick standing directly over him, the modified Schofield aimed directly at the outlaw's face.

"Be smart and toss the gun," Nick warned.

The man glared up at him and swore under his breath. He surprised the hell out of Nick by doing exactly what he was told.

TWENTY-SIX

———— •◆• ————

George stumbled through the general store, knocking blankets off their tables and tipping over barrels of flour along the way. He had a gun in his hand, but had forgotten all about it as he strove to distance himself from the door.

"What's going on out there?" the silver-haired store owner shouted. "I thought you men were leaving!"

"Shut up," George snapped. "Just shut up!"

A moment later, the door swung open again and Joseph stomped inside. He, too, seemed to have forgotten about his gun. In his case, however, it wasn't because of panic.

"Who're you?" the old man asked. "Jesus, how many more are there?"

Joseph ignored the store's owner completely as he lunged straight for his former ranch hand.

George's efforts to move away were blocked by a table stacked high with brushes and blocks of soap. His back knocked against the edge of the table, and he pushed himself on top of it so he could scuttle backwards over it.

"Trying to run off again, Georgie?" Joseph said, knowing how much the younger man hated to be called that. "Or are you just trying to set up another party in my honor?"

George swung his arm around, preparing to finally fire his gun. In his haste to be rid of Joseph, he pulled his trigger way too early and his wild shot hit one of the store's glass display cases.

"God dammit!" the owner shouted as he fixed his distraught eyes upon the shattered case.

Joseph remained focused upon George. He lifted his gun and took a shot, which caught the ranch hand in the hip. Joseph kept moving forward until he was close enough to grab hold of George's shirt. "You son of a bitch! You're the one that killed my family!"

George's eyes grew wide and he wildly shook his head. "No! No! I didn't fire a shot that night!"

"But you got everyone out of there so those bastards could ride right in! You watched as my wife was killed! You watched my little girl die!"

George's mouth flapped open and shut as he tried desperately to say something in his defense. When he heard the shots being fired outside, George remembered the gun in his own hand. He tried to take aim, but Joseph slammed the handle of his gun into George's wrist.

The slender bones of his hand snapped on impact and George let out a high, feminine scream.

"You!" Joseph snarled as he pounded his gun down once more in the same spot. "You let them kill my family!" With tears burning his eyes, Joseph brought the gun up, pointed it at George's eye and stared down its barrel.

Not only was George crying, he was sobbing. It was a pathetic mix of pain, fear and regret as he slowly shook his head while muttering, "I didn't know it would be like that, I swear. I thought they'd just take your herd."

"You told them about the money I was saving."

"I saw you take some money into your study and told them about it. I thought I knew where it was hid, but . . . I didn't know they'd treat An—"

"Don't," Joseph snapped, "say . . . her . . . name."

George was still shaking his head as the last shot from outside faded away. "I wouldn't have done any of it if I knew, Mister Van Meter. You gotta believe me. You folks were good folks. Anne was so nice to me. Laurie was the cutest—"

He was interrupted by a single shot from Joseph's gun.

That shot roared through the store just as Nick pushed the side door open. He stepped into the store with his gun drawn, taking in what was going on. "How many are here?" he asked the old store owner.

"Just them two. Jesus, they destroyed my new cases!"

Seeing Joseph staring down at George, Nick

pointed his gun at the ranch hand and slowly stepped forward. He felt the anger poring from Joseph in waves. Approaching him then was like inching up to a rattler that already had its fangs bared. When he saw the smoke pouring from Joseph's barrel, Nick knew he was too late.

"Don't say their names," Joseph whispered to the dead man beneath him. "I told you not to say their names."

Holstering his gun, Nick reached out to carefully place a hand on Joseph's shoulder. Joseph swung his gun around reflexively.

"It's just me," Nick said. "It's over. They're all gone."

Joseph looked around in a daze and lowered his gun.

"Get some supplies so we're set for the next couple of days," Nick said. "In fact, get as much as we can carry. We'll need to move fast."

Seeing the recognition in Joseph's eyes, Nick knew that the man's reasoning had come back to him. He then grabbed George by the collar and belt so he could heft the dead weight over his shoulder. For Nick, carrying the body was just another day at work, and he lugged the corpse outside while Joseph started gathering up food.

Outside, the gunman Nick had left flopped onto his belly and began inching toward the gun that he'd tossed. His hands were tied behind him and his ankles were bound, forcing him to move like a caterpillar. He could hear the rusty hinges squeaking and the thump of heavy footsteps behind him, but kept inching his way on the ground while straining his wrists against the ropes.

Suddenly, the footsteps came to a stop. Next, the unlucky gunman heard the heavy crash of something being dropped in front of him. He had to pull his head back a bit to get a look at what it was. "Jesus Christ!" the gunman hollered when he saw the gaping hole in George's head.

Nick squatted down beside the body he'd dropped. "There's one of your friends," he said. Grabbing the gunman's hair and wrenching his head around to face the first corpse, he added, "And there's the other. If you want to keep from joining them, you'd best tell me how many men you and George hired on."

"Four," the outlaw replied. There was no fear in his voice. Instead, there was just resignation. "They already rode ahead to meet up with the rest."

"Where at?"

"Some ranch named the Busted Wheel. It's about twenty miles or so from here, due south."

"You're a cooperative sort."

"What the hell I got to lose? If you were gonna gun me down, you wouldn't have trussed me up like a goddamn steer."

Nick studied the bigger man's face and then nodded. "All right."

When he saw Nick walk over to pick up the gun that had been tossed away, he asked, "Ain't you gonna untie me?"

"Nope."

The gunman was still grousing outside when Nick poked his head into the store. "You got a firearm, old man?"

The store owner looked around as if he didn't know whom Nick was addressing. He then pumped his head up and down. "'Course I do. I ain't stupid enough to make a move against armed killers, though."

"How many of them were here?" Nick asked.

Scrunching his eyebrows thoughtfully, the old man replied, "Them three you already met and four more. There were a few others who came by a few days ago, but that was just to conduct some business."

"What kind of business?" Nick asked carefully.

The store owner nodded toward a narrow hallway behind his counter. Standing there, huddled together, were three women in various stages of undress. They appeared to be a little frightened, but curious nonetheless. "That kind of business," the old man said.

"You run a whorehouse as well?"

"And sell liquor. This is the only store for miles, so's I figure on taking advantage. I just hope to hell those bastards don't kill the girls I sent out to them camps when they hear about what happened back here."

"When are they due back?" Nick asked.

"Tomorrow. Maybe I should bring them back sooner, though."

Nick blinked a few times and glanced back to Joseph. When he looked back to the old man, he said, "We might just be able to help you with that."

"How?"

"We'll go and make sure they get back here without you or anyone else having to risk yourselves."

"Why would you do that?"

"Because that way you can forget it was us who shot these men and you can let anyone who asks know that we're just working for you."

The old man squinted at Nick carefully as his face slowly pinched up. "You ain't the law. Are you bounty hunters?"

"We want to get close to those killers," Joseph said. "That's all you need to know."

Finally, the old man shrugged and said, "Fine. If you can get my girls back, that's all I care about. You two sure got a better chance of walking into them camps and getting out alive than me and the kid who normally runs my whores. You make it back and I'll even forget about the damage you caused to my place. It ain't gonna cover the cost of all that food and supplies you're takin'."

Just then, Joseph walked up to him and handed over a small bundle of money. "That should be enough to cover the supplies."

The owner counted up the money he'd been given and stuffed it in his pocket.

"You'd better find that shotgun of yours," Nick

said. "There's someone out there you might want to keep an eye on. He's tied up, but you still should be careful around him."

"What should I do with him?"

"Call the law or feed him to the coyotes, I don't give a shit which. We just don't have the time to waste on him."

As Joseph dragged the bags he'd packed out the door, the shop's owner looked around as if he'd been thrown into the middle of a whirlwind. Clenching his fist around Joseph's money, he shrugged and wandered over to collect his broom and shotgun.

TWENTY-SEVEN

The gang was divided into two small camps with just over a mile between them. In the main camp, Dutch talked to the men who'd gathered up the fresh recruits and discussed their next move. He'd looked in on the other camp before returning, like a field commander making the rounds among his troops.

"Lot of new faces," said one of the veteran gang members.

Dutch nodded and picked up a stick off the ground. With his other hand, he pulled a hunting knife from his belt and started whittling away the tip. "There should have been more, Bertram. You know that."

Bertram nodded. "Yeah, I know."

"What happened?"

"It's too soon after the raid at Van Meter's place. Some law's been poking their noses into it after all that ruckus and—"

"No law's been looking into it," Dutch cut in. "No more than usual, anyhow, and you know it."

Bertram shrugged and said, "Then I don't know why. We got more'n enough to pull the next few jobs, though, so what's the problem?"

"The problem is that you've been getting lazy. You've also been getting sloppy. You took too much time at the Van Meter ranch."

The memories brought a smile to Bertram's face. "That bitch wife of his was mighty fine," he said in a slow, breathy manner. "I wouldn't have minded fucking her even after we sliced her up."

Dutch's eyes shifted in their sockets and fixed upon Bertram. When that wasn't enough to dim the smile on Bertram's face, Dutch barked, "Shut your damn mouth!"

"What's the matter, Dutch? Jealous because we got to have the fun? That herd must be sold off by now. Maybe you can buy yourself some pussy." Licking his lips, Bertram added, "That younger girl at that ranch, though . . . she was the kind of sweet meat that you can't even buy. At least, not without looking real hard for it."

Dutch looked down for a second, snapped his eyes back up and then grabbed Bertram underneath his chin. Pinching Bertram's throat between his fingers, Dutch pulled the other man forward and said, "I put up with a lot of your shit because you get results. You fucked up at that ranch and it may have cost us money."

"Them bitches didn't have any money. I searched 'em real good."

"The rancher did, but he was shot before he

could tell us the rest of what we needed. Seeing as how we haven't heard from the man I left behind, the rest of that money is probably gone for good."

"We can always go back."

Dutch's grip tightened around Bertram's throat. His eyes narrowed a bit more and his lips curled back to reveal a set of perfectly straight teeth. "Now you're just talking like a goddamn fool and I don't tolerate fools."

"You're gonna have to tolerate me a bit longer," Bertram said. "I'm the most experienced man you got."

"Keep that fucking tone in your voice and the next thing you'll experience is the grave."

The smile on Bertram's face didn't fade, but it did lose a good amount of its cockiness. It was a subtle change, which made a world of difference.

When he saw that shift in Bertram's manner, Dutch loosened his grip and finally opened his fingers wide enough for the other man to slip free. "Maybe I should stay to oversee these new men," he said.

"My boys are doing fine," replied Bertram.

"Your boys are like you. They think with their dicks at the wrong times and it may have already gotten some of them killed."

"What's that supposed to mean?"

"You heard from those men who stayed behind at San Trista?" Dutch asked.

"No, but it hasn't been that long."

Dutch shrugged. "They should have been back

today and they're not. They're probably rolling around with some of those whores you found. Either that, or they're wasting time shepherding them whores back and forth between here and town instead of doing what they get paid to do. Or there could have been some trouble," Dutch added. "Trouble like whatever J. D. ran into."

"They're a day late," Bertram reiterated. "I wasn't even starting to worry about them. Besides, if there's trouble, they can handle themselves."

Dutch stared silently into the distance, his face resembling a portrait. While other men were known for how they collected their scars in various fights, Dutch was known for being in twice the number of fights without getting scarred once. His eyes were cold and calculating; they gazed off a little too long before blinking.

"Any word from J. D.?" Dutch asked.

"Not since we heard he was out of jail. Most of us didn't even know he was in jail."

"So where is he now?"

"I couldn't tell ya. Probably trying to catch up to the rest of us."

Judging by Dutch's expression, he didn't care for that explanation one bit. His annoyance only grew when he saw Bertram shifting from one boot to another without a care in the world. "Where's Bill?"

"What do you need him for? All he ever does is herd cattle."

Dutch answered that with a burning gaze that shoved Bertram a few steps back.

"Fine, fine," Bertram said, raising his hands. "I'll get him. Jesus Christ."

After Bertram had been gone a few minutes, another man walked up to Dutch. He was lean and had the look of someone who'd been raised on the floor of a desert. His skin was tough and creased. His hair was dark brown and stringy. When he approached Dutch, he did so with a respectful nod and then waited for the other man to talk.

"What's been going on here, Bill?" Dutch asked.

"Same bullshit you'd expect. Bertram shoots his mouth off day and night when he's not fucking some whore he brought in from God knows where."

"Is he getting his job done?"

"I suppose. All he needs to do is say 'howdy' to a bunch of wet-behind-the-ears gun hands who aren't much better than he is, so there isn't much of a way for him to mess up. At least they all kiss his feet on account of the women he brings in."

Dutch laughed under his breath and nodded. "You seem bored, so I got a job for you to do."

"As long as it involves me getting the fuck out of here, I'm plenty willing."

"I don't know if you heard, but I got a telegram from J. D."

"J. D.'s alive?" Bill asked.

"Yeah, and he was in and out of jail. He was headed to meet up with us, but nobody's heard from him since."

"How long ago was that?"

"We got the telegram almost a week ago. Anyhow, he should have caught up with us a few days ago. I want you to backtrack and see if you can find J. D. He was taking the Silver Gorge trail, so take that all the way back to Ocean if you have to."

Bill winced and commented, "That's an awfully tall order, isn't it? I mean, there's a lot of ground to cover and plenty of spaces for one man to get lost. He could have just fallen off his horse and I'd never find him."

"I know. We also haven't heard from George. This was the last day for him to wait for any more men looking to sign on, and there's been no word."

"I know. Bertram didn't seem too worried."

"Bertram's got shit for brains," Dutch said. "That's why I want you to ride through San Trista on your way out. Make that your first stop and send word to me at the normal spot. You know where I mean?"

Bill nodded.

"Don't wait for a reply. Just head on across to the Silver Gorge and start looking for J. D. Got it?"

"You think something happened to George and J. D.?"

"I don't know, and that's the part that gets under my skin. You find out for me and do it quick. If something is going wrong, we need to know about it and take care of it before it gets out of hand."

"What if the law's the cause of these problems?"

"Then you kill any law dog that's sticking his nose in our business. Things are going too good for that kind of bullshit to trip us up."

Bill kept nodding, but had let his eyes wander away from Dutch.

"You got something else to say?" Dutch asked.

He started to shake his head, paused and reluctantly said, "There's been talk about some of the men at that Van Meter place getting killed by some gravedigger from town. What if he's the one that got to J. D.?"

Dutch's eyes burned holes through Bill's head. His jaw shifted back and forth, slowly grinding his teeth together. "Did you see this gravedigger?"

"Not up close. I was rounding up that rancher's herd when the rest of you were shooting up the man that owned that spread. I heard the shots and tried to get there, but was too late to be of much help. Still, someone did shoot the hell out of the men that were going after one of that rancher's kids."

"And it wasn't the rancher, himself?"

Bill shook his head.

"If you hear about someone that killed one of our men," Dutch said, "gravedigger or not, I want him dead. Kill him in a way that'll make anyone else think twice about stepping up to anyone who might even be a distant acquaintance of ours. Kill his family, too. There's no reason that rancher should be the only one to get special treatment.

"Anything less and we look weak. Men in our line of work start looking weak and we might as well invite the law or other cocky little pricks to try their luck with us."

"And what if someone off that ranch is still alive and trying to hunt us down?"

"Then make him wish he was killed right along with the rest of that family."

TWENTY-EIGHT

───────◆───────

Four whistles cut through the air outside of the northernmost camp. The first two whistles were short, followed by one long and one more short. Hearing that combination, the camp's lookout lowered his rifle and raised his hand in a slow wave. Before too long, he got another wave in return from one of the two riders who were approaching.

"Looks like our friend with the wet pants was good for his word," Nick said as he waved toward the camp.

Joseph rode beside him and let out a short acknowledging grunt.

Both of the horses were breathing heavily and walking slowly after covering the ground between the camp and San Trista.

"Hold on a second," Nick said cautiously.

Joseph looked along Nick's line of sight and saw what had caught his attention. A single rider was thundering toward them, kicking up enough dust to make a black cloud in the early-evening shadows.

"Maybe we should have waited a bit longer before coming here," Joseph said. "Looks like all of them aren't settled in just yet."

"Don't get too riled up just yet. Let's just wait and see what's on his mind." His voice was calm, but Nick still placed his hand upon the grip of his gun.

Joseph didn't go near any of the guns he'd collected, but sat up tall in his saddle as if he could stare down whoever was approaching no matter how much distance was between them.

As the rider got closer, Nick raised his hand in a similar fashion as the wave he'd gotten from the camp. Racing by with his back hunched along his horse's neck, the rider returned the wave and kept on riding north.

Nick shifted and watched until the only remaining trace of Bill's horse was the echo of its steps. "All right, looks like we got someone looking out for us," he said.

"How many men you think are in that camp?" Joseph asked grimly.

"I don't know, which is why we're not riding in there with guns blazing."

Joseph snapped his head around to look at Nick. "What do you mean by that?"

"I mean, you may not care if you get killed, but I don't particularly fancy the idea."

They kept their horses walking toward the camp at an easy pace. Already, the other man who'd waved to them had turned and walked out of sight.

"When we get there, just follow my lead," Nick said. "I'll do the talking, and if you need to say something, make it short."

"I should only speak when spoken to?" Joseph asked sarcastically.

"That's exactly right. And don't draw your gun unless I do it first. Do you understand me?"

"If things go bad, I'm not about to wait and—"

"If things go bad, taking one step out of line will only make them worse."

Joseph let out a disgruntled breath and worked a kink out of his neck. "Are you going to tell me what you have in mind or should I just wait to be surprised while you talk to me like I'm a child?"

"So glad you asked," Nick replied with a grin.

As Nick and Joseph rode into the camp, the smells of burned coffee and cigarette smoke hung in the air and drifted among the four tents that were set up in a circle around the fire. Five horses were tethered nearby, and three men sat on the ground with their legs stretched out and their backs against a log. One of them got up, dusted himself off and ambled over to Nick. "You fellas are damn lucky if you're here about them jobs. You're late, but we wound up staying here a bit longer. You can call me Bryce."

Nick put on a friendly smile and shook Bryce's hand. "We're not exactly here about the jobs, so does that mean we're not lucky?"

"Uh . . . no. What are you here for?" Bryce asked as he nervously glanced from Nick to Joseph.

"We're here to collect the women and bring them back to San Trista," Nick said.

"Ain't no women here. Hasn't been for a day or two."

"Other camp's having all the fun?"

Although the man nodded, he didn't seem at all happy about it.

"There's something else you might want to know. Fella by the name of George asked me to pass it along."

"Let's hear it," Bryce said.

Ignoring the man's request, Nick looked over Bryce's shoulder at the fire. "You still got some of that coffee I smell?"

Raising his voice to make sure the men behind him could hear, Bryce said, "If you can smell it, I'm surprised you want it."

One of the men still seated by the fire flipped a rude gesture over his shoulder and grunted, "Kiss my ass, Bryce."

"If I don't get something in my gut soon, I'm about to fall off this horse," Nick said as he casually surveyed the camp.

"Sure. Come on over."

Nick climbed down from his saddle and nodded toward Joseph to do the same. As he walked over to the fire, Nick counted up the men he could see as well as what kind of guns they were carrying.

"Your partner don't have much to say," Bryce said as he squatted down next to the fire and used a dented kettle to fill two equally dented cups.

"I'm not supposed to talk," Joseph muttered.

Two of the other men sitting at the fire laughed at that. One of them said, "We keep telling that to Bryce, but he don't listen."

Bryce rolled his eyes and handed Nick and Joseph each a cup of coffee. The brew tasted every bit as bad as it smelled.

"You want some food?" Bryce asked. "I think there's still some stew around here somewheres."

Nick sipped the coffee and shook his head as the bitter sludge went down his throat. "Thanks, but no."

Bryce sat down and rubbed his hands together next to the fire. "So what's the word from Georgie?"

"There's been some law dogs poking around, asking about stolen cattle being driven across state lines. You're supposed to head for an old fort southeast of here."

That caught all the men's attention. They shifted so they could each look at Nick's face. "What?" Bryce said.

"George and the other one in town already headed over there. He was in a rush, so he made sure I knew your signal so I could tell you where to meet up with the others."

"The law ain't been a concern for Dutch before," Bryce said.

Joseph lowered his coffee cup and quickly added, "There're Federals with this bunch. A cavalry unit meant to trap rustlers trying to slip out of Texas."

"God dammit," one of the other men said before he was silenced by a quick wave from Bryce.

"One of Dutch's men was just here. How come he didn't tell us about this?"

"Because he didn't know about it," Nick replied. "This is the first place we stopped."

Bryce reflexively glanced in the direction that Bill had ridden only a few minutes ago. He then looked south toward the other camp. When he shifted his eyes back to Nick, he was nodding slowly. "What's this fort you're talking about?"

"It's not far from here, but it should put you well out of that posse's way." As he spoke, Nick could see Bryce shifting more and more. His eyes wouldn't stay still and he hardly looked at Nick directly.

"And you're sure them laws don't know about it?"

Feeling Bryce's growing nervousness, Nick kept talking until it seemed Bryce was about to bust. "If they do, you men should be able to handle them. It is a damn fort, after all. Look, we're just the messengers. We're going to the other camp and tell them the same thing. We can come through here on our way back to let you know what they said, but don't expect us to waste too much time. Those whores need to get back."

Joseph raised his eyebrows and looked over at Nick. "They could stay here if they want, but I don't want to meet up with all them Federals. Not if these are the boys they're after."

"I'll go with you to talk to Dutch," Bryce finally said.

Nick sipped his coffee as if he was sitting on a veranda. Keeping his cup up to his mouth, he shrugged and said, "If you want. The more I think of it, though, the more I like the idea of trading lead with that posse. Those sons of bitches killed a dozen men last time they rode through here."

"Just a dozen?" Joseph asked. "I know more than twenty holes in the ground that were filled by them Federals."

After listening to that, Bryce was more than anxious to leave.

Twenty minutes later, Nick and Joseph were halfway between the two camps, dragging Bryce's unconscious body into some bushes.

"You think those men will miss our friend here?" Joseph asked.

Nick laughed and lobbed Bryce's gun into the shadows. "Are you joking? Those men were wound so tight, they'll be a mess by the time we get there." Pulling himself onto Kazys's back, he added, "All we'll need to do is say that Dutch told them to follow us and they'll do it. Just mentioning a blood-hungry posse was enough to make a few of them twitch."

Joseph climbed into his saddle and shook his head. "If I didn't know any better, I would have sworn you were enjoying yourself."

The grin on Nick's face was plain enough to see.

TWENTY-NINE

"You sure that other camp is up ahead?" Joseph asked.

"That's what Bryce told me. I guess I should ask for that fellow Bertram. His name came up a few times."

Joseph nodded and rode ahead into the shadows. The landscape had thinned out to more desert than trees, reminding him of the open spaces that had surrounded his own ranch. It was easier to think of his place as simply gone rather than how it was when he'd last seen it. Picturing those charred frames and trampled grounds only made it harder for him to stand patiently at Nick's side when he did his fast-talking.

The moment they glimpsed the fires of the second camp, both men saw there was a difference between it and the other one.

"That camp's bigger," Joseph said. "A lot bigger."

"Yeah," Nick replied. "It sure is. I'd say double the size of the other one. Maybe more."

"Two of them are headed this way."

Nick patted the modified Schofield strapped across his belly. "I see 'em."

"You think you can talk your way through this?"

"I can give it a try. If not, be ready."

Joseph gave a quick nod rather than say anything out loud. The approaching pair of riders was already close enough for them to be heard over the rumble of the horses' hooves.

The moment Nick picked up the motion of the men reaching for their guns, he whistled the signal as clearly as he could. Although the men eased up a little bit, they kept their hands near their weapons.

"Who the hell are you two?" the first man asked as he came to a stop directly in front of Nick.

"We just rode in from San Trista to pick up the girls that were brought here. They're due back in town. We stopped at the other camp and were told to pass along a message to you fellas."

The second rider stopped in front of Joseph and said, "Who sent the message?"

"His name's Bryce," Nick said. "He told us to let out those whistles so you wouldn't gun us down."

The first rider's hand closed a bit tighter around his pistol. "We ain't gunned down anyone bringing us whores yet."

"I need to tell you about a posse headed this way," Nick said with just the right amount of nervousness in his voice. "The men at the other camp already packed up and headed to an old fort northeast of here. They're scouting ahead and clearing the way in case those Federals manage to find the place."

"Federals?"

Noticing that the men were eyeing him suspiciously, Joseph spoke up. "Some of the local law around here are riding with a cavalry division on the hunt for rustlers."

Judging by the looks on their faces, the riders bought into the story just as well as the previous men. There was a mix of suspicion and confusion on their faces, but not enough to make Nick worry. Finally, the first one told his partner, "You start getting everyone around and I'll go check with Bertram."

"We'll come with you," Nick said. "We do still need to collect them whores."

"There's only one here, but she may not be ready to go. You'll tell Bertram the rest."

Nick and Joseph followed the first rider deeper into the camp while the second rider started making his rounds at all the smaller tents. Within the space of a few seconds, preparations were being made to move out. It was plain to see that the men were ready to break camp at the first signal.

The tent where the first rider stopped was separated from the others by about twenty yards. It was larger than the rest, but still not quite big enough for anyone to stand up inside. Judging by the heavy breathing coming from it, the two people in there weren't worried about standing up.

"Bertram," the rider grunted as he swung down from his saddle. "Someone's here to see you."

The rustling inside the tent continued and was soon followed by a woman's giggling. By this time, Nick and Joseph were also on their feet and keeping an eye on the rest of the camp. The few men there were tossing supplies onto the backs of horses and starting to wander to the west.

"I'm already seein' someone," Bertram replied from inside the tent. "A whole lot of someone."

"It's important."

Bertram muttered a few quick words to the woman in the tent with him before crawling out and tugging his pants up over his waist. "What the hell's the problem that it's important enough to drag me outta that lady in there?" he asked amid the stench of his liquor-soaked breath.

"These two say we gotta pick up and head north."

Bertram was still fidgeting with his belt and dealing with the playful hands that were trying to pull him back into the tent. When he finally took a moment to look at Nick and Joseph, he stopped and said, "Hey, I know you."

Before Bertram could react, Nick drew his gun with a flick of his hand. The modified Schofield cleared leather and was aimed at the head of the rider who'd escorted Nick and Joseph to the tent. Meanwhile, Joseph had his own pistol in hand and pointed it at Bertram's face.

"Get in the tent," Nick said under his breath. Jamming the gun in their escort's ribs, he added, "And do it real quick."

The rider sighed and hunkered down so he could fit through the tent's front flap. Nick removed the gun from the rider's holster and shoved him into the tent with the heel of his boot. The rider fell face first onto a pile of blankets that were bundled up between a busty redhead's legs. She scooted to the back of the tent and tried to take the blanket with her, but her legs were too weighed down for her to budge. With one foot snagged under the blanket, she draped one arm over her generous breasts and the other across her lower half.

Bertram kept his eyes on Joseph and nodded slowly. "Yeah, I know you. You're that rancher from California."

Joseph's eyes were narrowed and seething with rage.

"Van Meter? Ain't that your name?" Bertram asked.

Nick busied himself with tying up the rider with whatever he could find. The woman's skirts weren't being used at the moment, so he quickly knotted them around the man's wrists. "You," Nick said to the woman. "Tie up his ankles. And you," he said, looking at Bertram, "shut your mouth."

"I'd suggest you do what he says," Joseph said quietly.

Bertram ran the tip of his tongue along his upper lip. "I remember your wife a whole lot more than I remember you. She tasted real good. I buried this tongue of mine so far into—"

Joseph lunged forward like a rattlesnake. He kept himself more or less upright with one hand braced against the ground inside the tent as he shoved the barrel of his gun against Bertram's chest. When he pulled his trigger, only a muffled thump could be heard.

The woman's eyes grew wide as saucers and her mouth dropped open when she saw Bertram's body flail under the point-blank gunshot. Nick's free hand shot out to clamp over her mouth and he leaned forward far enough to wind up on top of her.

The man at the wrong end of Nick's gun had been shoved halfway outside the tent and had somehow pulled up half the stakes along the way. As the dirty canvas settled on top of them, Joseph pulled his trigger again. The sound of the gunshot was absorbed by Bertram's chest in the same way that the redhead's scream was absorbed by the palm of Nick's hand.

Nick kept his gun pointed at the other man. "What's your name?" he asked.

The confused look on the man's face only got worse as Nick thumbed back the hammer of his Schofield.

"Your name," Nick repeated.

That metallic click did its job and the man spat out, "Eddie."

"Stay real quiet, Eddie, or my partner will put you to sleep just like he did your friend."

Eddie glanced over at Bertram's unmoving body, but didn't have the courage to meet Joseph's eyes. It was plain to see he couldn't make much of a sound even if he wanted to.

Nick pulled the body in under the partially collapsed tent. Looking at the redhead, he said, "Come along with me and I'll get you out of here. Be sure to look happy about it, or this won't work."

She nodded quickly and was all too anxious to get out from under the canvas.

When Nick stood up, he put a big smile on his face. Dropping his gun into its holster, he met the eyes of a few other men who were staring at the tent from their horses' backs. "If you boys are gonna sleep with guns under your pillows, we might not bring our girls out here anymore."

The men had begun to work their way over to the tent, and their faces brightened unanimously when they saw the naked redhead behind him. She brushed the dirt off her plump backside and legs. Remembering what Nick had told her, she put on a smile and did her best to cover herself with her hands.

Nick took off his jacket and draped it over her shoulders. "Good job, honey," he whispered. "Just keep it up and we'll all be out of here. Where are the other girls?"

"These boys must not've touched a woman in a good long while, because they finished quicker than you please. I'm the only one that needed to stay." Nodding in response to the whistles and hoots that had started coming her way, the redhead added, "I haven't gotten my fee yet, you know."

"Earn it by smiling to these men and keeping your mouth shut."

The other rider who'd met Nick and Joseph outside the camp rode toward them. Although he also took a long look at the redhead, he wasn't as amused as the other men behind him. "Where's Bertram?" he asked.

"He heard my message and left. He said the rest of you should do the same," Nick replied. "Eddie headed out and told me to take this lady into town. He also paid me to show you men to that fort. I'll gather up this tent and all for free."

"I didn't see Eddie ride away."

"Weren't you getting the rest of these boys moving?"

"Yes."

"There you go," Nick said confidently.

"What was going on in Bertram's tent?"

Looking over his shoulder, Nick laughed and said, "Just a little argument over who got the last kiss. It's all in good fun, though. You got a problem, take it up with Bertram once we get to where we're going. Otherwise, you'll be arguing with a posse riding up your asses."

The man nodded. "I sure as hell will take this up with him."

Just then, the redhead stepped up to the rider so she could reach up and run her hand along his chest. She went all the way down to his crotch and let her hand linger there for a few seconds. "Don't worry. Have I ever let you boys down?"

"No," the man said honestly. "You sure everything's all right?"

"It's just like he said. Eddie told him to show you men the way, and I'll make certain he does that. In fact, I can ride back to town on my own."

Eventually the man nodded and shot a quick glance at Nick. He turned in his saddle and shouted, "Everyone stop gawking and get moving. We're meeting up with the others, and I don't want to take all night getting there!"

The redhead strutted over to a light brown mare and pulled a set of britches from the saddlebag. She slipped them on, pulled off Nick's jacket and tossed it back to him. "If I don't get my money right now, I'll catch up to those assholes and set them straight," she said, taking a dress from the saddlebag and pulling it over her head.

Nick reached into his pocket, took out a chunk of the money he was carrying for Joseph and handed it over. "There's just under a hundred dollars here. For that, I expect you to keep quiet and back up our story if anyone asks."

She took the money, counted it and smiled. "I didn't intend on seeing these cowboys again, anyway."

"Good."

"You mind telling me who you are?"

"It's best that I don't."

"Don't worry about what your friend done," she said. "I've seen worse, and that Bertram fellow was the worst kind of pig. He had me brought out here the last three nights and always tried to cheat me." When she reached out to straighten Nick's collar, it was plain to see that she hadn't buttoned her dress all the way up just yet. "I was just hoping to earn the rest of this money."

Nick's hand closed around her wrist. Her skin was warm and smooth. She pulled in a quick, expectant breath that made her breasts strain against the fabric of her dress. Before long, Nick eased his hands away.

"You've earned it," Nick told her. "And then some. Just ride home and forget this whole night ever happened."

Shrugging, the redhead let her eyes move up and down Nick's body. She then turned her back to him, climbed onto her horse and flicked the reins. True to her word, she pointed the animal's nose to the west and never looked back.

When Nick walked back to the camp, he found the collapsed tent was the only one that remained. All the other men were either busy stuffing their saddlebags or had already ridden away. Joseph squatted next to Bertram's tent, cleaning the barrel of his gun against the canvas.

"What'd you do with the whore?" Joseph asked.

"I let her go. By the way, I had to give her some money."

"You think she'll tell those others about what we did?"

Nick shook his head. "She's got no reason to. If she gave a damn about anyone here, she wouldn't have cooperated so easily." Nodding toward the tent, he asked, "What about them?"

"That rapist cocksucker is dead."

"And I took care of the other one."

Eddie was covered by the canvas. Peeling back the tent, Nick tied Eddie more securely and shoved a wad of material into his mouth. Making a few unhappy grunts, Eddie strained to look up at Nick.

Even though the makeshift gag muffled most of what Eddie said, Joseph heard enough to make him point his gun down at the man's head. "This son of a bitch was there, too," he said as he tightened his grip on his gun until his hand started to shake.

"Are you sure about that?" Nick asked.

Joseph pulled in a breath and let it out through clenched teeth. "Even if he wasn't, he's riding with these killers now!"

"We don't have time for this," Nick snarled, looking around. "We're damn lucky those men are riding away from here. Do you want to draw them all back by firing a shot that'll be heard for a mile in every direction?"

Joseph hesitated.

Nick stepped forward, dropped the heel of his boot against the side of Eddie's head, and then covered him and Bertram with the tent. "There," he said as Eddie let out a groan and slumped into unconsciousness. "Now holster that gun and let's get the hell out of here."

THIRTY

———◆———

Only a few words passed between Nick and Joseph before they were on their horses and leaving the camp. Nick set Kazys moving at slightly faster than a walk, while Joseph tore away as if his horse's tail was on fire. Fortunately, Bertram's men had just enough faith in what Nick had told them that they waited a while before getting too anxious.

"Where's your partner?" one of the horsemen asked as Nick made his way to the group gathered away from the camp.

"He went ahead to make sure the others made it to the fort without getting lost, which is exactly what I intend on doing with you fellas."

"What took you so long in getting here?" the other man asked as he craned his neck to look around. "And where's Bertram?"

"Bertram and Eddie already left. They told me to give them a little distance so they can scout ahead to make sure that posse isn't setting up an ambush."

"How long are we supposed to wait?"

Nick let out a strained laugh. "If you want to keep busy, you can ride on ahead and chew Bertram's ear about it. He told me to give him a head start and that's what I intend on doing. You've dealt with him a hell of a lot more than I have, so you must know what to say to make sure he doesn't shoot you like he did those others I heard about."

There were no others and Nick wasn't even certain that the man he was speaking to hadn't grown up with Bertram. He could just feel the anxiousness among all the other men, who reeked of inexperience. But Nick's gamble paid off: The grousing horseman nodded and shut up. By the looks of them, the others were new to the gang. They waited for Nick to give the command to start moving.

Hoping that Joseph had had enough of a lead, Nick flicked his reins and announced, "I guess we should set out. We're headed northeast for about five or six miles. Our associates should have already led the men from the other camp by now, so we'll have cover once we get there."

"How big's this posse supposed to be?" one of the other men asked.

Nick shrugged and looked around. To his delight, almost all of the men were staring back expectantly, doing their damndest not to look nervous. "Hard to say. Could be five . . . could be a dozen."

"What the hell are we waiting for? Let's get moving."

"I'm with you," Nick said. "If Bertram sees any

lawmen headed toward us, we'll hear the shots."

"You'll hear shots all right," said the horseman who'd appointed himself the spokesman for the group. "I'll be shooting those assholes right out of their saddles!"

That got the rest of the men worked up into a hollering mob. Nick pointed Kazys northeast and snapped the reins. Although he was wincing on the outside, he couldn't have been happier on the inside. Riding with a vigilante group had taught him plenty about using a mob to his advantage. Nick figured he could work with this one just fine.

Joseph was so anxious that he almost forgot to whistle the signal when he approached the first camp. He remembered real quickly when he saw at least five rifle barrels gleaming in the dim moonlight. The horsemen kept their guns where they could get to them in a pinch even after Joseph gave the signal.

"Where's the other one?" someone asked.

Joseph's voice was tense, but that worked in his favor as he quickly recited what Nick had told him to say. "Bertram wanted to ride ahead to the fort to make sure it was clear. We're to follow right behind him."

The man who'd asked the question had a long face and a mustache that hung down past his chin. His eyes were narrowed as if they were constantly fighting the sun's glare. "I been around these parts for a while and I never seen no fort."

One of the other riders was younger and looked

about ready to start running if his horse didn't get moving soon enough. "I seen a lynch mob ride from out of nowhere once and they blasted the hell outta a gang of horse thieves! They come from the south just like he says."

Joseph nodded. "The fort's five or six miles to the southeast. Anyone that would rather take their chances on their own can do what they like. Bertram told me to bring you men to the new camp and that's what I aim to do. If you stay behind, I suggest you keep on riding and forget about any sort of job."

As Joseph was starting to ride away, he heard something that he hadn't been expecting.

"To hell with this," the young horseman said. "That lynch mob hung those men from a pole and left 'em there for days with piss stains on their pants for the world to see. I ain't getting strung up like that." With that, the young man lowered his head and steered his horse away from the rest so quickly he almost twisted the poor animal's neck.

"You damn coward!" the man with the long face said. "What the hell did you expect you was gonna do to earn yer pay?"

Despite the harsh words pouring from the older horseman's mouth, a few of the younger ones followed the kid, who had yet to look back. That only left four men with Joseph.

"Are you men with me?" Joseph asked.

"Yer damn right."

"There may be some trouble along the—"

"If there is," the horseman interrupted, "we ain't a bunch of snot-nosed kids, and we can prove that to Mister Bertram."

When Joseph looked around at the other men, he saw intense faces and angry eyes. The anxiousness hanging in the air over the men's heads reminded Joseph of a herd working itself up into a stampede. "All right then. We've wasted more than enough time already."

"Lead the way."

Joseph snapped his reins and got his horse moving, quickening the pace until all five horses were charging into the shadows. He shook his head in amazement. "This might actually work," he thought.

Kazys chomped at the bit to run faster. It seemed the horse could sense what was coming as surely as if Nick had whispered it into his ear. All nine men riding with him were anxious as well, but they were more than happy to let Nick stay up front and lead the way. In fact, when he looked over his shoulder to check on them, it seemed he'd lost a few along the way. Nick grinned and faced front. He was surprised that some of those kids hadn't ducked out sooner.

After riding a few miles, Nick strained his eyes toward the northwest. The shadows were thick, but the stars and moon allowed him to make out shapes from a fairly good distance. Just when he was starting to worry about Joseph being found

out and overtaken by the men in the first camp,
Nick spotted a few shapes moving at a quick pace.
Nick kept a close eye on the figures until he was
certain they were headed for the spot that he and
Joseph had agreed upon. A little bit longer, and
Nick was able to make out the rough shapes of
men on horseback.

Nick breathed in to steady himself and then
turned around in his saddle.

"Looks like we might have some trouble!" Joseph shouted to the men following behind him.

The horseman with the long face trotted up next
to him and asked, "Where?"

Joseph pointed to the south at the shapes he'd
spotted a minute ago.

The rider twisted and looked in that direction.
Soon, his eyes were able to pick out the same shapes
that Joseph had been searching for the entire ride.
"Holy shit! Is that the posse?"

"It's not anyone I know," Joseph said. "The
other camp's been cleared out already. Besides, the
fort is to the southeast. Those men are riding in
the opposite direction."

"They sure are. They're headed straight for us!"

Two of the other men joined them. "What're
you talking about?" one of them asked.

"Someone's riding straight at us," Long Face said.

"It's got to be that posse," Joseph added. "They
must have been on their way to the fort when they
heard us coming."

"Or they've already been there," one of the others offered.

"Wherever they've been, they're headed this way now!" Joseph shouted. "And it looks like they've already got their guns drawn."

"How the hell can you see that?" Long Face asked. "I'm lucky I don't steer my horse into a goddamn hole."

"I ride this stretch of land all the time. I know a damn posse when I see one, and I know what a gun looks like. Can't you see them?"

"Jesus Christ. I see 'em, all right!"

Nick drew his gun and held it pointed upward. His throat was straining after getting the others riled up so far, but he wasn't about to let up now. "Posse's riding straight for us! Get ready!" he shouted.

While most of the men drew their guns and held them at the ready, a few of them glanced back and forth as if they didn't know what to do. Nick sized them up in an instant, guessing they would either bolt now or after the first shot had been fired. He knew better than anyone that it was always easier to talk like an outlaw than ride like one.

"They sure as hell ain't turning," Long Face said to Joseph. "You think we can outrun them?"

"If you don't mind giving them your back," Joseph replied. Seeing the way the men were squinting ahead at the approaching horses, he drew his own gun and pointed it toward the other group. "It's the posse!" he shouted. "That's one of them right up front!" Before anyone could say a word or do a thing, Joseph pulled his trigger.

The shot cracked through the air, but Nick didn't hear the hiss of a bullet come anywhere close to him. Even so, he took a shot of his own. "They're shooting at us!"

That was all the rest of the men needed to hear before they took aim and started firing wildly.

Nick gritted his teeth and kept shooting well above the other riders until he could make out which of them was Joseph. As return fire started coming back at him, he prayed that Joseph's men were as rattled as the ones behind him.

Joseph didn't need to act in order to look rattled. He'd heard about men riding into battle during the war and always figured it was terrifying. This scene was more than enough to prove those stories right.

Glancing over his shoulder, he could see the hardened faces of the remaining riders as they squeezed off shot after shot. The bullets flew in a steady stream, most of which came from pistols. Long Face had enough presence of mind to draw the rifle from his saddle and take his time before pulling his trigger. Joseph kept firing and then eased his horse slightly away from the rest.

"One of them's bolting!" Nick shouted. "Let him go. Try to get the rest before they get too close."

Even though he repeated himself a few times, Nick knew his voice was being swallowed up in the growing crackle of gunfire.

As the two groups drew closer, the gunfire intensified. A few men around Nick let out pained grunts as some of the bullets found their mark. None of the men had fallen, but with the shots hissing closer and closer, that would change soon enough.

THIRTY-ONE

———◆———

Nick steered Kazys away from the group, but a few of the horsemen followed. He knew that, soon, men on either side might recognize a familiar face or two. He wasn't certain any of the new prospects had met each other, but it was always better to assume the worst.

As if reading his mind, Joseph let out a piercing whistle that could be heard over the gunshots and thunder of horses. A loud holler followed as Joseph snapped his reins and steered his horse back around to the group, which turned their horses directly toward Nick's group.

Recognizing an experienced cattle driver when he saw one, Nick snapped the reins and touched his heels to Kazys's sides. The horse responded immediately and put some extra steam into his strides. From there, all Nick had to do was guide the horse with an experienced hand and hang on for the ride as he used the same tactic to get his own men charging faster.

The groups rushed toward each other like steam engines on a collision course.

Shots blasted between them and men screamed curses back and forth.

The chaos lasted for a few seconds before building to a peak. After that, the men closed to within a pistol's effective range. Two riders from Nick's group were ripped from their saddles and one from Joseph's bunch fell. One of Nick's boys pulled his horse to one side and tore away from the fight as fast as he could.

"There's no way I'm going to that fort!" Long Face said as he sighted down his barrel and shot one of their opponents off his horse. "Lord only knows how many more lawmen are coming."

Joseph tried not to look angry that the other man was sticking so close to him. "Then get as far from here as you can! Just go!"

"To hell with that! I'm riding to that ranch. Mister Bertram may be mad now, but he'll take all the help he can get when they start that raid." Shifting in his saddle, he shouted, "Come on with me!"

One of the men jerked back as a bullet ripped through his shoulder, but he managed to stay on his horse and nod to Long Face.

"You coming along?" Long Face asked.

Joseph heard a bullet hiss past him and got his horse running in the opposite direction from the others. "That's not my dance," he said.

Long Face waved him off and got moving. He

switched to a fresh pistol from his double-rig holster, fired at the other riders and headed west.

"Dammit," Joseph muttered, as more and more bullets were aimed in his direction.

"They're running!" Nick shouted to the three men that were left in their saddles on his side.

A few more shots were fired, but those quickly tapered off. After that, there came the metallic clicks and rattles of cylinders being emptied and fresh rounds being put in their place.

"I say we go after them," one of the horsemen shouted. He was a thick man with a head so bald that it shone like a wet rock in the moonlight.

"We ain't even getting paid yet!" the youngest of the horsemen replied. "This was just to keep from gettin' strung up!"

"They're already gone," Nick said. "That fort's probably full of dead men by now. You men should just get the hell away from here."

"The fuck I will," the bald horseman snarled. "Those goddamn law dogs killed my partner and tried to kill the rest of us. I don't let nothing like that pass."

Nick shook his head and tried not to feed the other man's fire, but he could tell that at least one of the others was starting to be swayed. The third horseman was the youngest. He hadn't spoken either way on the matter, but was already maneuvering his horse next to the bald man.

"Look there," the bald horseman said. "One of 'em's coming this way."

Nick had to squint, but he could see that one horse was circling back. Despite the great pains Joseph was taking in riding as stealthily as possible, the terrain was simply too open for a rider to go unnoticed for long.

"He is coming back," the youngest rider said. "He might be scouting so the rest of them can attack us again."

"Or his horse is scared," Nick offered anxiously. "If they're lawmen, we can't stand around and let this one see our faces. If they're vigilantes, I sure as hell don't want to give them another reason to come after us. Just get the hell out of here and be done with it! He won't be able to spot any of us if we cut out now."

As he fixed his eyes upon the horse in the distance, the bald horseman switched his pistol into his left hand while taking up his rifle in his right. "Fucking lawman. Fucking vigilante. Whoever this asshole is, he's gonna regret not running with his chicken-shit friends when he had the chance."

"Let him go," Nick said sternly. "We shouldn't push our luck."

Even the younger horseman picked up on the change in Nick's tone. All of the remaining three riders now watched him as carefully as they were watching Joseph closing in on them from the shadows.

"What's the matter?" the bald one asked. "You gone sweet on those fellas?"

"No. I just want to get out of here without having to dodge any more bullets."

"I think you gone sweet on them. Or maybe you're with them. You sure seemed to lead us straight into this shit storm."

The young horseman started to nod as his eyes grew wider. "Yeah! Yeah, he did. Holy shit!"

"This is crazy," Nick groaned. "They were shooting at me just like they were shooting at you."

"But they didn't hit you."

"They didn't hit you, either."

"But I'm not the one that wants to let 'em go." Turning to address the other two, the bald horseman said, "You know what Mister Bertram would like? If we dropped this cowardly asshole right here!"

Just as the other two horsemen started to raise their voices in agreement, three shots blasted through the air: one for each of them.

Nick had drawn and fired all three shots from waist level before any of the others even knew what happened.

The young one died so quickly that he took his surprised face into the afterlife.

The silent horseman caught his round in the stomach and crumpled over the back of his horse while letting out a slow, pained groan.

The bald horseman had reflexively hunkered down low and therefore positioned himself so his arm and ribs absorbed most of the impact of his bullet. Even so, he was in a world of hurt.

Nick raised his gun arm so he could aim more carefully. "You should have left when I gave you the chance," he said as he rode Kazys closer to the other three horses.

Gritting his teeth, the bald horseman fired a shot that was quick but not even close to accurate. He straightened up so he could take better aim, which also presented a much bigger target.

Nick put a round straight through the gunman's heart and then fired again to knock him off his horse.

The gunman landed with a heavy thud, which forced his last breath out in a powerful gasp.

On his way over to meet Joseph, Nick used his last round to put the gut-shot horseman out of his misery.

Joseph had his gun in hand and at the ready when he finally rode to a stop in front of Nick. His horse fidgeted nervously and looked as if it might give in to a shaking fit at any moment.

Nick sat in his saddle, calmly replacing the spent shells in his gun's cylinder.

Finally Joseph holstered his gun and took a breath. "Well." He sighed. "That turned out better than I expected."

Nick laughed once and holstered the Schofield.

THIRTY-TWO

———•———

The Busted Wheel ranch was an impressive spread by anyone's assessment. It was situated on a portion of land close to the size of Joseph's property, but had almost double the number of buildings at its center. Nick and Joseph rode straight over the fence at the property line and stormed through the open terrain as if they were trying to wake the dead.

Finally, the two of them came to a stop and waited. After a few minutes, they still couldn't see any sign that they'd been spotted.

"This makes me sick," Joseph said as he shook his head. "Any man who'd let someone get this far into his property without getting a look at him deserves to be robbed."

Nick shrugged and stood up in his stirrups so he could get a better look around. The night was clear enough for him to see fairly well in every direction. "I guess Dutch must have gotten someone on the inside of this place just like he did with yours. We haven't passed a single steer, though, so the herd's probably not even here. They must be after a hell of a lot of gold." Fixing his eyes upon a spot in the distance, Nick lowered himself back onto the saddle. "Well, it looks like we're not as alone as we thought."

Joseph eventually spotted the same rider Nick had seen. After a few seconds, he said, "Looks like there's only one."

The rider came to a stop several yards from Nick and Joseph. He tipped back his hat and propped a shotgun on his hip so it couldn't be missed. "You two lost?" he shouted.

"No sir," Nick replied. "We're looking for the Busted Wheel ranch."

"You found it."

"Good. I need to speak to the owner."

"You found him, too."

"I'm Nick Graves and this here's Joseph Van Meter. Can we have a word with you?"

The longer the rider stayed quiet, the more Nick thought he and Joseph were going to be turned away. After a while, Nick even began to wonder if he might have to deal with the business end of the shotgun in the rancher's hand. Finally, he lowered the shotgun into a pouch on the side of his saddle.

"Follow me," the rider said.

Before Nick or Joseph could respond, the rider had turned around and headed deeper into the property.

The owner of the ranch was in his late fifties and

had a head full of thick, silver hair. His large, friendly eyes were set closely together over a bulbous nose. He rode straight to the middle of the property, where most of the buildings were clustered together like a small village.

One of the larger buildings was a wide, flat-roofed house with a porch that spanned the entire front. Climbing down from his saddle, the owner waved for Nick and Joseph to tie their horses to the same post where he'd tied his own. Once both men had complied, he walked up the two steps leading to the porch.

"You said your names were Nick Graves and Joseph Vandemere?" the silver-haired man asked.

"Van Meter," Joseph corrected.

"Right," the man replied, tapping his ear. "These don't work like they used to. I'm Brad Hofferman. Pleased to meet ya both."

Nick shook Hofferman's hand, but climbed only one of the two porch steps. "Good to meet you, too, sir. We really need to have a word with you."

"Talk away. Sorry about the reception. I don't usually meet guests with a shotgun, you know."

The front door to the house swung open and a slender lady stepped out. Her smile was bright and her dark hair was streaked with some gray. Glancing back and forth from Brad to the other two men, she asked, "What's all the commotion out here? It's past midnight."

"I know," Hofferman said with a crinkled smile,

"but I heard the dogs barking, so I went out to have a look-see. Found these two out skulking around in the dark."

"Do you know them?"

"That's Nick and that's Joseph. I was just about to ask if they're hungry."

"We didn't come for food," Nick said. "We need to warn you about—"

"Nobody asked if you came for food," Brad scolded good-naturedly. "I asked if you were hungry."

Nick looked over his shoulder at Joseph and got a roll of the eyes in response. Seeing that both Brad and the woman were waiting expectantly, he said, "You might have some company soon and they won't want food. They'll want to rob you blind."

Brad's eyes widened. "What makes you think something like that?"

"Because we just drove most of them off," Joseph snapped. "Not that there's anything stopping them if they did decide to turn around and ride through here. Don't you have any men riding your perimeter?"

"Not when there's nothing to steal. The herd's already up to Kansas by now and the boys won't be back with the money anytime soon. Most of the ranch hands that did stay behind took work moving steers for some other fella. Me and the missus here were just enjoying the quiet."

"I might know where those cattle came from,"

Joseph said bitterly. "Do you have anything else of value here? Anything at all?"

Brad scowled a bit, but still couldn't get himself to look too threatening. "Why would you want to know something like that?"

"We crossed paths with some men who were known to raid spreads like this one here. We know for a fact they've had their eyes set on this place."

Shrugging, Brad said, "There's always someone out to take what you've got. I've learned that ever since I started running my own outfit."

"So does anyone want some pie?" the lady asked. "I baked it fresh this morning."

"I want some," came a little voice from inside the house.

The lady stepped to one side and allowed a little girl with bright blonde pigtails to step into the doorway. She couldn't have been more than six years old and was rubbing her eyes sleepily.

"This is our little granddaughter Sandy," the lady said. "She's waiting for her daddy to come back home with the rest of the boys, isn't she?"

The girl nodded and clung to her grandmother's dress.

For a few seconds, Joseph couldn't take his eyes off that little girl's face. When he saw her shrug away from his intense glare, however, he snapped his eyes toward Brad and said, "You need to listen to us, old man. Get your head out of your ass, for God's sake!"

Brad walked forward and stood between Joseph and the front door. "You'll watch your tone, mister."

"We've had a rough night," Nick said. "Please, just give us a moment to explain."

"You'd best explain and be on your way, then."

"I will. Just give me a second with my friend, here." Turning to face Joseph, Nick shoved him away from the porch until there was a bit of room between them and the rancher. "What in the hell is wrong with you, Joseph?" Nick hissed.

But Joseph's eyes were still fixed upon the front of the house. The anger had subsided, but there was still plenty more going on inside of his head. "Those folks don't know what's coming. Jesus Christ, they don't even seem to know what kind of wickedness is out there."

"We're here to warn them, but we'll be run off this land if you keep barking at them like this."

Joseph kept shaking his head. "They don't even guard what they've got. It's like they just roll on their backs and let anyone on a goddamn horse ride in and do what they please. They worry about their fucking pies or where that little girl's daddy is when they could be dead right now!"

"Dead like your wife and your little girl, is that it?" Nick asked.

It was a harsh question, but it was the only thing to snap Joseph out of the bloody memories that were washing over him. When he looked at Nick this time, he seemed to be fully aware of his sur-

roundings. "Yeah." Joseph sighed. "Like them."
He started to look toward the house, but couldn't
meet the eyes that were looking back at him.
"Maybe you should talk to them on your own."

"Do you think you're going to give our host another tongue lashing?"

"No."

"Then you're coming with me to apologize. Besides, these folks need to hear what kind of men
they might be up against, and you're the man to
tell them."

Joseph nodded and took a few deep breaths. He
started walking toward the porch, but stopped
when he saw the silver-haired man rush down the
steps to intercept him.

"I think you two should leave," Brad said.

Nick was about to step in, but held off when he
saw Joseph calmly wave him back.

"I spoke out of line, Mister Hofferman," Joseph
said. "But these men we told you about are out
there and they nearly killed both me and my friend
earlier tonight. They've done a whole lot worse to
people much closer to me. We've followed them
this far to try and put them down, but there's still
some left and they'll probably be headed here to
finish the job they started."

The silver-haired man glanced back and forth
from Joseph to Nick. "That would explain why
you're wound up so tight. Come to think of it, I
have seen some fellas roaming at the edge of my

property. I figured I'd keep an eye on them, but thought they'd lose interest once they saw there's no herd for them to steal."

"They're not out to steal a herd," Joseph said. "They stole enough cattle to keep them busy for a while. In my case, they bought one of the hands who worked for me and found out where I kept some money I'd been saving. That's the sort of thing they're after, Mister Hofferman. They know about the gold you have. I know this sounds crazy, but—"

"But that's how some folks are," Brad interrupted. "Some men are civil and some are just animals. I didn't get this many gray hairs without dealing with my share of animals, you know."

"Has there been a problem with rustlers in these parts?" Nick asked.

"Oh, sure. Real nasty ones, too. From what I heard, they're the type who spill blood for the sake of spilling it. Now that you mention it, some of my own workers have been caught poking around where they shouldn't be." Brad gave a single, solid nod and then turned toward his house. "You boys come in and have something to eat."

"We were hoping to get something ready in case anyone tried to make a move on this place," Nick said. "They're probably going to make it soon."

"Then you'll need something on your stomachs to make it through the night," Brad insisted. "All of my men are gone, but if these killers are after what I got stashed, they'll be coming to this house.

It'll be a long night, so head inside and get a bit of food while you can. The devils will still be out there when you finish eating."

Nick and Joseph looked at each other and knew they were thinking the same thing: Suddenly, the old man didn't seem so careless, and he was far from stupid. His wife was regaining her smile and the inside of the house looked awfully inviting compared to the growing chill of the night.

With nothing else left to do, they shrugged and went inside to have some pie.

THIRTY-THREE

When they heard the thunder of approaching horses, the morning was just a promise smudged across the bottom of the sky in a few streaks of orange. Dawn would arrive in an hour or less, but the darkness wasn't about to give up its fight.

They rode straight across the property as if they owned it. Dutch rode at the front of the formation with five men following behind and flanking him on both sides. His murderous eyes were focused upon the ranch house, and he charged forward until he was almost close enough to ride straight through the front door.

One of the other men was in his late twenties and had a lanky frame. He was breathing so heavily that one might have thought he'd done all the running for the last few miles. "They should be in there," he said. "I'll go in and bring them—"

Before he could finish, Dutch interrupted by drawing his pistol and sending two shots through the front window. The sound blasted through the early morning air, shattering what little remained of the almost sacred silence. By the time the glass stopped falling, Dutch and three of the other men were off their horses.

"Anyone in that house better come out!" Dutch shouted. "Because I'll just be coming in after you!"

The three men standing around Dutch were the same three who'd ridden in Joseph's group during the charge he and Nick had orchestrated. Long Face stood closest to Dutch. He had a gun in each hand and looked plenty anxious to use them.

"I'll go in," Long Face said.

"Fetch the old man, Ross," Dutch shouted over his shoulder. "You'll know where to look."

The lanky young man climbed down from his saddle, but paused as if he thought Long Face would do the job if he only waited long enough. Before Dutch had to ask again, Ross took a deep breath, drew his gun and walked toward the front of the house. Before he could get up the steps, the front door swung open and Brad Hofferman stepped out.

Shaking his head solemnly, the silver-haired man put his hands on his hips and met Ross's eyes without taking much notice of the other men. "We treated you as good as the rest of our hands, Ross," Brad said. "What would possess you to do something like this?"

"I . . . I . . ." Ross stammered.

"We know about the gold you took out of the river that let you buy this spread," Dutch cut in. "Hand it all over and we'll leave."

"I will not," Hofferman said defiantly. Even though he carried a shotgun in his hands, the weapon seemed like more of an afterthought. His arms hung loosely and the shotgun was positioned across his body at waist level.

"Stand aside, old man," Dutch said. "You don't want to push me right now."

When he saw that Hofferman wasn't about to move, Long Face surged forward and shoved him away from the door. "You heard the man! He said move!" Grinning with his easy victory, Long Face started to walk into the house, only to be stopped by the man who was standing behind Brad.

Nick stood with his hands at his sides and his holster strapped across his belly, waiting for Long Face to spot him. He took hold of Long Face's shoulder and buried a punch in his gut that forced the air from the man's lungs.

Long Face stumbled backward and sucked in a few shallow breaths. Seeing that Dutch and the others were watching him, Long Face raised his gun.

Nick's eyes remained fixed on his target and his hand effortlessly plucked the modified Schofield from its holster. He fired once and then shifted his aim to the rest of the men, knowing Long Face was already done.

"Fine," Dutch said calmly. "We'll do this the hard way."

The moment he went for his gun, a shot went off over everyone's heads and knocked Dutch off his feet.

The other two men who'd ridden on Joseph's side of the charge drew their pistols in a rush and immediately began pulling their triggers. Hofferman raised his shotgun and emptied one barrel after another, the first of which sent a gunman sailing into oblivion. Although his second barrel only grazed one of the other gunmen, that man got knocked down by another shot from Nick's Schofield.

As the men were falling beside him, Dutch pulled himself up and searched for the gunman who had put the lead into the meaty part under his arm. That bullet hadn't come from either of the two men on the porch, so he knew there was another shooter. Sure enough, when he looked upward, he saw Joseph on the house's flat roof, sighting along the top of a rifle.

"God . . . damn . . . you!" Dutch shouted as he lifted his arm to take a shot at the roof.

Joseph squinted behind his sights and took aim. He pulled his trigger again with every intention of punching a hole through Dutch's skull. Instead, he tore a section from the man's cheek and knocked the back of his head against the dirt.

Nick could feel panic building in the air just like he could smell the burned gunpowder hanging in front of him. He stepped through the acrid cloud, kicked the gun from Dutch's shaking hand and then took aim at one of the two other gunmen who were still standing. Hofferman was right beside him, aiming his freshly loaded shotgun at his former worker.

Ross shook his head wildly and tossed his gun. He might have fired a shot or two, but wasn't even collected enough to hit the house. "I swear I didn't want anyone to get hurt!" Ross said. "You weren't even supposed to be here!"

"Guess it's a good thing I decided not to go along on that drive, then," Hofferman said. "Otherwise, I never would have seen for myself what a sorry piece of trash you are." Hofferman looked to the other young man standing nearby. "And you, Peter? You sided with these men, too?"

Peter was a man in his thirties with a round face and dull eyes. Letting his gun drop from his hand, he said, "A man's gotta make money however he can."

Hofferman shook his head and tightened his grip on his shotgun.

Just then, Joseph stormed through the front door of the house with the rifle in his hands.

"Cover this one here," Nick said, indicating one of the two gunmen, before Joseph could do anything.

Joseph complied and stood at the edge of the porch.

Nick walked over to Dutch, squatted down to his level and said, "Things aren't so easy when you don't have a dozen men backing you up, are they?"

"Go to hell," Dutch wheezed.

Joseph's rifle barked once to send a round into Dutch's face and out the other side of his head.

Dutch lay sprawled on the ground, twitching for a few seconds before his end finally came.

When Joseph spoke, it was in a soft, almost disbelieving voice. "That man killed my family," he said as if reciting it to himself. "He killed them."

Hofferman's eyes were wide and he shifted nervously on his feet while keeping his rifle aimed at Ross. "What'd he say?"

"He's speaking the truth, Mister Hofferman," Nick told him. Looking to Joseph, he said, "Put the gun down now, Joseph. It's all over."

But Joseph shook his head slowly while shifting his aim to Peter. "No it's not. It's not over until they're all dead. Every last one of them."

"You've done plenty," Nick said. "You and me have tracked these bastards down and put an end to them. It's over, you hear?"

Joseph kept shaking his head as he put his rifle to his shoulder and took careful aim at Peter's head. Seeing the cold, haunted look in Joseph's eyes, Peter couldn't breathe. Moving was entirely out of the question.

"Jesus!" Peter said. "I didn't hurt no one! I swear!"

"Not yet, maybe," Joseph said. "But you would have."

Joseph's finger tightened around the trigger just as someone suddenly shoved his rifle barrel toward the sky. Fire roared from the barrel, scorching the mangled hand that held it.

Gritting his teeth through the pain, Nick tried

to pull the rifle out of Joseph's hands, but the heat from the barrel made him give it up. "What in the hell are you doing? Stop this!"

"That's a fine way for you to talk, Nick. You've killed more men than I have, and now you want to start preaching to me?"

"Those men we tracked down were killers who meant to kill us. I did as much dirty work as I could so you wouldn't have to."

"I didn't need your help. I didn't even ask for it!"

"The hell you didn't!" Nick snarled. Since he'd let go of the rifle, it had been aimed directly at his chest. He didn't seem to care about that in the least as he glared into Joseph's eyes and shouted in the hopes of being heard. "You charged into this thing looking for revenge and if you couldn't have it, you would've been more than happy to die. I recognized that look in your eyes the first night I took you in, and you had every reason for it to be there. That's why I decided to help."

"You want to help? Then step aside, Nick."

"I may not know what it's like to lose a wife and daughter the way you did, but I know what it's like to want to kill as badly as you do right now. I felt that taste in my mouth when I was shot to pieces in Montana. I tasted it when those good folks who helped me were threatened, run off and . . . God only knows what else."

"That wasn't the same," Joseph said bitterly. "Not by a long shot."

"It was brought about differently, but killing is killing. The men who killed your wife and daughter deserved to die. It's only right that you got to take the first shot at them, eye for an eye, just like the Good Book says.

"I spent years of my life digging through the same pile of shit until it was all dug up and the men that wronged me got what they deserved. More than once, I wondered what it would have been like if I would have just turned my back on it all and got on with my life when I still had the chance. Turn the other cheek, just like the Good Book says," Nick continued with a wry grin. "It's too late for me. I spent years healing up and gunning down anyone who even talked about that Committee. From there, I kept living by my gun because it was all I knew. I've been like that since I was old enough to shoot straight. But you haven't."

As he listened, Joseph's eyes darted from Nick to the two men behind him. They were still too frightened to move, and if they tried or so much as flinched, Hofferman and his shotgun were there to change their minds.

"You have every right to be angry," Nick said. "And you always will. What happened was terrible, and the men that hurt your family deserved what they got. Folks are hanged for stealing horses. Hell, I arrange the parties they throw afterward. Sometimes, killers get away just because they're smarter than the men trying to hunt them down. I know both sides of this argument too damn well."

"So what?" Joseph said with a little less venom in his tone. "I've killed, so I guess I'm no better. Is that it?"

Nick shook his head. "You could have let the law take a run at these men, but you didn't. I don't really blame you for that. The men you killed, as bad as they were, will haunt you. I tried to give you some time to simmer down and have second thoughts, but you kept going. I can't blame you for that, either. You'll carry this with you your whole life, but these two boys here," Nick said, pointing behind him, "they didn't have a damn thing to do with what happened to you or your family."

"They would've hurt this family right here."

"Maybe, but they didn't. I'd wager you can live with putting bastards like this one down," Nick said, gesturing toward Dutch's body as if it was a dung heap.

"I couldn't have lived with myself if I didn't," Joseph replied solemnly.

"What about this boy here?" Nick asked while stepping aside to let Joseph look at Ross. "He wasn't there that night. He doesn't know you. Kill him and you'll be stepping into some territory that you don't want to get into. You'll lose sight of the man you were and you'll become a killer without any bit of righteousness behind you. You'll be a stone's throw from the assholes who drove you to this. You'll be an outlaw, and there's no angels for outlaws. Those words become truer to me every day. Maybe you should think about them before you get so far into hell that you won't be able to find your way out."

Although Joseph didn't say anything, the fire in his eyes was dimming a bit. Nick stepped forward until he bumped his chest against the end of Joseph's rifle barrel.

There was no fire in Nick's eyes.

There was no emotion whatsoever.

There wasn't even a flicker of humanity when Nick took his modified Schofield and pointed it directly between Ross's eyes. It was that same icy glare that had gotten Nick further in his days as a bad man than whatever gun was in his hand at the time.

"I could pull this trigger right now, send this boy to his Maker and sleep just as well as if I'd spent the day picking daisies," Nick said evenly. "I've spilled too much blood for another few drops to make a dent anymore. All it would have taken to keep me from losing so much of my soul was for someone to tell me when to stop. Every man is entitled to his justice. You've gotten yours. Now . . . stop."

The longer Joseph stared at Nick's face, the more he felt like he was looking into a cold, bottomless pit. He couldn't hold that gaze for too long and when he finally looked away, Joseph felt as if he'd been shaken out of a fever dream. The anger was still inside of him, but it no longer had the teeth and claws that had been ripping his guts apart.

When he let out his breath, Joseph felt as if he'd been holding it for weeks.

"Put the gun down, Nick," Joseph said. "It . . . it's over. This is all over. I just want to get back home."

Nick holstered the Schofield and lowered his head. Even after Joseph had turned and walked toward the house, Nick kept his head down and his eyes open as the coldness slowly worked its way under his skin.

THIRTY-FOUR

———— ◆ ————

The ride back to Ocean was quick and quiet. Although Joseph told Nick a bit about the son who was waiting for him to return, he didn't ask about anything from Nick's past. After what he'd already heard, it was obvious that he didn't want to hear any more.

That suited Nick just fine. He enjoyed listening to the few words that Joseph had to say. Those words were enough to show that Joseph was a changed man. There was a shadow in his eyes, but not the genuine darkness that had been there before. More important, Joseph preferred to talk about the future rather than the past. Joseph sometimes bowed his head in reflection as if thinking about his wife or daughter.

They rode into Ocean early one afternoon. Rain from the night before had left the grass wet and green. A few flowers bloomed here and there, but most of the flowers they could see were already cut and lying at the base of a few tombstones. The graveyard smelled of warm air and freshly turned soil.

Joseph asked Nick to stand with him next to the specially carved markers of his wife and daughter. The two carved angels were still looking at each other as if no time had passed, and Joseph looked down on them as if he were peeking in on a private conversation between mother and daughter. Nodding once, he turned to Nick and said, "Sammy should be here with me."

The expression on Joseph's face, shadows and all, was a good sight for Nick's sore eyes. He led the way to his cabin, anxiously awaiting his own reunion with Catherine.

When they got there, however, they found the cabin's windows broken and its door knocked off its hinges.

"What in the hell?" Nick snarled as he swung down from Kazys's back and ran to the doorway. His gun was in his hand before he even knew his arm had moved. When he saw the mess that was inside, he stormed into the cabin in search of an excuse to pull its trigger.

"Good Lord," Joseph said as he took a step through the doorway. "What happened here?"

"I don't know, but Catherine's gone."

"What about my boy?"

Nick wheeled around to look at Joseph as if he didn't know whom he was referring to. He then blinked a few times and dropped his gun back into its holster. "I don't know. There's nobody here."

"By the looks of it, there was a hell of a scuffle. Is there any blood or . . . ?"

As Joseph's unfinished question faded away, Nick took a slower, more careful look around. "No. There's no bodies. I don't see any blood. In fact, it looks more like someone tore through here just for the hell of it."

"Maybe they were looking for something."

"Where did you tell your son to go if Catherine didn't agree to look after him?"

Joseph snapped his fingers, already turning to go outside. "His uncle's place. I'll take you there."

Nick practically flew out of the cabin and onto Kazys's back. He and Joseph raced through town.

They had nearly left Ocean's limits again before Joseph reined his horse to a stop.

"This is the place," Joseph said.

The moment Nick's boots hit the dirt, his hand was resting upon the grip of his pistol. His eyes darted to and fro, looking for any suspicious movement or any face that he didn't like. When the door to the little house swung open, Nick planted his feet and prepared to draw the Schofield. The face he saw, however, was far from threatening.

"Pa! You're home!" Sam shouted as he rushed outside.

Nick didn't relax until he saw Catherine step through the door. Fixing her hair, she smiled and started to say something, but couldn't make a sound before Nick ran to her and swept her up into his arms. She laughed and tried once more to speak. This time, she was cut off by an urgent kiss.

"Well, well," Catherine gasped, once she had a chance. "It's good to see *you*, too!"

For the next few moments, all Nick wanted to do was hold on to her tightly, pressing his face into her hair and nuzzling her neck. Once he'd filled his lungs with the sweet scent of her, he allowed himself to loosen his grip.

"I thought something happened to you," he said.

Catherine winced and asked, "You were at the cabin, weren't you?"

"Yes. What happened?"

"Someone came into town and made that mess," she replied while shaking her head. "It's not as bad as it seems. Sam and I weren't even there at the time."

"Who did it?"

"I don't know who it was. The sheriff says he was probably just after money or food."

"Sheriff Stilson saw him?"

She nodded. "He saw more of him than I did. In fact, he ran him out of town."

"And you weren't hurt?" Nick asked. "Or the boy?"

Catherine looked over to where Joseph was swinging his little boy around and happily wrapping him up in his arms. "We weren't hurt. Sam was so lonely after you and his father left that I thought it best to bring him here. Seeing as how you two were probably headed for some trouble, it seemed best if I stayed with him to make certain we were safe until you two got back. It is just Alice here by herself, after all. Sam's uncle had some business in Sacramento."

Nick looked toward the front door and saw a thin woman with short black hair for the first time. Alice was so skinny that she looked like she could be snapped in half by a strong hug, but her smile was friendly enough and she waved to Nick the moment she made eye contact with him.

"Before you ask, I also brought the shotgun," Catherine whispered.

"You're one hell of a woman," Nick said while brushing the back of his hand against her cheek.

She smiled at him and patted his hand. "I'm glad you realize that."

As the wagon rattled up to the sheriff's office, Stilson opened the door and ambled outside. His thumbs were hooked over his gun belt and he nodded with mild surprise when he saw who was driving the noisy rig.

"Sorry, but I don't have any deliveries for you today," Stilson said.

Nick set his brake and climbed down. "I'm on my way to my parlor and wanted to stop by and have a word with you about what happened to my home."

The sheriff raised his hands and said, "I did what I could. By the time I got there, most of the damage was already done."

"I don't intend on being cross with you. I wanted to give you my thanks."

At first, Stilson looked at the hand Nick offered as if it might reach out and slap him. He grasped it hesitantly at first, but then responded amicably when Nick shook it in friendship.

"We've never been good friends, but I wanted to tell you I appreciate what you did."

"Just doing my job."

"Can you tell me what happened?"

Stilson walked around as if he was inspecting the wagon. "It was lucky that I was making my rounds when I heard the noise. I thought it was someone's roof collapsing or maybe a horse got a burr under its saddle and was kicking in a wall. Turns out it was your door getting kicked in. Far as I knew, you were nowhere to be found, so I went and had a look for myself.

"I saw two of them as I rode up to your place," Stilson explained as he tapped his foot against one of the wagon's wheels. "One of them bolted before I could even bring my horse to a stop. The other took his sweet time coming out, even after he saw me, but walked away from your cabin soon enough once he saw I wasn't just some nosy neighbor."

"Did you get a look at them?"

Stilson walked over to examine Rasa and Kazys as if he intended on purchasing the horses. "One of them might have been the fella that me and Miguel found in the graveyard that night when the

Van Meter place was raided. Come to think of it, I'm almost certain it was him."

"Jesus," Nick muttered as he felt a knot tighten in his stomach. "And the other one?"

"Didn't recognize him," Stilson replied while checking to make sure the bridle was secure on both horses. "But he was a different breed from that first one. The fella that ran first, the one that was in my jail, was skittish and moved like he was hurt or scared out of his mind."

Nick kept quiet, but knew that J. D. was both of those things the last time he'd crossed paths with him, on the Silver Gorge trail.

"The second one was still around after I'd taken a look inside your cabin. I thought I might have to take a shot at him since he didn't clear off your property right away."

"What happened?"

Shrugging as he walked around to examine the other side of the wagon, Stilson replied, "He asked where you and your missus were."

"What did you tell him?" Nick asked, while silently dreading what the answer might be.

"I said you both had moved on."

Nick's eyes snapped back into focus and he fixed them upon the sheriff. "What?"

"I said you and Catherine were in a rush to get out and that's exactly what you did. I made up some story about how folks were talking that you two just up and left without packing more than some clothes and food into a few carpetbags. The more I told them," Stilson said, chuckling, "the more I started believing it, myself."

"What made you think to tell a story like that?"

"There was just an opportunity, I guess. Nobody was home and the damage was done, so I spun the first yarn I could and hoped it would be enough for them to move on. There wasn't anyone inside your place, so I just figured on getting him to leave of his own accord.

"Men like that are like stray dogs. You show 'em there ain't nothing to gain from being somewhere and they'll stay gone. Don't you worry, though," Stilson added. "I bowed up and chased him off, just to be certain."

Nick could imagine it hadn't taken much to chase off J. D. If Dutch sent another gunman along for the job, however, it was probably a man who didn't frighten so easily.

His inspection of the wagon completed, Stilson wound up standing next to Nick with his arms crossed. "That fella from my jail was off like a shot. That other one, though . . . he wasn't in no hurry. He left, but he made sure I knew he was leaving of his own volition. He seemed pretty happy with himself, though. My guess is that he didn't have any trouble believing what I told him."

As Nick listened, he also didn't have any trouble believing what Stilson told him. In fact, the only reason for those gunmen to think Stilson was lying was if they already knew better. If that was the case, they would have known where to find who they'd been looking for. Since Catherine wasn't harmed or even rattled, Nick could only conclude that those two gunmen were long gone.

"I think you might have saved my wife's life," Nick said. "And the life of Joseph's son right along with her."

Stilson shrugged. "I did my best."

THIRTY-FIVE

———◆———

When Nick returned to his cabin, his wagon was fully loaded. The top was covered by a tarp, which was strapped down to keep all the things secured in the back. Catherine busied herself that entire day with cleaning up and putting their home back together. That evening, she fixed Nick a dinner that was more like a banquet and served it to him at his regular table in the back of her restaurant on Ninth Street.

Although the cabin was still a mess, they spent the night there enjoying each other's company in their own home. They didn't notice what was broken or what shelves still needed to be straightened, since neither one of them spent much time out of the bedroom.

Catherine woke up to an empty bed, threw a robe on and searched for Nick. She found him outside, staring up at the stars that were scattered overhead like a mess of silver dust. He wore his rumpled trousers with the suspenders hanging loosely from the waist. The scars that crossed his naked back and chest showed up like streaks of water in the shimmering starlight.

"Why are you up?" she asked. "What time is it?"

"It's late," replied Nick. "That's all I know."

Stepping in front of Nick, she leaned back against him and nuzzled in close until she felt his arms wrap around her. "After all we've been doing, I'm surprised you have the strength to get out of bed."

"I wanted to soak in as much of this place as I could . . . before I left."

Nick could feel Catherine shrink a bit in his grasp. Her head lowered, but quickly came up again so she could look up at the sky. "Why would you want to do that?"

"You don't sound surprised."

"I'm not. Actually, I'm just surprised you let me see you before riding off. I always feared waking up one night and having you just be . . . gone."

"You've been through so much just to be with me," Nick explained. "And just when things seemed to be settled, this happened."

"But it didn't happen to us," Catherine said sharply. "You took it upon yourself to ride off with Joseph. I think it was a good thing, and Joseph seems like a whole different man now that he's back, but this was your choice. It's over now," she said, gripping Nick's forearm. "We can get back to the way it was."

"Do you know how close you were to getting

hurt? Jesus, Catherine, I didn't even know those other two were coming back here. They could have . . ." Nick trailed off as the terrible speculations ripped through his mind. Not wanting to put a voice to those images, he just said, ". . . and I wouldn't have even known until it was too late."

"There's always something bad that can happen, Nick. If anything, you should have learned that from Joseph. Bad things can happen just like good things can happen. There's no way to know what's coming next or when it'll get here."

"As long as I'm here, I know something else will be coming," Nick said. "Usually, it ain't good."

"You'll be able to take whatever comes. And if you think that I can't handle myself, you really haven't been paying attention all this time we've been together."

Nick grinned and held onto her a little tighter. "I know you can handle yourself. That doesn't give me the right to keep putting you to the test, though."

"If I didn't want it, I would have left you by now."

"I'll only be gone for a little while, just until I know this thing is over and there isn't anyone left trying to find me. Sheriff Stilson did a real good job of covering up for me and if I stay here, I'll ruin it."

"Did he tell you to leave?"

"No."

"And what happens the next time something comes along?" Catherine asked. "I would think you'd do what you need to do, but I would never think you'd just run away."

"That won't work on me," Nick told her. "I know you're just trying to rile me up."

"I think it is working."

"Not a bit." A few seconds slipped away before Nick added, "Well, maybe a little. Either way, I thought this would be a good night to give you something."

Taking his arms from around her, Nick reached into his pocket. When he took his hand out and opened it, there were two gold rings sitting on his palm. "I didn't want us to wear these because I was afraid you'd be marked as a target if someone else came looking for me."

"And since they came around anyway, you figure we might as well wear them?" Catherine asked.

"No. I want to always know you're with me . . . no matter how far away I might go. I've hidden from a lot of things, but having you as my wife isn't gonna be one of them."

Catherine's eyes locked upon Nick as he took her hand and carefully slid the ring onto her finger. He then slipped his own ring on and flexed his hand to get the feel of it.

"Don't go," Catherine whispered. "You've got a good business here and I'm not about to leave my restaurant now that it's up and running. Most folks would call that a life worth keeping."

"Most folks don't have gunmen, vigilantes and a

few determined lawmen out to nail their hide to a wall."

"Then at least give me the chance to try and talk you into staying," Catherine said as she took Nick by the hand and started pulling him back to the cabin. "After all, this is sort of a second wedding night."

Although Nick grumbled a bit, he allowed himself to be dragged into the cabin and toward the bed. Once he got there, the furthest thing from his mind was riding away.